The Bethany Road

The inspirer and organizer of a small party which sets out for the Holy Land is the genial Bishop Brakewaite, but the true source of his inspiration is not revealed till the last chapters of the story. Jonathan Palmer – the narrator – has had, in middle age, an unhappy love affair with a girl much younger than himself. For him this is an attempt to rediscover his lost Anglo-Catholic faith. For almost every member of the group, in fact, the venture has some profoundly individual significance. It is Mr. Prender, a famous orientalist, who emerges as the unofficial guide, treating them on the slightest pretext to thrilling discourses on every aspect of Eastern religions, but he is also battling with an inner despair and seems to bear the burden of some secret guilt.

The narrative develops as the pilgrimage proceeds, through Lebanon and Jordan, to the Dead Sea, Qumran and Jerusalem. . . . Three of the men make a tremendous detour to work even further back towards the origins of religion; to see Babylon, the Tigris, and, in Persia, the Royal Road of the King of Kings; even to camp for a night beneath Mount Behistun, under the figure of Ahura Mazda, Zoroaster's god, on the great mountain-inscription of King Darius.

With The Bethany Road, *Ernest Raymond has produced one of his very finest novels. It is a story which has depths and a subtle sense of narrative. The relationships of the characters evolve during the journey and are described with humour, warmth and understanding. Above all Mr. Raymond writes with authority on one of his favourite subjects: the search for faith.*

BOOKS BY ERNEST RAYMOND

NOVELS

A London Gallery *comprising:*

We, the Accused	*Was There Love Once?*
The Marsh	*The Corporal of the Guard*
Gentle Greaves	*A Song of the Tide*
The Witness of Canon Welcome	*The Chalice and the Sword*
A Chorus Ending	*To the Wood No More*
The Kilburn Tale	*The Lord of Wensley*
Child of Norman's End	*The Old June Weather*
For Them That Trespass	*The City and the Dream*

Other Novels

The Mountain Farm	*Morris in the Dance*
The Tree of Heaven	*The Old Tree Blossomed*
One of Our Brethren	*Don John's Mountain Home*
Late in the Day	*The Five Sons of Le Faber*
Mr. Olim	*The Last to Rest*
The Chatelaine	*Newtimber Lane*
The Visit of Brother Ives	*The Miracle of Brean*
The Quiet Shore	*Rossenal*
The Nameless Places	*Damascus Gate*
Tell England	*Wanderlight*
A Family that Was	*Daphne Bruno I*
The Jesting Army	*Daphne Bruno II*
Mary Leith	

BIOGRAPHIES, ETC.

Paris, City of Enchantment	*In the Steps of St. Francis*
Two Gentlemen of Rome	*In the Steps of the Brontës*
(The Story of Keats and Shelley)	

ESSAYS, ETC.

Through Literature to Life	*Back to Humanity*
The Shout of the King	(with Patrick Raymond)

PLAYS

The Berg	*The Multabello Road*

Wakefield Libraries
& Information Services

Ernest Raymond

The Bethany Road

CASSELL · LONDON

CASSELL & COMPANY LTD

35 Red Lion Square, London WC1
Melbourne, Sydney, Toronto
Johannesburg, Cape Town, Auckland

© Ernest Raymond 1967
First published 1967

Set in 10-on-12 point Monotype Imprint type, and
printed in Great Britain by Cox & Wyman Ltd,
London, Reading and Fakenham
F.167

With admiration
to
R. C. Hutchinson and Margaret

.

Contents

1 At Bishopscourt 1

2 Through the Clouds 16

3 Alethea 27

4 Over the Mountain 39

5 A Dream of Hebrew, Greek and Latin 51

6 Mr. Prender in Some Disgrace 57

7 Qumran 68

8 The Name of Names 76

9 Metamorphosis of Mr. Prender 84

10 Ozymandias is Everywhere 95

11 The Infidel Prophet 104

12 The Great Road 114

13 Under Bisitun 129

14 On Olivet 144

15 Beth-muri 148

16 'When the Hidden Things are Told' 155

17 The Summing Up 180

18 Homeward 192

Author's Note

The quatrains from the Persian Sufi poet, Jalālu'l-Dīn Rūmī, in Chapter 13 of this story are taken from the translation by A. J. Arberry in the *Everyman Anthology of Persian Poems*.

My gratitude to him for these lovely lines and for his permission to make use of them.

E. R.

1

At Bishopscourt

'I TAKE it bishops will fly,' I said.

'We shall all fly,' said the Bishop.

This was no part of an eschatological discussion on the Four Last Things, or on the habits of the Faithful in the Hereafter; it was to do with a pilgrimage to the Holy Places which Bishop Brakewaite was organizing. 'Back to the springs of it all' was his definition of this pilgrimage. He had told me about it, enthusiastically, in the smoking-room of our club of which he is the only episcopal member. We are proud of him in the club. A man of wealth, he entertains generously, but it is not for this that we are so pleased with him, nor because he is an imposing figure in our public rooms, but because he is the only bishop who has preferred our friendlier clubhouse to the academic shades of the Athenaeum. When, large and well-rounded beneath his apron and cincture, with buttoned gaiters below and ribboned hat above, he descends our steps into the view of the world, and is ushered into his large car (ecclesiastically black) by his waiting chauffeur, we sometimes feel that an ironical bow in the direction of the Athenaeum would not be misplaced.

'My dear boy, what else could we all do but fly?' he asked me now in his large drawing-room at Bishopscourt, pacing back and forth while I lounged on the flowered chintz of an easy chair. 'Rail would take days. A ship weeks.'

I had no map of the Levant in my mind's eye and could not remember what railways or ships' routes ran towards it.

'A flight would do it in hours, dear boy. Five hours.'

'But the expense? I am but a poor man.' This was not quite true, but it's the sort of thing one says. As a 'Master Printer', and director of our family firm, Palmer, Sands and Hume, my salary is no sweater's wage.

'Don't make me laugh, Jonny.' My name is Jonathan Paul Palmer. '*You* poor! But anyhow, it won't cost any of us much if we fly through the night. We shall be a bunch of fly-by-nights.' And he rubbed his hands together with pleasure at his little joke. 'I've the finest agents in London working it all out for us.'

He is a handsome figure of a man, our Bishop Brakewaite: with his sculptured features and suitably silvering hair though he can only be in his mid-fifties. No nonsense in this bishop about walking the world dressed like a layman or junior cleric in a subfusc suit with nothing but a purple stock to blazon his rank. As he stood in front of me now, halted before his imposing marble fireplace he looked all that a prince of the Church ought to look—or nearly so. Not quite, but so very nearly so. He measured more, I suppose, around his middle than around his broad breast, but sash and apron modified this enough, while the gold pectoral cross lifted the eye above such imperfect matters. And, of course, in divine service when he walked in rochet and chimere or, better still, in a magnificent cope, this small unevenness was annihilated; it was as though it had never been.

A grandee among men, surely, but . . . the thought occurred to me while he stood there beneath his huge Arundel print of Dürer's 'Adoration of the Trinity', 'Is it possible to have an appearance like that and to live as a humble Christian? If it is difficult for him, as a rich man, to get through the needle's eye, is he not equally obstructed by so admirable a face, figure—and voice?' Because his voice, by the grace of God—or perhaps by the wiles of the Devil—was an almost ideal instrument for pulpit and platform.

I had got to know him well in the club and liked him immensely. Liked him with all of a largely imperfect layman's tolerance of a somewhat imperfect bishop. I thought of him as a 'professional' ecclesiastic, far too untroubled by any inadequacies in his religion, far too unconscious of any hypocrisies, and altogether too happy

2

enjoying the good things of this world. When he lunched at the club his Austin Princess waited outside not only with the uniformed chauffeur at the wheel but also with some heraldic device above its radiator. Whether this shield carried the arms of the House of Lords or of his diocese I do not know, but I suspected (for I have a highly critical, if forgiving, nature) that he liked the passers-by to see it and to think 'That car's waiting for someone important inside. I wonder who he is.' Often, too, his letters to me came under the heading 'House of Lords, S.W.1', rather than 'Bishopscourt, St. Brigid's'. In my suspicious way, I was pretty sure he preferred this of the two addresses. He had just acquired seniority enough for membership of the Lords.

But if I laid these weaknesses to his account I knew him as a man of abounding goodwill towards all his fellow-men, and there's a good deal of Christianity in that. After all, Abou Ben Adhem's name led all the rest. And may his tribe increase.

Percy Brakewaite is only the third Bishop of St. Brigid's. This new diocese was only founded in 1927, when it was hewn out of the ever-spreading built-up areas of North Middlesex and Hertfordshire, and no doubt my good and genial friend liked to forget at times that Rochester was founded in A.D. 607 and Lichfield (formerly Mercia) in 664. The Church, when it created St. Brigid's, bought the large Edwardian red-brick house, in which we now talked, for the episcopal home. No old stone castle or palace this, but a place of large comfort with a pleasant garden around.

'How many other bishops will be coming?' I asked.

'Only two. Don't be alarmed, my dear boy.' So he persisted in addressing me, though he was barely ten years older. 'Two more. Three is as much as any company can stand. Four would sink the plane.'

'Which are they?'

'Stourminster and Solomon Islands.'

Now, in my fervent Anglo-Catholic youth, twenty years in the past, I would love, as a pretentious and all-knowing young 'spike', to refer to bishops by the names of their sees; I would say 'That's what London said in the Lords,' or 'I see that Bath and Wells has

3

put his foot down on Benediction.' So I understood Stourminster, but what about Solomon Islands? I was not clear whether he was a diocese or a converted Jew.

My host removed the mist for me. 'Freddy Parrett is on leave, and well he deserves it after years in that impossible diocese, a spatter of islands all miles apart, somewhere off New Guinea. A delightful chap. I love him. Years younger than me, and infinitely better in every way. Why, the man's an absolute saint. Dear me, wish I were more like him. But I don't come within twenty miles of him; he's everything a bishop ought to be. So far, there are just these two of my brethren, you, if you come, two parochial church councillors, and—'

'But your wife'll come with you, of course?'

'Oh yes. Hester and I and . . . and a friend.' Had there been a small hesitation, very small, a note of doubt or even guilt, a looking away towards the light of the windows, as he said 'and a friend'? Had he himself observed this hesitation and regretted it? I thought he instantly changed his tone to one of brisk cheerfulness. 'Yes, a good friend of mine. And a wonderful man to have with us. There's nothing he doesn't know about Eastern literature and religions. I suppose he's one of the greatest Orientalists in the world. Absolutely.' The Bishop was easily driven by his gusto and friendliness to effervescing with enthusiastic superlatives. 'He's a . . . a Mr. Prender.' But again he appeared to have hesitated before uttering this name and to have instantly smothered the hesitation with another enthusiasm. 'He's a superb lecturer and quite the finest exponent of Eastern thought I've ever heard—' a halt, a stumbling, on the word 'lecturer', and thereafter he seemed to skirt quickly away from all talk of his friend as a lecturer. 'You should get on with him famously. "Prenders"—as all his friends call him—is an ardent Anglo-Catholic, just as you are.'

'Just as I *was*,' I corrected, not without sadness, and a smile to cover the sadness.

'And may well be again. Old Prenders has . . . er . . . been away for some time but in the past he did magnificent work for the Calborne College Mission—Calborne was his old school. The Mission's in one of the least savoury parts of my diocese, and he

4

gave it that dedicated work you sometimes get from a devout lay-man. He simply *was* the Mission—especially where its work with young people was concerned. Oh yes, we're lucky to have him. He'll be the eyes and the brains of this expedition. I've no brains.'

'So there'll be eight of us,' I began. 'You and your wife and—'

'But what about *your* wife? Won't she come too?'

'No, no . . . there are the children. She won't leave them.'

That would do for an answer. He couldn't see the ache in my heart as I spoke it. It was credible, and all that the world must ever know. I might act an ease, a carelessness, as I uttered the words, but really I was hearing my poor wife's all too generous, unbearably generous, decision, after the disaster, 'Yes, *you* go. We shouldn't be happy together just now. Go and try to enjoy it. I have the children.'

So easily the Bishop accepted the excuse. 'Of course. I understand. The children. You must try to do something very nice for her when you come back, poor dear.'

But if he only knew! . . .

What was known to me sank me into a minute of silence, and I was relieved when, before the minute ended, the door was pushed by the point of a tray, and the Bishop's wife came bustling in behind a tray spread with silver and china, sandwiches and cakes. Hester Brake-waite was a short, large-bodied, heavy-featured woman, given to loud gay speaking and loud gay laughing. 'My God! . . . Percy!' she exclaimed as she carried the tray to a coffee table. 'Oh, my God!' but before she justified these despairing cries she said to me, 'I'm parlour-maid today, Mr. Palmer. It's Heaton's afternoon off, and Mrs. Gittings isn't feeling well, so I packed her off to bed. Percy, my God, Olivia wants to come too. And *with* Maureen!'

'Maureen?' At this even the Bishop was moved to murmur a 'Good God!' which he quickly toned down to 'Gracious. Gracious. . . .'

'Yes, Maureen of course, darling. Certainly Maureen.'

'But not—' the Bishop had halted where he stood. He stood quite still, staring at Hester, as if a sudden rue-laden thought had pro-duced a catalepsy— 'not with Alexander?'

'With Alexander, beyond question. With Alexander, naturally.'

'Oh, my G—' but he saved himself again with an 'Oh dear, dear, dear. . . . Well, well, that'll make ten of us. Or shall we say nine and a half?'

Hester explained, as she set out the tea-cups. 'Olivia, Mr. Palmer, is the Dowager Lady Lampiter, and Maureen Applebie is her daughter. Unfortunately she's separated from Eric Applebie, her quite delightful husband. Why any woman alive should want to separate from Eric I can't imagine, but perhaps *he* did the separating. Yes, that's much more likely. That would be quite understandable. There's a child.'

'Is there not?' sighed the Bishop.

'Yes. One. Alexander. Seven years old and a—'

'Let's speak nothing but charity,' laughed the Bishop. 'Let's stop at the statement that Alexander is seven years old.'

'But what a pity to stop there. Still, if you say so, Mr. Bishop. . . . How do you like your tea, Mr. Palmer?'

'I propose,' the Bishop interrupted, 'that we now stop calling him Mr. Palmer, though it's a marvellous name for anyone going to the Holy Land. He'll be entitled to carry a palm branch wherever he goes, for the rest of his days. He must bring it into the club one day. It would do our more pagan members quite a bit of good, I think. But while he's with us Mr. Palmer's Jonathan. Or Jon. I see you've brought four cups. Who else is coming?'

'Mr. . . . Mr. Prender.'

Not a doubt of it: she too had hesitated, flinging a nervous glance towards me. 'He said he might look in since you and Mr. Palmer— you and Jonathan, I mean; or you and Jon—were discussing arrangements.'

There was a silence, brief but beyond my understanding, before the Bishop said over-briskly, 'Good. Splendid. I want Jon to meet him. They should have much in common.'

'I know nothing about Eastern philosophies,' I submitted, as I took tea from Hester and a cucumber sandwich from the Bishop.

'No, but all about Anglo-Catholicity.'

'Once upon a time,' I amended again. 'And all rather long ago.'

From now onward Hester's loud gay voice monopolized most of the

6

talk. Her talk was far less scrupulous than the Bishop's, whether it was about Lady Lampiter or Maureen and her separation from the delightful Eric, or Alexander, 'that frightful brat'. She was happiest, I thought, when discharging a loud and bruising wit at the expense of anyone she mentioned. About Mr. Prender her tone, if never her words, suggested potently that she could tell me something fascinating, but mustn't. Because of the fascination she tended to bring the talk constantly back to Mr. Prender. I had no very high opinion, as I have told, of the Bishop's moral stature, but I could see scruples in him that were missing in his wife. He had been happy and at ease in the loyalty of holding back something dark or melancholy in the story of a friend. She strained against these fetters.

Rather than leave the topic of Mr. Prender she repeated her husband's words that 'he should suit you since you're both such keen Anglo-Catholics'. To so resolute a talker it seemed to matter nothing that this opinion had been offered less than five minutes ago, and denied. Or, perhaps, interested in her own talk rather than that of others, she had not heard what we men had said. 'Foolish woman, and rather blind,' I was thinking, as she rattled noisily on. 'Does it never cross your mind that a man may lose the easy certainties of his youth? Are you one of those natural believers who, never ceasing to believe themselves, cannot imagine that a man who was an ardent believer in the bright years of youth can slowly shed it all to his sorrow and depart into a wilderness?'

We were at this stage when the door-bell rang. It rang once and dubiously, I thought; irresolutely.

Hester sprang up. 'That'll be him. That'll be Prenders. Excuse the parlour-maid, Mr. Palmer—Jonathan—while she attends to the door.'

She bustled out and I heard her noisy, hearty voice in the hall. Someone had spoken low, and it was as if she were lifting her voice high in opposition to such quietness. 'Nonsense. Everything's going to be quite all right. You go in, Prenders dear, while I dash for more hot water. I'm the acting, unpaid parlour-maid today—a kind of *au pair* girl. They're in there talking.'

Presumably the unheard voice asked 'Who are "they"?'

7

'Percy and Mr. Palmer whom we're instructed to call Jonathan. Or Jon. Go in and make yourself nice to him. You'll quite like him. He's something big in the printing world. Palmer, Sands and Some-one Else. Enormous firm, I believe. A Combine, whatever that is.'

Our door, which was not quite shut, opened and a man came in. He was short, broad, perhaps fifty, but with all his boyish dark hair thick upon his head. His eyes were large and dark too; and sad or wistful as a dog's. But what struck me most was his pallor. It was a sick, off-white pallor. This, and the changing expression in the dark eyes, sad and defeated at one moment, then anything but defeated—angry, rather, and aggressive.

Was it these, the pallor and the hunted look in the eyes, or what was it, that made us all feel embarrassed, anxious and suddenly shy of one another? For I could detect a disquiet in both bishop and wife—a moment of anxiety as if they feared lest something untoward should happen.

The moment passed. It faded away. But I remember thinking then how tiny is the well-lit area that any of us sees in any of our brother men, and how vast an area remains in darkness.

When Mr. Prender was seated in a huge chair and taking his tea-cup from Hester, the Bishop rose and shut the door which his wife had left ajar. It was only April and the days were still cold. As the door struck the jamb and clicked home I saw Mr. Prender turn quickly towards the sound as if in dislike of it.

We all talked now about the route of the Bishop's pilgrimage—though Prenders contributed little. The Bishop described it jovially, perhaps to disperse that moment of unease. 'Fly by night to Beirut, then over the mountain of Lebanon to the Bk'aa valley and the astounding ruins of Baalbek. On from Baalbek to Damascus, that city of paradisal gardens on the desert's fringe, and thence to Amman, which may be Jordan's capital, but to me, Prenders, is the place where Uriah the Hittite was set in the forefront of the battle and shot down by the archers on the wall. And so to Jerusalem, Jon, surely the most haunted spot on the world's surface—'

Here we were interrupted again by a ring of the hall-door bell, and a knock on the door. To our surprise the knock was repeated

8

with a single bang that made our hearts jump. One guessed that the knocker had been lifted high and allowed to drop. It was a slam like an exclamation mark.

Hester was out to it before our hearts had settled down. We heard women's voices in the hall, all talking more or less together. I distinguished one voice, a young voice, saying, 'I *am* so sorry about that second knock. Alexander *would* do it before I could stop him—and such a bang!' The Bishop went out to this conversazione, leaving the room door unclosed. I saw Prenders look at it and release (as I thought) a sigh of relief before he turned to me.

'You going on this hajj?' he asked.

'This *what?*'

'Hajj. Arabic. This pilgrimage to the Christians' Mecca.' Strange the faint derisory note in one whom the Bishop had described as a devout, even a dedicated, layman.

'I hope so. You too?'

'The Lord Bishop wants me to.'

'And you will, I hope.'

'I suppose I shall. But listen.' He leaned towards me and spoke softly. 'Before they come back, what are we doing about visas?'

'The Bishop's agents are looking after them.'

'Well, listen.' He looked towards the door. 'Get on the quiet a visa for Iraq.'

'Iraq? But we're not going there.'

'You never know. One might slip across the frontier. Get a visa for Iraq. And for Iran. Yes, slip a word to the agents about Iraq and Iran. Might be worth it. Well worth it, believe you me.'

'Iran? *Persia?*'

'Yes.'

'But why?'

'You never know. The Bishop talks of "going back to the springs of it all". But the springs are far further back than the first century A.D. Centuries further back. And they lie far beyond Israel and Jordan.' He seemed now to be speaking sadly, as though his thoughts were far from this room. 'They lie in Mesopotamia and in the old land of Shinar. Between Tigris and Euphrates. And they are certainly to be found up among the Persian mountains on the old Iranian tableland. With Zoroaster and his Great Spirit of Truth, Ahura Mazda. If we've got to have a pilgrimage I'm for doing it in greater depth. Anyhow, visas are often useful. No harm done.'

I didn't know what this remarkable person was trying to say, and he went on, 'Of course they're to be found among the Hindus and Chinese as well—' but here I interrupted, 'Good God, you're not going to make me get visas for India and China too?'

'No, no.' He did not laugh. Manifestly his thoughts were remote from laughter. 'All one can do is to bear them in mind. They're all one magnetic field. Buddha. The Upanishads. Sudden breaks of light in the universal darkness of man. But keep all this under your hat. It's just a few ideas in my mind. Keep it from the women for heaven's sake. Women are a curse on any worthwhile exploration. Talk all the time. About their friends and relations and each other. And their doctors. Especially if the doctor is an osteopath or herbalist or something. Never about ideas. Listen to 'em now. Hester!... My God!... Consider Hester Brakewaite. With Hester around, even my Lord the Bishop has a task to get his words in.'

At this point the others came into the room: Hester, the Bishop, an old lady with a high white coiffure like the turban of a Sikh, and a much younger woman with hair henna'd to a violently unnatural bronze. She held fiercely by the hand an unengaging little boy. Obviously the Dowager Lady Lampiter, Maureen, her daughter, and the seven-year-old Alexander. Alexander in some disgrace about that knock and held firmly lest he erred again.

The Bishop presented us. It was then I knew that this woman, Maureen, had brought with her, besides an unengaging little boy, a powerful fragrance. Whether it was Frangipani or Parma Violet or perhaps Paris-at-night or Harem Roses I could not know; I knew only that it advanced before her, clouded around her, and followed behind her to no small distance. Talking to me from within this enclosing fragrance, she gushed, 'You must forgive that awful bang on the door. Alexander jumped up and did it before anyone could stop him. Not only was it unnecessary, but, as I told him, no gentleman knocks at a door like that; only somebody who wants to sell you something.'

'Not to worry,' I comforted her, adding, I think, 'Boys will be boys,' or something equally trite.

Lady Lampiter, in a voice deep as a man's, which seemed to suit well with her patrician coiffure and large domineering nose, announced, 'His father was a fool: one of those cranks who won't have their child beaten. The back of a hair-brush on his bare buttocks up till about four years old and a handy cane in a cupboard thereafter would have done Master Alexander no harm. But no: Eric wouldn't hear of it. And look what he's left us with.'

'There's still time,' laughed the Bishop, glancing at the seven-year-old boy.

'No, there isn't,' snapped the Dowager. 'Women can't do it properly. Alexander just fights Maureen. It needs a man. One who has a nice pliant cane in a cupboard and really knows how to use it.'

From this condemnation of Eric's softness she passed, easily enough, to the proper treatment of criminals. She was all for the birch and indeed the cat, she said. Something that really hurt.

And as she said this the voice of Prenders came sharply from the hollow of his huge chair. 'If what you fancy, dear lady, is something that really hurts, why stop at the birch and the cat? Why not return to the thumbscrew and the rack? I should think that would be an excellent idea.'

She looked towards him in his chair, as if surprised that anyone should dare to contradict her. And so sharp was the surprise that it partly discomfited her. 'I don't know that I'd advocate the thumbscrew and the rack,' she temporized, 'but I'd certainly keep the gallows. Indeed I often think hanging's much too good for some people. I never see why we should go out of our way to make it painless for them. They didn't spare their victims any pain.'

'Why not crucify them?' His voice was quiet and even enough, but was there something unusual in this heated sarcasm spoken on behalf of criminals?

'*Really!*' Shock. Shock that left her speechless . . . for a few seconds.

'Yes. A man, properly crucified, doesn't die for hours, sometimes not for a day and a night, so he has plenty of time to suffer agony and think of his sins. Excellent in every way.'

'I think that's blasphemous,' said the Dowager, turning away from it. This of course was no answer to the argument, but a good vent for her fidgeting indignation that anyone was arguing with her at all.

'It could be that the blasphemy lies elsewhere,' suggested Prenders, ruthlessly quiet in his deep chair. 'I prefer to think it lies in Christians advocating merciless cruelties. If it's blasphemous to crucify, but we want something that really hurts, why not tear chaps' limbs from their living flesh, as was done to the assassin of Henri Quatre? That should really hurt.'

'I never heard such—'

'*Alexander!*' A cry from his mother. And for once a misbehaviour by Alexander was of help to us all in bringing down the guillotine upon this untimely disputation. You would have thought that Alexander might have taken a personal interest in an argument that had begun with his buttocks and a hair-brush, but no: he had left us to it and was ambulating around the large room, picking up objects of virtu from occasional tables. Perceiving that the Bishop was watching his more valuable objects anxiously, his mother called, '*Alexander!* Come here at *once.*'

Alexander took no notice but struck a succession of notes on the open keyboard of the grand piano at which he had now arrived. Lady Lampiter, grim-lipped, shot to his side and brought him back to base where he stood, grounded, between grandmother and mother. You could see in the large-nosed face under that white turban of hair that she was thinking regretfully of the hair-brush which had lain so sterile on Eric's dressing-table.

I have a foolish mind which must ever find descriptive titles to sum up my friends or acquaintances. It had already provided 'The Wandering Fragrance' for Maureen, and now it chose 'The Hanging Dowager' for her mother. This latter was an unloving title, because, like Prenders, I react away from keen churchwomen who, however frequent their churchgoing and devout their prayers, remain self-righteously and violently vindictive, harbouring no perception at all of Christ's real teaching, which is that you can never conquer darkness and evil by themselves but only by their opposites. For me this is a blinding light, however feebly I live with it.

Most of the talk now danced between Hester and Lady Lampiter, with even the Bishop getting few sentences inserted, and then only after repeated starts. It might have been, of course, that he was anxiously watching Alexander who was pursuing his detailed examination of ornaments and souvenirs displayed about the room. The next cry of '*Alexander!*' came when Maureen observed the worry lying in a wrinkle between her host's eyebrows. '*Alexander!*' she called. 'Come here. Don't *finger* things.'

Generously the Bishop said, 'Let him be happy if he's interested. But I shouldn't touch things, old chap.'

As for Prenders and me, we had withdrawn from any hope of entry into the chatter. Once or twice I had leaned forward with the opening words of a surely valuable or even witty sentence only to sit back defeated. Prenders stayed silent, only turning to me once with a shrug of humorous despair and a wink. He was able to do this because nobody was looking at us or interested in us. We were spectators on a side-line. After a time he beckoned to me with his head and with an inconspicuous thumb, down on his lap, to come and sit on the chair beside him. I did so, and nobody commented on my movement. Nobody was interested in it. Probably nobody observed it.

Since it was now obvious from the talk that Lady Lampiter and her daughter, complete with Alexander, would be coming on the pilgrimage, he murmured to me, in a voice pitched only a little lower than usual, the women's voices in their fine entanglement providing screen enough to hide his words, 'Don't you think we'd better back out of this? Can you stand two or three weeks in the company of Alexander? Or of this Maureen and her lady mother? Shall we retire?'

I shook my head. 'Too deep in it now, I'm afraid.'

'So'm I. Oh well . . . perhaps the mighty ruins of Baalbek and the Great Mosque of Damascus will outbalance Alexander. But only just. And when we get to Jerusalem, we may effect an escape. I have my ideas. Do you think there'll be any more women coming?'

I knew of none, I said. I'd heard only of two bishops and two parish church councillors.

'Two more bishops! Two parish councillors! Good God. Will there be anybody who's not a Christian? Anybody to keep me company?'

I expressed no surprise at this remark, so unexpected after the Bishop's description of him. I felt I did not know him well enough to probe with intimate questions. I said only, 'Perhaps I could fill that part for you.'

'How? Aren't you a Christian?'

'I was once. Red-hot. But not now. Not for years now. And probably never again. Just a doubter apparently beyond hope of healing.'

'Then I think you'll suit me down to the ground.'

I felt driven to add, 'But a doubter who'd love to be back where he once was.'

To this he offered no comment. It seemed to have sent him away into some place of his own, very private. After a while he emerged from this shadowy place with no more than a sad 'Oh . . . well . . . .'

When it was time to go Lady Lampiter offered to drive me part of the way home. Her car was waiting outside. I accepted gratefully. Prenders remained in the drawing-room, the Bishop having persuaded him to stay for dinner. Unconsciously—or consciously perhaps, fearing the draughts on a cold day—the Bishop shut the drawing-room door as he came out with us into the hall.

In the hall, with two such *perpetuum mobile* talkers as Hester Brakewaite and Lady Lampiter both at full stretch, it looked like taking no small portion of an hour to get the lot of us out of the hallway, on to the threshold, down the two steps, and along the garden drive to where the car waited—and where there would certainly be further talk. And it was while we were yet in the hall, and the Bishop had just opened the front door (perhaps to help matters on) and Maureen was seizing Alexander by the hand lest he attacked the knocker again or perhaps attempted the bell—it was then that I, while I stood listening impatiently to the protracted farewells and thanks and invitations and newly recollected gossip, heard the drawing-room door softly, secretly, unlatched.

It opened again, an inch, no more; and I heard Prenders' steps go no less softly back to his chair.

2

Through the Clouds

FOUR O'CLOCK in the afternoon at the Airways Terminal. Among the fifty or sixty people seated or standing in the expansive hall as they awaited their coaches to the airport, I easily distinguished the Bishop's bevy of pilgrims. Easily because the Bishop, standing amid them, was still in full episcopal array: frock-coat, apron, gaiters and ribboned hat. When I joined his party he took an opportunity to tell me, 'Had to come dressed like this, because I may have to visit the Catholic Bishop of Bethlehem, or the Patriarch of the Greek Orthodox Church, or perhaps the Armenian Patriarch, and quite the cheapest way to carry such garments in an aeroplane is on one's person. You can thank your stars, my dear boy, that you're free of all this clobber.'

So he said, but I thought my own thoughts, suspecting other things. Our leader was certainly the most imposing figure among the wandering crowds in this vast ambulatory. He was smoking the latter half of a long cigar, which rather surprised me at four in the afternoon, unless he was in the habit of smoking cigars one after another from lunch-time onward, at ten shillings a time.

The women clustered around him: Hester, Lady Lampiter, Maureen (with Alexander in a secure hold and grumbling) and someone else: a long lean stringy woman in loose tweeds and flat-heeled shoes. She had a sharp, eager nose, and every now and then sprang up and down on her toes in a show of jolly excitement and suitable gaiety. I assessed her as a spinster who desired to be sporty.

It soon emerged that one of the two parish church councillors was a woman, and that this was she.

The men of the party stood near, but aside from the women laying siege to the Bishop. Only one of them was a bishop too, a tall, fair, bronzed and unexpectedly young man, hardly more than forty and looking younger. He wore an old and rather worn grey suit with nothing to show his rank but the purple stock. Solomon Islands, without a doubt. Only a missionary bishop would be as young as this. So it was: in conversation he told me that Stourminster had been unable, after all, to leave his diocese, and he, Freddy Parrett, would be the only other bishop, but he would do all he could to help our distinguished leader. I liked him at once: he seemed a gentle, modest and wise young man; even perhaps—but only in the hidden eyes of God—a saintly one. I thought he would be an admirable member of our company, ready with help or guidance for any of us at any time; and my mind had already found a title to describe him: 'The Spare Bishop'.

Prenders stood near this new bishop, but in silence. And yet again I was struck by his pale hunted face.

I went towards him, and, coming out of his silence, he introduced me to a third man, a Mr. Oslow, who was the second parish church councillor. This introduction curtly and summarily performed, he grumbled, 'Oh, for Christ's sake let's go and sit down somewhere. Away from these cackling women and that blasted whining child,' which seemed hardly the true note for the opening of a Christian pilgrimage.

The three of us, he, Oslow, and I, found seats on a long red bench, and as I was seated next to Oslow I got into talk with him. And quickly, as with Bishop Parrett, I knew that I was going to like him and enjoy his company. Much my age, he was a man of figure rather too short for the big head and the fine face with its large strong features and its large dark laughing eyes. He pleased me at once by saying, 'I may be a parish church councillor because as an accountant I can be of some use as treasurer, but I'm only a very muddled Christian. Nothing but the incredible old C. of E. with its amazingly generous and catholic temper would tolerate me as a councillor. I go regularly to church, trying to believe what I can. I'd love to believe it all, but . . . but . . . but . . .'

'You mean, then, that you're not really a full member of the Party.'

He laughed. 'I'm certainly a fully *paid-up* member, technically, but it'd be more to the point to call me just a fellow-traveller. Just a very frail Christian in the pews. However, do understand that when I say I don't believe this or that, I'm not saying I *dis*-believe it; I just mean that I can't yet say I believe it. I can't stand up and sing "Firmly I believe and truly", as everyone else seems able to do. With no trouble at all. Women all round me singing it at the tops of their voices. Men too, an octave or so lower. I stay silent. I can sing some things quite cheerfully, but nothing so precise and certain as this. If only they'd let me sing, "Firmly I desire belief, But, Lord, as yet I am not sure; I simply do not know," that'd be fine. Pausing, he tried to improve his verse. " Greatly I would love believing But I'm not quite sure as yet." I just don't *know*. Like the Great Bell of Bow "I do not know". And sometimes I suspect I shall never know.'

So here we were: two of a piece, though I had to say, 'I'm afraid you can no longer call me even a fellow-traveller. I don't go to church any more but, like you, I long to be a fellow-traveller and much more.'

'Well, the old Bishop—he knows all about my muddles—seems to think we may find something to help us out of our doubts if we go back to the places where it all began—but I don't quite see how. Why should we?'

'He knows all about me too,' I said. 'But I don't think he has any idea how stubborn a case is mine. He and Hester believe so easily themselves. They seem entirely without trouble in their faith or their consciences. One would like to be like that.'

'Well, anyhow,' he laughed, 'here we are. And we don't quite know why we're here, or what we are waiting for. Or what is waiting for us. So let's fellow-travel together.'

An accountant he might be, giving his days to the harsh literalism of mathematics and money, but there was clearly a small poet imprisoned within him. There was nothing of the accountant, occupied solely with the cold finances of earthbound business-men, in that 'What is waiting for us', as we sat together in this noisy atrium, side by side, with anxious or bewildered travellers streaming back and forth.

I asked, did he know the other parish councillor in the party.

'Do I not!' he said, and swung his head towards the tall stringy, tweedy woman, springing up and down on her toes, whom I'd assessed as a sporty spinster. 'That's she. Millicent Hilder, and quite a girl. She's on my council. Millicent is her real name but she likes to be known as Jimmy. I don't quite know why, but Jimmy Hilder she is to us all.'

Jimmy. It suited well, I thought, with that long mannish figure, the tweedy skirt, and the low-heeled, square-toed shoes. And the springing up and down.

'Yes, Jimmy. And this seems the moment,' he said, 'to ask you your name. Here we are, having exchanged detailed analysis of our lamentable spiritual conditions, and I don't even know your name.'

'Palmer,' I supplied. 'Jonathan Paul Palmer, generally known as Jon.'

Immediately he made the Bishop's joke, 'What a name for a pilgrim to the Holy Land.' And he quoted, ' "The faded palm-branch in his hand Showed pilgrim to the Holy Land." Well, Jon, I'm afraid you can get nothing out of my name, Clement Oslow.'

Pat came Prenders' voice from his other side, where he'd been sitting in silence. 'Clemens Alexandrinus,' it suggested. 'Clement of Alexandria. One of the greatest and sanest Christians of all time. He was *Saint* Clement for a long time till a fool of a pope, Benedict XIV, completely misinterpreting him, kicked him out of the calendar. Clement had all the splendid catholicity and humble comprehensiveness which I heard Clem attributing to the old C. of E. just now. He taught that the truth could be found in every quarter—in all good philosophers, all good pagans, all good heretics and doubters, because anything that is good must come from God, and if Christ is the Logos, or Reason, he must be in them all. His date was somewhere about A.D. 190, and I doubt if we've had so sane a Christian since. He saw that the aim of the old philosophers was no less the attainment of holiness than is the Christian's aim. In his *Stromateis* he describes one of his favourite teachers, Pantænus, as "the Sicilian bee plucking flowers from every prophetic meadow to produce a wonderfully pure knowledge for the souls of his—" '

'May I have your attention, please?' A charming voice, coming from the loud-speakers, echoed everywhere in these spacious halls.

'Damn!' said Prenders. '*I* wanted your attention.'

'Will passengers for the flight to Beirut please board the bus at the south exit.'

'Never do I get to my punch-lines,' Prenders objected, 'but what the door-bell rings, the telephone lets fly, or a blithering loud-speaker starts to blare—'

'The south exit. Have your tickets ready, please. Thank you.'

'Still, there must be someone rather ravishing behind that voice,' he allowed, as we all rose to obey. 'Perhaps, after all, it's a pleasure to be interrupted by her.'

We trooped out, Clem Oslow and I among the last. A few paces in front of us I saw Jimmy Hilder springing along towards the coach and swinging her handbag in time with her springs. She stopped of a sudden and stood dead still. 'Oh, hell!' she said. 'Hell and be damned.'

I asked what was the matter.

'The devil! Needless to say, I've left my boarding ticket. On the table where we were sitting, bugger it.'

I allowed myself no sign of surprise at this last imprecation from a parish church councillor and Christian pilgrim, for I like people to remain at ease with themselves. I asked only, Could I go and get it for her.

'No, no. Lord, no. I'll go. I'm the idiot.'

And as she went pushing back through the following crowd I guessed quite a little about Jimmy Hilder. I guessed that her dashing slang and these masculine oaths had some relation to her eager springing walk, her preference for 'Jimmy' to 'Millicent', and at the same time—in contrast with all this semi-masculine behaviour—to the brilliant geranium lip-stick on her mouth.

I thought it wise to halt till I saw her returning safely, which was not long to wait, for here she came, waving a triumphant hand to me and then holding up two triumphant thumbs—one supporting the sling of the bag—and finally calling out, 'All okay. Blasted thing lying on the floor under the table. Don't wait. Don't wait. Tell the blasted bus not to go off without me. Coming like a bomb.' Nevertheless I waited and let her pass me. Greatly relieved at having found the ticket, she hurried past me, swinging the bag on its long sling at her side, with a new vigour, like the pendulum of a clock suddenly pleased. But my polite hesitation made me last on the bus. Standing on its deck, I could see no empty seat anywhere.

And while I stood puzzled I heard that call 'Alexander' again, but this time it was appealing rather than desperate; it was, so to say, without its exclamation mark. And I saw that the boy had secured quite the best seat in the bus, a solitary seat by the window to the left of the driver.

'Get up and give that seat to Mr. Palmer,' ordered his mother from a seat four rows back.

The boy remained where he was, lips sourly compressed.

'Come along,' she commanded. 'Do what you're told. There's room here.'

'Oh, no,' I protested. 'It's a shame to disturb him.'

'Not at all,' she announced. 'He's pleased.'

Never in my life have I seen a statement more emphatically disproved by an out-thrust under-lip. Never a mouth showing less of pleasure.

'But I bagged this seat,' he complained.

'Never mind that. Now you give it up to someone older than you. Come along. There's a good boy.'

'But I shan't be able to see out of the window,' he explained very sensibly.

'That can't be helped. You can see London any time. And you'll see plenty in Jerusalem.'

'I wanted to watch the driver,' he further expounded.

'You can see all you want of him from here.'

Again I objected. 'No, no. A pity to—' and again she assured me,

'Not at all. He's pleased,' while he rose sullenly, taking with him a mouth that proclaimed she lied.

When I had taken his place, shrugging a helpless protest, I realized that Clement Oslow was behind me, for he leant over my shoulder to whisper, 'I should say that child was a muddled Christian too.'

'A very frail Christian,' I agreed.

The coach started and was soon a speeding van of voices, mainly feminine, two of the most audible and perpetual being Hester Brakewaite's and Lady Lampiter's. The sound from these two embattled talkers seemed as ceaseless and uninterrupted a noise as the murmur of the engine all the way to the airport.

§

In the aeroplane, as it flew through the early evening, leaving the day behind and cleaving into the eastern dusk, I was seated next to Prenders. The two bishops and the two older ladies, Hester and Lady Lampiter, had advanced straight up to the foremost seats, the Dowager carrying her turban of white hair proudly and declaiming as she passed me, '*I'm* not afraid of fire. If you've travelled in an aeroplane as often as I have, you realize that the chances of dying in a crash are considerably less than those of being done to death on a London road.' I had turned into this seat at the back, near the exit, because I had been talking to Prenders and had followed him there. For a long time he spoke hardly a word, and I noticed that he continually turned and looked back at that single means of egress, while the fingers of one hand kept clasping tightly those of the other. His face when I turned a sidelong eye towards it was strained. He fidgeted in his chair, almost as if he'd like to get up and walk about. And then it was I remembered that furtive unlatching of the Bishop's drawing-room door after it had shut on him.

Claustrophobia? Was it that there was now no chance of gently unlatching these doors? Was he, none the less, finding a relief in constantly seeing his nearness to an exit? Had he made for this seat with this purpose in view?

When there was no more to be seen through the window except a million stars spangling above us, and an Alpine continent of clouds stretching from sky to sky beneath us, he turned towards me and gave himself more to talk. He admitted, 'I'm afraid I rather hate being shut up in any place where there's no chance of opening the door and getting out. An Underground train, for instance. But that's better than this because the doors do open at every station. We're in prison here for six hours. But it's better when there are others locked in with you. I was alone in an Underground carriage late at night, once, and didn't like it at all. I got out at a station and changed into a compartment where there were other travellers.' He turned again and looked at that oval doorway beyond its curtains. 'Can't get out of this compartment—' and he laughed, but not easily.

Was it that he wanted to talk so as to keep his mind off those doors behind him, hermetically sealed? Better if other people were about? Better if there was someone to talk to? But astonishing his talk was, some of the most bemusing I'd ever listened to, because I could not gauge the truth of him. Had not the Bishop described him as an Anglo-Catholic who'd laboured magnificently among the youth in his college mission; had not he himself, just now in the Terminal, praised the catholicity and generous, humble comprehensiveness of the old C. of E.; hadn't he held forth on the splendidly eclectic Christianity of Clemens Alexandrinus? And yet here he sat, attacking any and every religion hotly and bitterly. Mumbo-jumbo, hocus-pocus, witch-doctoring, were some of the stock epithets he applied to the sacraments of the Church which I had once so loved—and, God help me, loved still in my arid place of exile. Were we not supposed to be pilgrims to the springs of Christianity, and yet here was one you could only describe as an Infidel Pilgrim.

'Listen, Jon.' So quickly he had turned to Christian names, to 'Jon' and 'Clem', almost as if behind a misanthropic bitterness was a longing for the warmth of friends. 'If there's one thing we can be sure about, it's that the Church is doomed. A century ago Newman wrote that the new scientific thought had increased alarmingly the territory of the natural at the expense of the supernatural. Well, now another century has gone by and the supernatural has hardly an inch on which it can stand.'

'Infinitely more,' I protested, 'because, Heaven help us, we dwell on the borders of the Unknown, and God alone knows how far the Unknown stretches or how odd a place it may be.'

This retort rather pleased me—and it still does—but he only hurried on. 'To any modern intelligence all the prayers and practices of the Church are gradually being seen for the mummeries of superstition which they are. I give the Church a few generations more in which to fade out, and then it will be like a thousand other religions, a tale that was once told.'

'But no—wait,' I persisted. 'Can't you believe in God without the mummeries as you call them?'

'Not in a God of love. God, no. For my part I agree with the merry Frenchman who said Nature could be summed up as a conjugation of the verb *manger*.'

I begged him to explain.

'Well, the active mood of that verb runs *je mange, tu manges, il mange*—fine—but there's also a passive mood, *je suis mangé*. Happily we men are usually on the *je mange* side, but just you chance to get on the *je suis mangé* side, meeting a lion, say, in the jungle, and you'll have lost most of your faith before the meal's got very far. Though, come to think of it, I've read that in some cannibal tribes it's considered an honour to be eaten by their mates.'

So he spoke in bitterness and satire but then suddenly his tone seemed to change. I thought it changed because he was not really confident in his arguments but was talking for show rather than in certainty. It changed to a sadness of loss. 'There was Matthew Arnold,' he reminded me sadly.

'Yes?' I encouraged. 'Matthew Arnold?'

'Years before Newman he said "The Church as it now stands no human power can save," but he said it with sorrow because he loved Christianity, calling it a beautiful though fond dream. I suppose that goes for me, really.'

'Not for me yet. Not quite yet. Beautiful, yes, but how far a fond dream I'm not sure.'

'You're an Anglo-Catholic, old Brakewaite says.'

'Was.'

'So was I.' And here, most remarkably, followed a passionate, even,

24

one might say, a loving assertion of what Anglo-Catholicity ought to be. 'Absurd,' he said, almost spitting in his indignation, 'to say that the Church of the twentieth century should be no more than what it was in its first days. Either it believes that the Holy Spirit dwells within it and guides it towards all truth, ever unveiling new facets of truth, or it doesn't. Did the Holy Spirit go to sleep at about A.D. 100 and stay asleep for two thousand years? Or did he just come down to get the Apostles going, and then hurry home? Of course he didn't. Okay, if he still abides in the Church it is still the slow discoverer and discloser of all truth. It is still *Ecclesia Docens*. And that goes for the old C. of E. which is undoubtedly the old historic Catholic Church in our country, even if it's in some error, as I'm sure Rome and Constantinople are too.'

As he poured all this out I began to suspect how like to me he was, in that while his head could no longer say 'I believe' he had left his heart behind him in the old Church.

I said something like this; I said, 'I believe you haven't dragged your heart away from the Church yet.'

He looked through the window at that world-wide continent of starlit clouds beneath us which must be screening all the stars from a darkened world below.

'*Nephelococcygia*,' he said. 'What a gift to the world Aristophanes was. Cloud-cuckoo-city. Don't you read his glorious comedy, *The Birds*, as a loving, laughing satire on all religious excesses?'

Never having read *The Birds* I could offer no comment, and left him to continue.

'Didn't Peisetaerus and Euelpides set forth to conquer Heaven by establishing with the help of the birds a city in the clouds—possibly just where we are now; I guess we're somewhere over Greece—a city which would be a buffer-state between mankind and Heaven, and so enable it to hog all the worship of men and all the power of the gods? Admirable notion! So, properly naturalized with feathers, they and the birds built Nephelococcygia. Aristophanes ought to have lived to see Pope and priests, in their fine feathers, claiming "Whosoever's sins we remit they are remitted, and whosesoever sins we retain, they are retained. Whatsoever we bind on earth shall be bound in heaven." God save us! Slightly arrogant, don't you feel?'

I looked at our two bishops sitting happily among the ladies in the forefront of the plane, and after a time asked him, 'So you call our two holy fathers cuckoos in the clouds?'

'If they can believe that—yes.'

I did not comment, and he proceeded impatiently, 'Ach! Most Anglican priests, if their goal is preferment, tread the Broad High Road because it's the easiest and quickest avenue thereto—certainly our good Bishop Brakewaite does—but I've no use for any broad easy road in the old *Ecclesia Anglicana.*'

Extraordinary. One would have thought he had no use for, or further interest in, any *ecclesia.* Surely this was a heart speaking instead of a head.

Somewhere here our talk ended. We had been flying more than four hours, it was nearly eleven, and a weariness had silenced many voices in the plane. Those that spoke at all now spoke in murmurs. Some had switched off the lights above their heads, and slanted the backs of their chairs so as to sleep. In the silence our ears apprehended again the stable roar of the engines of this ship in the clouds. The night must be brighter now in the world below because the cloudscape was breaking up and its fragments travelling slowly under the stars.

3

Alethea

I LOLLED deeper in my chair and closed my eyes, not to sleep but to dream. Certainly to dream of past and future. Prenders' talk had plunged me deep into old memories of a lost religion and into a frail hope which had brought me to this reclining-seat up in the skies.

In my young manhood, the son of protestant parents, I had rejoiced in my violent conversion to the Anglo-Catholic Movement. How I had loved the sudden radiance it had flung around our drab old humdrum C. of E., claiming that it was no protestant creation of a gross and lascivious king but, with all its faults, the original and only Catholic Church in our islands, descended direct from Christ himself through its unbroken episcopal succession. No human handiwork, but the 'Daughter of God and the Bride of Christ'. New and wonderful idea for a young man ready for a fervour! It put its torch to some tinder within me, and I was alight. The radiance of its new Solemn Eucharists (or High Masses, as I began defiantly to call them), the priest in glorious chasuble, deacon in dalmatic and subdeacon in tunicle forming at the altar a central jewel with the tall candles above and beside them and the censer swinging slowly behind them, its smoke ascending in columns or crescents and filling the church with an aromatic odour which had accompanied men's worship for three thousand years! Had not God himself ordered that 'the sweet incense' should be burned before and over the Mercy Seat in honour of his godhead? 'And when Aaron lighteth the lamps at even, he shall burn incense upon it, a perpetual incense before the

Lord throughout your generations.' So I argued happily, excitedly, with headshaking parents or scoffing friends. The sacred and heart-stirring moment of the Elevation when a lonely and distant bell, high in the tower, told the homes around that Calvary's sacrifice was being pleaded again on behalf of them all. The radiance glowing around the heroes of our Movement, those who had gone to prison rather than abandon teachings and rituals which they believed to be the heritage of their Church. Rioting gangs had broken up their services, over-thrown their ornaments, and assaulted them. Remember Father Mackonochie, of St. Alban's, Holborn, who, harried by his bishop, reviled and persecuted by the anti-papists, had wandered away into the snows and there died with his two dogs beside him.

'Spikes' they still called us ardent young partisans in those days, and we wore the title like a gay robe. I was the very Spike of spikes. How happy I was in my eager, excited, unthinking allegiance to this brilliant uprising in the Church. Sometimes, I wonder, is there any joy greater than that of a zealous partisan in a rebellious uprising—in a *Résistance* behind the barriers or under the banners of a Libera-tion.

My childhood had been spent in a religious home—at least my mother and sister, Louise, both enamoured of our local Low Church vicar, were ardent churchgoers, and I was one under compulsion. My father, a typical business-man, left this aspect of things to us. Save that, while never going inside a church himself, he was warmly opposed to 'ritualism' in other people's churches. Louise, at thirteen, vehemently devout, would sometimes yell at me from the top of the staircase, or from our playroom window to me in the garden, for the neighbourhood to hear, 'Jonny, have you said your mid-day prayers?' I had not, and did not intend to, being, at ten years old, a lapsed Christian if out of these women's sight. But Louise had nothing on me with her mid-day prayers after I had discovered Anglo-Catholicity. Why, in the first sunny days of my conversion I would try to say Sext in my lunch-hour, and None perhaps in the train coming home, and certainly Compline at night before getting into bed. This at first only; no young man not a postulant for a monastic order could sustain such piety. I settled rather soon for speedy morning prayers and Compline at bedtime—sometimes gabbled. There was no more enthusiastic server and acolyte at my new-found church, St. Aidan's, Elbury Gardens. I served three or four times a week at Daily Mass; at High Mass I was ever in my place, carrying a taper or swinging the thurible or even acting as ceremoniarius—and I would have you remember that a ceremoniarius can direct the very priests themselves when to sit down or stand up in the sedilia. In all this there was not only a young man's delight in ceremonial movement like the pleasure one can draw from drill or dance; not only a pleasure in my robes and my prominence on altar steps or pavement; there was something of these, of course; but there was more, much more; there was a real joy in worship and service, and all of a young man's longing to love given to his God and his Church.

§

But then I began to think. It was strangely late in my life when this happened, perhaps because love is blind. I had been happy for twelve years and more in an uncritical loyalty, but now—I was thirty, and I began to think, and it all fell away from me. Not my love for the enrapturing beauty of it all, the colour, the music, the singing, the tapers glimmering and the incense drifting—these live with me for ever—but my faith in the miraculous story which alone gave heart and meaning to it all. From virgin birth to resurrection there was hardly a miracle recorded that I could accept any more: walking on the water; feeding five thousand and having more food at the end than you started with; quelling a sea-storm with words; raising the dead. There were even sayings and deeds of Christ which I could no longer love. They overturned and flung down my worship of him.

But enough of these doubts. Their rightness or wrongness has been thrashed out in a thousand volumes; they've been ploughed up and raked over for all of two hundred and fifty years, ever since the German sceptics really got going; and only the fact of them has any place in this story of a sad doubter's search; only the loss of a joyous allegiance and an engrossing love.

I went to church no more. Still loving the memories of Anglo-Catholicity, still 'on its side' when ecclesiastical arguments arose—just like Prenders—I called myself for the fun of it an Anglo-Catholic agnostic. Never mind if the title was idiotic; it enshrined something; it enshrined a disharmony like that which I suspected in Prenders, a jangling discordance between heart and head.

Lolling, eyes closed, in my aeroplane chair I thought that the only difference between Prenders and me was that, while we were both exiles from an old faith, I would have loved to get back to it whereas he was glad, or apparently glad, to be done with it all.

The engines roared, all voices were low, some distant snoring competed with the engines as all ninety of us sat shoulder to shoulder within long walls of throbbing, quivering, patient noise. Eyes closed, I dreamed on.

§

Any day I might be seated in my study hardly hearing the music from my radio as I read newspaper or book—and then suddenly it was sacred music; it was Bach's St. Matthew Passion sung from a cathedral by a choral society; it was Haydn's Mass in D Minor; it was Purcell's Solemn Music for the Funeral of a Queen; it was Gregorian plain-chant sung by men's voices alone in some monastery or seminary; it was Evensong sung beneath the echoing roof of King's College chapel—any one of these, and I was lost to it; it forced my book to my lap that I might listen, the prey of a longing that did not heal.

Sometimes the music that could most surely still me in my chair to listen was no more than a choir singing 'Brother James's Air': 'In pastures green: he leadeth me The quiet waters by.'

Did this ever happen to Prenders, I wondered; this assault of a homesickness at once painful and desired?

With all practising religion gone, my central love lost, and the chains it had hung about me fallen to the ground, some of my moral life collapsed. It was not that I had ceased to believe in the grand Christian ethic—forgiveness and self-sacrifice and losing your life to save it—this still seemed to me, and it always will, the greatly glorious and utterly lovable truth, however hard, but where were the sanctions to enforce it now? With all the dogmas gone, and the difficult but happy Sacrament of Penance long abandoned, the sanctions were gone too. I was free. Free to indulge myself as I wished. Free for illicit loves with available women, one after another, though not one of them caught much of my heart—till I found Alethea. Alethea, when I was forty and she eighteen.

By this time my union with Charlotte, my wife, was no more than a merry friendship. We had jokes and fun together; to me she was always 'Charles' or 'Charlie' or 'Karl' or 'Lots'. Best of these pet-names was 'Lots'. 'Come along, Lots, jump to it. Look after your husband as a wife should.' Sometimes, in our friendly idiocy, it could be 'Lots P.'—for Palmer. 'Lots P., I beg to state that I've been waiting a solid hour. Could we start?' A lively friendship but a dead marriage. She had fallen in love with the phrase, 'I can't gush,' and now she was at its mercy, more and more its prisoner, till the full words of love or any warm unleashed caressings were impossible to her. In bed she offered me only a cold passivity that slew my heart so that I would often turn away from the business, neither wanting nor able to go through with it. Months would pass and still we were lively, happy friends in the daytime, while our nights were given to separate rooms, with only books for bed-fellows. Now, from being rare, it had become impossible for me to go to her room; the recoil was larger than the desire. I stayed where I was, put out the light, and slept.

Into this poor compromise our partnership settled. On the merry jesting level we were side by side or face to face; in the world of caresses and hunger we were in different countries.

Then Alethea. In that throbbing aeroplane, its engines sounding through the night, I saw her again as she was when we first met. A staff dinner for the chiefs of Palmer, Sands and Hume. I am there with 'Charlie'. Our art director, Bill Haven, whose wife is unwell, presents his daughter.

'This is my daughter, Alethea. She is so excited at coming instead of her mother.'

'Then she must always come. That's settled from now onward.'

'Oh no. . . .' A proper show of diffidence from Alethea.

'But oh yes. Most certainly. Bill, why have you never produced her before?'

'She's only a little over eighteen.'

'So much the better. We could do with a few younger ones.'

A dark head with (as it seemed to me that evening) a face of perfect features, and a beauty of tallness. The first sight of her shook me.

Oh, well; this is no story of her, for she had gone into the past now; no story of secret meetings in her single-room flat where she gave me all the love that any living man could desire—she eighteen, nineteen, twenty, I in my forties. She could have been a daughter—was there perhaps an incestuous sweetness in my rapturous love? I know I have never loved anyone as much as Alethea, and I dare to think, in spite of what happened—I shall think to the end—that she will never love anyone as she loved me. There was no difficulty in our meetings: as a student at the Art School where her father had studied, she had this flat, one of several, in a neighbouring Victorian mansion, where she could entertain whom she liked.

Three years of these stolen meetings but an end had to come. She could not stay the course, once Charlotte had discovered all and was suffering. She could not endure Charlotte's pain.

Nor I. Oh God, I remembered in that aeroplane an evening when I left home with the usual lying excuse about 'dinner at the club', and next morning learned how Charlotte, stricken and desperate, her old love for her husband having fired up again at the breath of a certainty, had followed me in the same train from Vintner's Cross to Marylebone, and from Marylebone along streets like a tailing detective to the house in Devonshire Place, there furtively waiting, sometimes half-hidden round a corner, poor lonely suffering creature, till Alethea and I had done with loving and I was bringing her out to find a taxi that we might go to the restaurant of our choice. At that time, as we walked on, Alethea was leaning against me and saying, 'So tall you are! I'm glad you're tall for me. I'm too tall.' And I: 'You're perfect.' Together we passed round a corner, and what was there then for Charlotte to do, my poor wounded 'Lots', but to wander back to the station and take the train home?

Some weeks after this, when I was dining with Alethea and had perhaps wined too well, I told her this story—and that began the end.

We parted on her threshold one winter night after a futile effort at a last happy evening together, with a dinner, a theatre, a supper and dancing at the Savoy, a hotel room and I fondling all her body and no more—she allowed no more and I asked no more; then, long after midnight, a walk home through empty streets to her threshold, many, many kisses, a 'Good-bye, Alethea, good-bye,' a silence from her, one last look at each other, she from her dark hall, I on her threshold, and a door closing.

We never met or spoke together again. Any letters or gifts I sent were returned unopened. She wanted the break to be as final as death: one terrible pain and then the road lying open to the mercy of a partial forgetfulness.

I made no attempt to walk along that road; rather would I wander of evenings from the offices of 'Palmer, Sands' in Fetter Lane to the corner of Cockspur Street, and the block of offices where, so I'd heard, she was now employed, in a hope that I might see the shape of her head at a window. Once I thought I saw it, bowed over a desk, and the thought was like a deathly pain. I hurried along Pall Mall to my club and there in its empty library I dropped my head on to my arm as it lay along the mantelshelf and gave myself to a spasm of tears.

Then, a year and more after our parting, and just when the pains of loss were becoming bearable, I encountered a girl in Piccadilly who'd been Alethea's friend and confidante in that Victorian mansion and she asked me quite carelessly—why should she suppose that a tall man over forty could suffer long?—she asked, 'Did you know that Alethea married a few weeks ago?'

'Married?' I showed her no sign of a heart's sickening fall. 'Really? And to whom?'

'The Honourable Rod McDonagh.' Was she so impressed with the courtesy title that she had to speak it? 'He's the son of the Earl of Islay.'

'Is he indeed? And how and where did she meet him?' You would have thought I had little more personal interest in all this than a reporter taking notes for a gossip column.

'They met on the boat coming back from France and he fell for her at once—'

'I can imagine he did.'

'—and he asked her to dinner and naturally she went and so it began.'

'You've met him, have you?'

'Oh yes, several times; he's a charmer.'

'Is he . . . young?'

'About a year older than she is. Twenty-three, perhaps.'

'Was she—' I asked the unbearable question—'was she in love with him?'

'Oh yes, I think so. You see, he's ever so sweet and absolutely adores her. Tall like you and reasonably good-looking too. And ever so generous. He gave her the most lovely engagement ring—all diamonds. It must have cost the earth. So he's really rather a Maiden's Prayer, in some ways.'

'Well, that's good,' I said with a smile. 'I hope they'll be very happy together'; and I went from her, middle-aged, forty-five, a Master Printer, and wanting to die.

I even walked homeward along Piccadilly, past the grandiose shops and the sauntering pedestrians, muttering idiotically, meaninglessly —but it was the only analgesic word anywhere, and a feeble word at that, 'Death . . . death . . . death.' That evening, walking on, I understood how younger men, all too often in their early unripeness, could kill themselves when they knew the loved one was lost forever.

Alethea. . . . So soon. So quickly. . . . I had heard it, I must accept it as true, but belief could only come limping hopelessly behind this truth. Alethea. . . .

So soon. If I must believe in the fact, need I believe in this new love? Need I ever? Ever? No, never, never believe in a fulness of love like that which she gave to me. This husband was second-best. Only second-best. But the entrance of this personable and decent young man had lifted my love and pain to all the heights they'd reached after we'd parted at her doorway. It was not a torment of jealousy but of loss. I felt no anger or hate against my supplanter, only against Fate or Life or Chance or my own Past—or whichever or how many of these—had made him my innocent supplanter—had put him into my lost bed there to—to—but I could never give this sentence its closing words; I shut them out; I ran from them.

And I had all the suffering lover's need to seek out more and worse of the pain. In the telephone directory I searched out their address, her home, their home together. Aldford Street, Mayfair, by the Park. And after office hours one evening I went secretly to spy it out—their numbered house in Aldford Street. After walking quickly past it, my eyes pretending not to look at its door, its curtains, its upper rooms, I loitered near the Grosvenor Chapel in South Audley Street to watch and watch her road. Evening: would she come out with him? My sense of completeness demanded that I suffered the worst, the climax and end of this story; my pain would be dissatisfied till I'd done this and seen them walking happily together. Over an hour I delayed by the chapel, watching, peering, spying; and suddenly I remembered that I was now suffering what my poor Charlotte had suffered when she spied on us from round a corner in Devonshire Place.

They did come out together. They walked away from me towards the Park, for the evening was fine. I watched till they were out of sight; then walked homeward down South Audley Street with my mouth shaking and grimacing as I, middle-aged, held the massing tears in check.

Never would I see Alethea again, I told myself then. I could not bear to. Never in any social gathering, if I could avoid it, would I meet her with her husband and possessor at her side.

§

Eighteen days later, and it was morning in our little village near Vintner's Cross. I was walking along its High Street which tilts up towards the square grey tower of its ancient church. The church's bells were sending their last few notes over the huddling roofs, for it wanted but one minute to eleven. I was not walking that way with a view to attending divine service. Not in fifteen years had I entered a church except for the wedding or funeral of a friend. And certainly there was nothing in that old church of what our villagers would have called 'high-church goings-on'; under its ageing vicar its services were the drabbest of the drab. And yet, as I looked up at the old square tower, and as the bells dwindled to a stop, leaving the Sabbath silence on the hill, there came upon me suddenly, unsought, unexpected, even unwanted, the consuming knowledge that if I could recover the pure essence of Christianity and could practise it, all these pains of self-seeking would fade away, and I would be able to say, 'May she be utterly happy with him, helped by forgetfulness of me.' Oh, it seemed very wonderful in that moment—the prospect of a life full of service for others and emptying slowly of self. It seemed to offer happiness instead of pain.

And of course the moment passed by, and I was my usual egoistic self again.

But within a week what should happen but Bishop Brakewaite, fine in apron, gaiters and cross, his long cigar in hand (an indulgence which was always there after lunch) walking into the Smoking-room of the club where I sat alone with my coffee, seating himself in one of the big leather chairs, leaning forward, and pouring out gaily, enthusiastically, with wavings of the cigar, his plan for a 'journey back to the springs of it all'.

'By which you mean exactly what and where?' I said.

'Oh, Jerusalem, Bethlehem, Capernaum, Galilee, a visit, a pilgrimage if you like, to them all.'

'Sounds splendid. But what exactly do you expect it to *do* to one's religion? Or lack of it?'

'Nothing much, perhaps. Something perhaps. I don't know. It must deepen the amazing fascination of the old story, if you walk where it all happened; and something might come of that. Who knows? Anyhow, everyone should see Jerusalem before he dies.' He was sitting beside me and slapped my knee. 'And you must come, my dear boy. You must come with us. Yes, yes. Don't tell me your firm can't function perfectly well without you.'

Now I might believe no more in miracles but in all my life I've never ceased to wonder whether odd things that happen, strange coincidences, oddly helpful words exactly apt to one's current state, read in a book or spoken in one's hearing, unforeseen but wonderfully fortunate meetings, may not perhaps be what believers in their God call 'guidance'. Could it be that God who refuses to reveal himself directly by miraculous 'signs from Heaven' yet works in these ways from behind a veil?

Gambling—why not?—that there might be 'guidance' here, I said, 'I might think of it.'

'You'll do more than think of it. You'll decide at once. Dammit, as your father-in-God and spiritual director I direct it. I prescribe it. Medicine for your soul.'

As he said this, the thought passed across my mind that, much as I liked him, with all his hearty goodwill, he was about the last person I should choose for my spiritual director; he seemed far too complacent about his creed and his character, as if both were little more than untroubled habits in him.

'Yes, yes,' he repeated. 'You're to come as a good pilgrim with us.'

I submitted that I was a sinner.

'So'm I. So'm I,' he declared enthusiastically. 'So are we all. But you're coming with us. I'm glad I've settled that. And, Jon—soft! A word with you.' He swung his eyes towards the closed door. 'Come to dinner with me here next Friday. In the Strangers' Room. D'you know who I've got coming?' On my shaking my head with a grin of ignorance, he mentioned two persons no less than the Leader of Her Majesty's Opposition and his Shadow Chancellor of the Exchequer. 'They know I'm not of their party but just one of the scattered remnants of the poor old Liberals, to whom I propose to remain loyal till the end of time—but no one, Tory or Lab, minds a Liberal these days; they rather like us; they feel a mild pity for us, and pity is akin to love. As a matter of fact, I intend to get a prominent Lib to come and meet them, so the talk may be fun. And I'll have a word with the Chef and see that he puts on something extra special in the food line. And I'll get Robby as well to dig out one or two of his more memorable wines. You will come, my dear fellow, won't you?'

Of course I said I would, and thanked him sincerely, even though I was thinking that his reputation for using his wealth to cultivate the great of the Earth was justified. The Leader of the Opposition was likely to be Prime Minister before many years had passed.

Had my good Bishop Brakewaite his eyes on an archiepiscopal throne? Or on one of the three great bishoprics, Winchester, Durham, and London?

'That's fine, Jon. That's magnificent. You come along and say something good about the Government just to annoy them and stir them up. Well, now I must go.' The great cigar went back into his mouth. 'Can I take you anywhere? I've got my car outside, and plenty of time. Run you anywhere you want. In reason. In reason.'

Yes, I'd seen his Austin Princess saloon waiting there with its uniformed chauffeur at the wheel and its coat of arms on the radiator.

I declined this invitation; he went with a gay wave of the cigar; and my dreaming in that aeroplane fell back upon Alethea.

It was after midnight, we were flying over the Dodecanese, so the cockpit told us, and must be nearing our destination. Night, and she would be in the arms of her young husband, twenty-three years younger than me. One must try to be glad if she was happy thus; glad if she got ecstasies now from the body of another; even able to bear that he should get an ecstasy out of hers. But not yet: even now, in this darkened and voiceless aeroplane, my body shivered and my heart sickened, as I thought of *that*; my heart was near to stopping with the pain of it; and the aeroplane went on. Still . . . one day, if not yet, I might achieve unselfishness enough to be glad, in my love of her, that he was becoming more and more to her while I faded more and more into a shadow, normally unremembered, unrecalled, till at last—

A hand touched my shoulder. 'Would you please fasten your seatbelt, sir. We're coming in to land.'

I must have been half asleep, for I'd seen nothing and heard nothing before this.

4

Over the Mountain

The Lebanon is a mountain. A sinuous mountain running parallel with the sea for a hundred miles. It is sometimes known simply as The Mountain. In one or two places, so close it comes to the sea, its feet seem to rise out of the waters of the Mediterranean; in other parts it recedes, to leave a ribbon of level and luxuriant earth. Here, watered by the mountain, flourish all the fruits of the earth: apples, peaches, citrons, almonds, figs, vines. Here, besides the fabled cities, Tyre, Sidon, Beirut and Tripolis, are orange groves and banana plantations and orchards of orange, lemon or lime trees. The figs and the trailed vines and the silver olive trees climb the mountain to about half its height; then come forest oaks, Alpine pines, junipers—and the famous cedars. The cedars of Lebanon that went to the making of Solomon's temple, the palaces of the Pharaohs, and those of the Great Kings in Persepolis. They are few now, and mainly to be seen among the snows that cap the summits, giving the Mountain its name of Lebanon, the White.

In the morning after our arrival at Beirut we set off in three Lebanese taxis to drive over the mountain and down into the valley of the Bk'aa. For there is Baalbek. And from Baalbek a way to Damascus.

I had gone to one car with Clem Oslow, having decided that I had more in common with him than with any other of our pilgrims, though I wouldn't have minded Prenders joining us with his curious, bewildering, but often learned, witty and fascinating talk. We were just about to board a car together when (oh, no! Was there no pity sitting in the clouds?) Maureen came up, bringing her most artificial smile, her head coyly to one side, and her Alexander held by the hand.

'Oh, may I come with *you*?' she said, beseechingly as it were; head on one side, girlishly.

'Why yes, if you'd like to,' I answered, producing a smile that was even more of an artefact than hers. I had no moral courage to say, or I could see no way of saying tactfully, 'Oh, please not, my good woman, I had a mind to talk sensibly with Mr. Oslow.'

'I would *so* like to,' she assured me, head still aslant, rather gracefully. 'I'm not awfully keen on going with Jimmy Hilder. It'd be much nicer with you.'

'Well then . . . please. . . .' No one more gallant. Holding open the door for her. Even bowing a little way.

'Alexander! Alexander, come here.' Alexander had flown from her hand and was in orbit somewhere. 'We're going with Mr. Palmer.'

'I want to sit by the window,' the child announced, as he returned after repeated summoning towards his launching pad.

'You'll sit exactly where you're told,' his mother announced on her part, and then turned again to me. 'May I sit by you, Mr. Palmer? There won't be room in front for both me and Alexander.'

This was untrue for these taxis were large American cars, and the driver's bench-seat could easily take a slim young woman and an awful little boy.

Clem, a kindly person, said immediately (to my dismay): 'That's all right, Mrs. Applebie. I'll sit in front.'

'Now that's sweet of you,' she told him. 'Then Alexander can sit in the back with me and Mr. Palmer.'

'But I want to sit by the window,' Alexander reaffirmed, that there might be no misunderstanding about it.

'Yes,' his mother agreed, 'you sit by the window, and I—'

'And you,' I provided, still gallant, 'shall have the other window.' Here was sacrifice indeed, because I had wanted to study the mountain's flora with Clem and, worse, it would put me next to Alexander.

'No, I'll sit in the middle,' she said. 'Between the two men.' Witty. And coy.

I had no doubt what had happened. I recalled her in the Airways Terminal, scanning the members of our party, with special attention to the men. Clearly she had been discriminating among the men, and I had guessed at once that for Maureen the next weeks were to be less a 'pilgrimage' than a 'tour' in which one 'got off' with one of the men for some days of dalliance. Here were five men: two bishops, Mr. Prender, Mr. Oslow and Mr. Palmer. The bishops were walled off from her by their clerical collars, those good white bulwarks; a pity because Freddy Parrett, of the Solomon Islands, was a young and attractive man. As for Bishop Brakewaite, he was protected not only by his collar but by a loud and lively wife. She was more than bulwarks; she was an army in occupation. Prenders was fifty and about as chilly and gusty as a February afternoon, so there were only Clem and myself, the nice Mr. Oslow and the nice Mr. Palmer. Of these I was the younger and Mr. Oslow, she had overheard, was a parish church councillor. Probably she had little idea what this implied but these three words suggested he might be less available than me. And therefore she had settled for the nice Mr. Palmer. I could well imagine her saying, 'I like a man in his forties.'

Well, nothing for it but to get into the car after her and Alexander, the boy having pushed in ahead of us to get the corner seat. And with us thus disposed—Maureen between me and her cub—the car set off. I had called her The Wandering Fragrance in the Bishop's drawing-room; she was now very much The Seated—or The Static —Fragrance, for the scent, whatever it was, commanded wide powers of radiation at this early and breezy hour of the morning. The mountain road was often contorted and I had no doubt that Maureen was pleased when the swinging of the car round a bend impressed her against me; nor that she hoped I was pleased with this too. She talked most of the way, and none of her talk was about the beauties of the mountain; rather it was about the reasons for her separation from Eric, her husband, and about her doubts what to do with Alexander, she being a woman alone (burn him, I thought). Once, dilating on her difficulties, she touched me on the knee with a finger, even letting the finger delay there while she elaborated a point. I would have liked to flick that finger away; instead, rather than hurt this unwanted woman, I discussed these tedious topics, leaving the finger *in situ*. In short I laboured for her comfort while wishing her, say, in the Solomon Islands. But how could the foolish woman know that it was only a few weeks since I'd learned that Alethea had married another, and that never was man less ready for dalliance, never a heart less free. Why, one of the bishops might have been easier country for a brief invasion.

Later, so helpfully was I responding to her talk, she laid the hand flat on the knee like a small but spreading pancake and left it there, beating a little time with its fingers, while she said, 'You're a wonderful person to talk to.'

'Oh, no,' I protested, not in reference to this tune on my knee but to this estimate of my talk.

'Yes, you are,' she insisted, this time squeezing my knee before she took the fingers away. (Surely, in taxis and other closed chambers travelling through the hours, it was usually the gentleman who was instructed at times to keep his hands to himself.)

I asked her if she was not excited to be visiting the shrines of three great religions.

'*Three?*' she repeated in surprise.

'Yes, Judaism, Christianity and Islam.'

This defeated her, as she admitted. 'I'm afraid religion means nothing to me,' she said, and patted me on the knee. 'I'm more interested in Lawrence of Arabia. He was in these parts, wasn't he?'

'In Damascus,' I agreed, with an inconspicuous sigh. 'Most emphatically in Damascus.'

At last I found a way which, while friendly and unhurtful, would yet bore her into silence. Glancing through the windows I pointed out all the flora on this tilted landscape, the umbrella pines, the myrtles, the planes, the azaleas that climbed with us half-way up to the pass; and then as we got higher the little Alpine flowers, the rock whitlow grass, the pearl-wort, the sand-spurrey. This was so successful in its purpose that I went further, giving her, when I could remember them, the Latin names. These bored her so that she went silent for a while and kept her hands to herself, folded on her lap.

Our fine American car took the pass in its stride, and now we were going down into the Bk'aa, an upland valley of reddish earth, with the true Mount Lebanon for one of its flanks and the Anti-Lebanon for the other. I was indeed excited now (though Maureen seemed quite unperturbed) because we were travelling quickly towards the mighty temple ruins of Baalbek; Baalbek, or 'Baal the lord of Bk'aa' and therefore a holy place in those times far beyond the sight of history when Baal first was lord of the Semites.

§

We were over the pass, but was the car still climbing? Yes, remembering my appropriate studies before we started on this safari into history, I realized that it must be climbing on to the ridge which was the watershed between the Litani and Orontes rivers. The Orontes! Even to Maureen I felt compelled to speak of the Orontes and, incidentally, to display before her and Clem some of my learning, without disclosing how recent it was.

'Are you aware, Mrs. Applebie—' I began.

'Oh, don't call me Mrs. Applebie. Call me Maureen.'

'Oh, well . . . yes . . . are you aware, Maureen, that we must now be near the head-waters of the Orontes?'

'The who?'

'The Orontes. Syria's most famous river.'

'Famous? Why famous?'

'Why?' I couldn't remember. So easily does recent learning retire into a mist or into the dark. Fortunately the answer came to me without too awkward an interval; and it came, full clad in excellent words. 'Because, like a mother, it created the famous city of Antioch. Antioch, "Queen of the East". They call it Antakieh now.'

'I'm afraid my geography is awful.'

For a second I was afraid this confession would induce an apologetic touching of my knee, so I hurried on, 'It was the old capital of Syria and figures often in the Bible. It—'

'I'm afraid I don't know the Bible really well.'

(I'll say you don't.) 'It was the scene of a first-class row between St. Paul and St. Peter, as to whether they could eat with the Gentiles. Paul says he withstood Peter to the face because he was to be blamed. It must have been quite an occasion.'

'Indeed?' said Maureen. Lifting her eyebrows in polite surprise rather than interest.

'Yes, the first anti-papal row,' Clem volunteered from his seat in front. And he added, 'Antioch was the site of some of the most famous ecclesiastical councils in the early days of the Church.'

I was grateful to Clem for this because I saw that some early Church councils would serve the same purpose as the flora of the mountain. They would quiet the lady with ancient history as a change from botany. It also provided me with a pleasing and amusing idea. 'If you want to know all about the early Church councils, Maureen, and a lot more valuable information, Prenders is your man. When we get out get hold of him. He's the great Orientalist.'

'Oh, I'm terrified of Mr. Prender.' Said girlishly, but without, thank God, any endorsing of this appealing humility by a sad little touch on my knee.

'Or try one of the Bishops.'

Bishop Parrett of the Solomon Islands, it came to me, was obviously the kindest of men and ever ready to take his share in 'bearing another's burdens'. And he, for sure, did she try on him, an attractive bachelor of forty, any of her coy seductions, would be well plated with the armour of his faith and, like St. Paul's Ephesians, able to withstand in the evil day and, having done all, to stand.

'Oh, he wouldn't want to be bothered with me.'

(Perhaps not, dear lady, but why should you imagine that I . . .? and so on.)

Only a little farther, and there beyond the fruit trees on the now well watered soil and among mean village buildings rose the incredible columns of the Baalbek temples, carrying high against a sky of middle-eastern blue their broken but magnificent entablatures, and shining, golden in the sun.

Maureen did get as far as a 'Golly!' No one is wholly dull.

When our car stopped, I got out and hoped to effect an escape with

44

Clem, for Alexander, having alighted last, was yelling 'Wait! Wait!' to his mother, as she sought to keep pace with us.

Pretending not to hear these distress signals, I accelerated my pace with every step.

'Come,' I encouraged Clem. 'This woman and Baalbek are an impossible mixture.'

'And not improved by a dash of Alexander,' he added.

I agreed there were pleasanter children. And together we walked towards the ruined temples, happily forgetful of Maureen and Alexander.

When I came nearer and really saw the Temple of Jupiter on its high stone platform, acres in extent, with its giant columns soaring into the sky so that people standing by the base of one of them looked no more than pygmies, and all around it the humble dwellings of the villagers, there hit me like a blow between the eyes the appalling might and ostentation of Imperial Rome as it advanced with pomp and power across the mountains of the East to the very fringes of the desert. I had seen the ruined forum in Rome but it could not stress for me, like these towering columns, the enormous contrast in scale between the exalted arrogance of Hellenistic Rome and the normal habits of men. Two hundred years, they said, it had taken the Graeco-Roman civilization to raise this temple, the most grandiose example of its architecture in the whole of the East; and one could believe it, because the Temple of Venus at its side appeared almost small, though larger than the Parthenon at Athens. And now—both of them stood among their own dust. And Baalbek, once a city of vast wealth and voluptuous splendour was but a lonely village among fallen columns and broken masonry.

How this village manifested yet again that contrast of scale: here was the life of the peasants lying permanent and unchanged beneath the marching and the falling of haughty empires which, proceeding one after another, left only the clutter and shreds of their passing to lie about the world. A little distance from the village on the dusty hill was the big black tent of a Bedouin family with their few black goats and their scrawny hens grazing or pecking in the scrub around. And so here beside the settled peasants, and near these tremendous

45

stones were the nomads, happy perhaps with their tents and flocks but the everlasting underlings of Time.

Last night I had been in an aeroplane cleaving through clouds and darkness; now the sky above these golden columns was a cloudless blue, and I imagined myself in an aeroplane seventeen centuries ago and looking down upon the magnificent city of Heliopolis, which was this Baalbek.

My aeroplane flew low that I might see in its fine streets the merchants from Tyre, Palmyra, Alexandra and Antioch with their camels and their caravans, the marching legionaries of the Roman garrison quartered here, the priests who served these amazing temples, some of the women dedicated to the licentious rites within, and, look, there in the vast colonnaded courtyard of the Great Temple, a crowd of worshippers like those which congregate today in the colonnaded Piazza di San Pietro, when the Pope, from the portico of his basilica, gives his Easter Benediction *urbi et orbi*.

§

Before we got back into the car I tried to do a deal with Clem that he should now sit in the back with Maureen and let her impress upon *his* knee the major points of her talk. But he said, 'Oh, no. She's chosen the better man. She's your girl,' and when I protested, 'Oh, but come! Fair shares,' he said, 'Not a bit of it. You've made a conquest there. I listened to all her advances and decided you were doing your part splendidly'; and he went on without mercy to talk of Bishop Parrett with whom he'd been walking while I strolled off to wander among the ruins.

He was full of admiration for our Spare Bishop but, as he talked, I thought that, while revealing the bishop's character, he was revealing more of his own.

'I'd give something to have a faith like his,' he said, 'or even one half as sure. You may laugh, Jon, but there's something in me that would really have liked to be a bit of a saint and to devote my life to others in disgusting circumstances, just as he's doing. I may be only an accountant, a mere sweeper in the courts of Mammon—' here spoke the poet in him—'but don't you think there's a buried

46

Franciscan in us all, believing in complete self-sacrifice and aching to go out and kiss the lepers?'

'In some,' I allowed. 'Not in all. Not in me. I'm afraid I'd be content with much less than that—just a full faith and enough strength to live up to it. I've no ache to kiss a leper.'

'Not sure I believe you. I'd rather bet the Franciscan's lying deep in you somewhere.'

'If so, he's much nearer the surface in you than in me, and since you feel so strongly about kissing lepers, why not take on Maureen and Alexander in the back of the cab? There you have the widow and the fatherless, waiting to be visited.'

'No, no; St. Francis is a lot deeper in me than that. A lot more inaccessible. You go on with your excellent work. You're doing splendidly. But just fancy, Jon, having a diocese lost in the Pacific, hundreds of thousand of square miles of it, and consisting mainly, I gather, of volcanic islands with a cathedral somewhere on a coral reef built up by long-legged coral polyps. Not only are all the islands steadily rising—which must be a bit unsettling, you'd have thought —but they're full of agues and alligators, and the Papuan Negroes who constitute his congregation have rings in their ears and noses and are still cannibals, some of them. So apparently he's come to terms with the *je suis mangé* aspect of things. Well, there it is, and as he told me all this I was thinking how I'd love to have had the guts to be a missionary bishop.'

One issue of all this warm enthusiasm for our young bishop's sanctity, was a growing certainty in me that he'd be of little use to Maureen.

§

Winding away from the crests of the Anti-Lebanon, down through gorges and ravines, travelling eastwardly towards the desert, there comes a stream not yet worthy the name of river. But it swells, fed by mountain springs, and by the time it meets with the main road to Damascus, which has come over the Mountain from Beirut, it is indeed a river, rapid and deep. Now it winds out of the foothills and creates around itself a fine circuit of orchards, gardens, vineyards, fields and poplars on what else would be parched and yellow desert. A large and luscious oasis this, and from its heart rise the slender minarets, the corpulent domes and all the towers and roofs of Damascus. Channelled in a hundred conduits this river brings coolness and beauty, and often the music of its waters, to the streets of this most famous city, which is its gift to the desert. For three thousand years it had been writing the turbulent history of Damascus on the parchment of the desert.

When it has done its business with Damascus, and left the city behind amid its paradise gardens it spends itself and is lost in a lake which in the scorching summer suns is no more than a morass. Thus after its one magnificent creation it dies on the desert's lap.

As it came into our view near the road Clem turned from his front seat in the car and said, 'The Barada.'

Barada is the river's name today. Long ago it had a different name.

Maureen had gone into a silence, made somnolent by seventy miles of mountain. Alexander had actually dropped off to sleep. So I was free to think my own thoughts, and Clem had hardly said 'Barada' before I remembered another voice. It was speaking nearly two thousand five hundred years before. 'Are not Abana and Pharpar, rivers of Damascus,' it was saying, 'better than all the waters of Israel? May I not wash in them and be clean?'

An attractive voice, I thought, from an attractive man, generous, courteous and magnanimous, if a trifle irascible: Naaman, commander-in-chief of the king's armies, his powerful favourite, and a very big noise in Damascus. But . . . a leper.

How these old Hebrews could tell a story, I said to myself in that sleepy car. What skill. Where in ancient scripts was there a story more delightfully told than this of Naaman and the 'little maid out of Israel' who waited on Naaman's wife—mightn't we say a kind of *au pair* girl? 'Would God' said the little maid in a chat with her mistress which one could almost hear after twenty-five centuries, 'would God that my lord were with the prophet that is in Samaria, for he would recover him of his leprosy.' And she speaks at length, one guesses, of her great prophet, Elisha.

Naturally Naaman's wife tells this to her husband, who thereupon comes with his horses and his chariot and a retinue of servants and gifts of silver and gold and garments, and stands at the door of Elisha's house. But Elisha, the austere man of God, sends only a servant to him with the message, 'Go wash in Jordan seven times, and thy flesh shall come again to thee.'

Jordan! *Jordan*, look you! 'What?' cries Naaman in some wrath, 'are not Abana and Pharpar, rivers of Damascus, better than all the waters of Israel?' And he goes off (though the Bible doesn't put it quite like this) in no end of a paddy.

But one of his retinue, obviously one of those sensible types who are impatient with melodramatics and spoil our pleasing wraths for us by pricking them with a simple pin, comes up and submits, 'My father, if the prophet had bid thee do some great thing, wouldst thou not have done it? How much rather then when he says "Wash and be clean".'

So Naaman, open to good sense (after a time) goes down and dips seven times in Jordan, and lo, his flesh comes again to him like the flesh of a little child.

Back, like the decent man he was, goes Naaman to Elisha and insists that he receives great gifts, but the stern and discomfiting man answers only, 'As the Lord liveth, before whom I stand, I will receive none.'

And Naaman, slightly incensed, no doubt, by such brusque treatment, he being a great man in Syria, 'departs a little way'.

Now enters Gehazi, Elisha's servant, who has seen and heard all. '*Vot?*' he thinks. 'My master lets this Syrian off, refusing all his gifts! As the Lord liveth, I will run after him and take somewhat off him.'

And he goes after Naaman's chariot, 'running', so well is the story told. The courteous Naaman, seeing or hearing him, stops his chariot, alights from it and asks, 'Is all well?'

'All is well,' says Gehazi, and, to be sure, it was looking well for him, as he spun a verbose account, probably with shrugs and gestures, of two young men, 'sons of the prophets', who had just come from Mount Ephraim and could perhaps be given, say, a talent of silver and two changes of garments. Not more.

49

'One talent? Take two,' says the munificent man. A nice fellow, this Naaman. He urges him to take these while Gehazi puts up a show of reluctance—with, I have no doubt, palms outspread and head on one side shaking—even as the two changes of garments for the sons of the prophets are produced and folded for him.

He takes the gifts home to his house and goes, the most innocent of servants, into the presence of his master.

And then the pay-off.

Elisha: 'Whence comest thou, Gehazi?'

Gehazi: 'Vot you mean?' Admirable indignation, no doubt, in Gehazi's eyes. 'Thy servant went no whither.'

Elisha: 'Went not my heart with thee when the man turned again from his chariot to meet thee? Is it a time to receive money and garments? The leprosy of Naaman shall cleave unto thee.'

And Gehazi went out from his presence a leper as white as snow.

What a story. What character, dialogue, and drama. And these waters of the Barada now running by the side of our road were once known as the river Abana.

Driven into this dreaming by the car's long journey, as I had been by the aeroplane's six-hour flight, I found my eyes engaged by the towers and gardens of Damascus which we were now approaching, and fell into a far different dream.

5

A Dream of Hebrew, Greek and Latin

IT was about noon, and somewhere near here, outside Damascus, a sudden blinding light, above the brightness of the sun, smote a young man named Paul and felled him to the ground. By that noonday light he was changed—and the whole world was changed. Near here.

Secretly I had come to these places from which sprang an enlightenment of the whole terrestrial globe in the hope, faint and probably fanciful, that I too might find some change, some renewal, some light to fill, or partly fill, the dim emptiness in my heart. A great light had shone for Paul of Tarsus; before our lively pilgrimage was over, would any illumination, however small, be vouchsafed to me?

They say our dreams in sleep seem to be long but in fact occupy only seconds. Maybe; I do not know; but certainly between a stretch of leafy road and our entry into Damascus only a minute or so later, I dreamed a dream which covered plenty, piercing deep into my memories and recalling much of my happy readings in the past.

In my years of bright faith St. Paul was my hero and my chosen patron saint—was not my name Jonathan *Paul* Palmer? More than my admiration for his world-shaking achievement, the spiritual and therefore far nobler counterpart of Alexander's or Caesar's conquests of the known world; not only because words written out of his great heart could nearly lift tears to my eyes—'It is meet for me to think of you all because I have you in my heart. . . . God is my record,

how greatly I long after you all in the bowels of Jesus Christ. . . .
Paul, an apostle of Jesus Christ, to Timothy, my dearly beloved
son . . . without ceasing I have remembrance of thee in my prayers,
night and day, greatly desiring to see thee . . . that I may be filled
with joy. . . . For love's sake I beseech thee, being such a one as Paul
the aged and now also a prisoner'—more than because of these, I
loved him for his frequent stumbling into weaknesses like my own,
a strong egotism, a quick temper, his small unconquerable resent-
ments, his compulsions to boast of his labours or his sufferings—so
often he stumbled thus but always with his conscience rebuking him
as he did so, and an apology following: 'Are they ministers of Christ
(I speak as a fool) I am more; in labours more abundant, in stripes
above measure, in prisons more frequent. . . . It is not expedient for
me doubtless to glory. I will come to visions and revelations of the
Lord.'

How one can love and forgive all these because of the great heart.

The dream began with a leap of words into my mind: 'Written in
Hebrew, Greek and Latin.' What had these to do with Paul? They
referred to the contemptuous title which Pilate caused to be nailed
on the cross—contemptuous of the Jews rather than of their victim
who hung beneath it. *Iesus Nazarenus Rex Iudaeorum*. Why had
these words appeared to me as I dreamed of St. Paul?

After a time I saw why. Here was a young man, small of stature,
'of bodily presence weak and his speech contemptible' (as he admits
himself, trying to glory in the weakness, but who knows?), a little
man handicapped throughout his life by some physical disability
that may have been epilepsy, 'the ugly little Jew' as Gibbon called
him, 'who turned the world upside down'—yes, but could he have
overturned the world if his whole substance had not been com-
pounded of Hebrew, Greek and Latin?

Hebrew. He was a Hebrew of the Hebrews: 'After the straitest
sect of our religion I lived a Pharisee'—do we ever consider the great
courage of his return from Damascus to come face to face with
Christian Jews whom he'd lately persecuted with threatenings and
slaughters?

Greek. I remembered his proud answer when the chief captain

arrested him outside the Temple because all Jerusalem was in an uproar against him. He asked, 'May I speak to you?' to which the captain answered, 'What, can you speak Greek?' And Paul in reply, bragging a little, 'I am a Jew of Tarsus in Cilicia, a citizen of no mean city.' No mean city? Indeed not. In the greatest hours of Greek history it was a famous city, and now, under the Roman emperors, it was a seat of learning on a level with Athens itself and Alexandria. When Paul was to speak at Athens on Mars Hill he would reveal his familiarity with Aratus and Cleanthes, philosophers of the Epicureans and the Stoics; to Titus he could quote Epimenides. To the Corinthians the poet and playwright, Menander.

Hebrew and Greek, then. How Latin? Again on the Temple stairs when the chief captain ordered him to be examined by scourging Paul turned proudly on him and demanded, 'Is it lawful to scourge a man that is a Roman and uncondemned?' Some panic in the centurion standing by, probably to supervise the binding of the prisoner to the whipping post. To the captain he says something like, 'For God's sake look out what you're doing, sir. This man is a Roman.' And the chief captain (who was having a surprising day) asks of his prisoner, 'Are you a Roman? It only was with a great sum that I obtained this freedom.' Proudly comes the answer, 'But I was free born.'

One of our best moments as we read the *Acts*.

A voice in the car. 'I suppose this is it, Mr. Palmer. We're there now. You're not saying much. You don't say anything.'

'I'm sorry, Maureen, but I was dreaming. A long journey in a car nearly always sends me into silence and a half sleep.'

'Me too.'

Thank God.

Hebrew, Greek and Latin. Jerusalem the spiritual capital of the world, Athens its intellectual capital, Rome its great material capital. And this young man, blinded by a light outside Damascus, was free of them all. It was in Rome, by all accounts, that he fell to martyrdom by the sword.

'Hebrew, Greek and Latin,' and, from Damascus onward, like that title, nailed to the cross of Christ.

'It is hard for thee to kick against the pricks.' What pricks? Could one doubt? Had he not come from standing by and watching the stoning of Stephen, first of all Christian martyrs, outside the walls of Jerusalem? The witnesses who according to the Deuteronomic Law must cast the first stones since they were responsible for the prisoner's condemnation had even, when they flung off their outer garments so as better to hurl their stones, laid these clothes at the feet of their young leader, Paul. And Paul stood watching the scene, he saw the staggering grandeur of Stephen's martyrdom, he heard as Stephen died under the stones his loud cry, 'Lord, lay not this sin to their charge' (Father, forgive them), and since in these words lay so much of the new teaching, I suddenly thought, there in my dream, that St. Stephen too, in another sense, laid his raiment at the feet of Paul. For never was Tertullian's word so true that 'the blood of the martyrs is the seed of the Church' as when the first martyr's blood stained the stones outside Jerusalem's wall, for it, in the heart of one watching, turned the world upside down. 'Lay not this sin to their charge'—these words, I thought, were pricking, pricking, pricking him as, like me today, he came near to Damascus, and they proved too much for that great heart. They broke it and made him ready for the light that blinded him.

In Tarsus this young man had learned a trade as all Jewish boys had to do, and it chanced that because the hair of the Cilician goats was particularly good for making canvas, he became a tentmaker. And on his missionary journeys over the whole Roman world he would, as he tells us (not without the faint bragging) ply this trade so as to earn his keep and be a charge on no one. Well, did he ever think, I wondered, as he plied his needle between preachings and travellings and writings (those letters must have taken a long time) that he was busy building a new tent, or tabernacle, for the whole world. For the horizon he had set for his message was nothing less than the rims of the known world. For him the Church of his Master was to be even more comprehensive and catholic than the empire of Rome.

That tent was in fair shape when in Rome the time came for him to lay his tools aside. For he was a prisoner now, chained to a Roman soldier night and day. He had perhaps made an impulsive mistake when, before Festus, a successor of Pilate as Procurator of Judaea, he claimed proudly, 'I have done nothing worthy of death and as a Roman citizen I appeal unto Caesar. I stand at Caesar's judgement seat where I ought to be judged.' Did not King Agrippa say afterwards to Festus when they were chatting together, 'This man done nothing worthy of death or bonds. He might have been set at liberty if he had not appealed unto Caesar.'

I knew well enough that there had been those who queried the authenticity of the Epistles to Timothy, *as they stand*, but even these questioners had allowed that large fragments of St. Paul's correspondence must be preserved in them. And was not all of this most lovable man present in his last words to Timothy, written from his prison in Rome: the affection, the dregs of his old egotism, the complete self-consecration, the sudden intolerances, the contrition, and the heart-breaking courage. The charge against him was one of 'endangering public order by inciting the Jews and fostering treason against the imperial cult', and it was probably on the eve of his adjourned appeal when he knew that judgement would go against him, that he wrote this last letter to Timothy, 'my own son in the faith'.

'I suffer even unto bonds, but the word of God is not bound.' Paul wrote his huge letters quickly, untidily and often obscurely, but Shakespeare does not surpass him when, in Erasmus's words, he is speaking pure flame. 'I am now ready to be offered, and the time of my departure is at hand. I have fought a good fight, I have finished my course, I have kept the faith. Do thy diligence to come shortly unto me. For Demas hath forsaken me, having loved this present world, and is departed unto Thessalonica, Crescens to Galatia, Titus unto Dalmatia. Only Luke is with me.' Luke, the beloved physician, as Paul called him; caring for Paul even in his chains, who can doubt?

'Take Mark and bring him with thee, for he is profitable to me for the ministry.' Here was full forgiveness, because he had been very angry with young Mark on an earlier occasion and would have nothing to do with him, because he'd turned back from Pamphylia, and not gone on with the task in hand. Paul had little use for anyone who turned back.

'The cloak that I left at Troas with Carpus, when thou comest, bring with thee—' was he cold in his prison?— 'and the books, but especially the parchments. Alexander the coppersmith did me much evil: the Lord reward him according to his works—' oh, dear! a lapse here into an unchristian vindictiveness, but the spirit of St. Stephen, who first won him, calls him home at the last. 'At my first answer no man stood with me, but all men forsook me; I pray God that it may not be laid to their charge.' Stephen's exact words.

Thus ran my thoughts on this road leading into Damascus, and with them went the old wish to believe again all, or much, of that which my late hero had lived, striven, and died for.

Rome, Athens, Jerusalem. At the hour of the Annunciation to Mary in Nazareth, Rome had conquered the known world and reduced it to order. Their roads were laid and made and, radiating from Rome, were ready for the feet of the messengers. The *pax Romana* brooded over the earth. The culture of Athens had spread over the Empire, and the Greek colonists had taken with them their language which was destined to be the vehicle in which the new thing should be given to the world. Lastly the Jews of the Dispersion had been scattered over the world that they might lay in every city the base on which Christianity could be built.

Everything was ready. And if all the great stories could be believed —and who would not wish them to be true?—it was as though Earth's greatest hours were striking, and first the heavens parted that Gabriel, spreading his wings, might sink to earth at the feet of the Nazarene girl; and that then, three or four decades later, the heavens broke again, here above Damascus, to release a great light, and in a new annunciation to commission a messenger. A messenger who largely combined in himself the Hebrew, the Greek and the Latin. A messenger who only ended his commission with his life, on the blade of an executioner's sword, as was the last right of a Roman citizen.

6

Mr. Prender
in Some Disgrace

I T was next day and twenty-four hours later, while our little party was strolling among the ruins of Jerash, so barely credible as to be like a dream, that I really began to assess my fellow pilgrims and assign them each to his or her compartment. We were walking and talking in a cluster around Bishop Brakewaite, and it was a series of extremely unfortunate comments by Prenders, and the responses of the ladies to these observations, which encouraged me to make these assignments.

This Jerash was nothing but an Arab village in a valley with a few strange tall columns standing erect and stark against the desert sky, when the excavators began to dig. They dug, and began to lift the ancient city of Gerasa from its grave where it had lain for a thousand years: a Graeco-Roman city with no less than three theatres, each seating thousands, two great Baths, a colonnaded highway leading to a column-ringed forum, a hippodrome, temples and a triumphal arch.

Much of this ruined splendour was already standing again, risen in loneliness from the dead, but as we walked and talked between the columns of the highway we could see that much more was yet to rise, for here and there, among the rounded hills of wind-blown dust that had buried the tumbled glories, the capital of a Corinthian column stood like the head of a human who'd been buried to his neck, or perhaps a part of a column's shaft was above the surface, and then it looked like a half-torso emerging from an earthy mound.

So here we were once again among the shreds of dead centuries and the debris of Rome.

The Bishop was doing most of the talking. He was telling us at length, and often in his fine pulpit voice, everything we ought to know about this 'long-dead city in a valley among the mountains of Gilead'. In parts he was truly eloquent and I suspected that cuttings from past sermons had got worked into his discourse. I thought I could identify the parts that came from old pulpit or platform utterance, because then his voice dropped for effect, as if he were reciting, and some of the original unction of the pulpit descended upon him. Pointing now to the circling columns of the forum at the end of this colonnaded street, he did not fail to speak of Time like an ever-rolling stream bearing all its sons away and to set against these deaths of cities and civilizations and religions the ever-enduring stillness of God. I expected the legs of Shelley's Ozymandias to appear at any moment standing trunkless in the desert, 'while the lone and level sands stretched far away'. But Ozymandias did not put in an appearance as yet. Later.

I thought that this picture of our good Bishop, happy to be the chief figure among a small congregation of admiring followers, and because happy, loving them, symbolized well enough the substance of him. It made a little picture of Satisfaction in Success, or of Peace in Conscience and Creed.

Just ahead of our group, though listening to all that was said, walked our Jimmy Hilder, springing as usual on her toes and swinging from one hand her shoulder-bag by its long strap. More than once I thought she looked like a thurifer swinging his censer before the Bishop's procession.

It was when the Bishop pointed to the really mighty columns of the Temple of Artemis and, saying that Artemis was worshipped here as the city's own goddess, asked, 'Where are the gods of yesterday?' that Prenders came in with the first of his extremely unfortunate remarks.

He said, 'Yes, and in a thousand years, or probably much less, where will be our gods of today?'

Promptly Lady Lampiter demanded, 'I hope you're not suggesting that our Christian God can go the same way as these heathen gods.'

'I am suggesting,' answered Prenders, not a man to be intimidated by any dowager 'precisely that'.

A gust of indignation from the Dowager. And from Hester Brakewaite. And Jimmy, springing along ahead.

These little gusts only blew up a dancing flame in Prenders. Palpably to rile the Dowager, and to a lesser degree Hester and Jimmy, he said, 'For my part, I've little doubt the time is not so far away when all our pomp of yesterday, St. Paul's Cathedral and all, will be one with Nineveh and Tyre. Just like this temple here.'

'Well, I think that's a dreadful thing to say,' declared the Dowager. 'In front of bishops too.'

Prenders, undisturbed by anything the lady thought, went on to quote Shelley (though not Ozymandias) for her further instruction. 'You may remember Shelley saying, "When London shall be—" '

'I've no interest in anything Shelley said. I never listen to anybody who attacks the Christian religion.'

'I can believe it. "When London shall be a habitation for bitterns, when St. Paul's and Westminster Abbey shall stand shapeless and nameless ruins in the midst of an unpeopled marsh, some Transatlantic commentator—" '

Lady Lampiter interrupted him. 'Shelley was an atheist,' she said, as though an atheist were an emissary of the Devil. 'I've no patience with these atheists and agnostics.'

'How regrettably unchristian of you.' This drew an astounded look from her but he only pursued, 'And worse: how profoundly unintelligent.'

Good! I thought. The old double for the Dowager. The old one-two. Left and right, on chin and nose. But if I thought Good! I also thought *God!* for what would happen now?

What happened at first was that Prenders went cheerfully on. 'And if Shelley was an atheist he had every right to be. If you believe in freedom of religion, as I suppose you do—or think you do—you must see that it necessarily involves freedom for irreligion. But I deny he was an atheist, even if he called himself one. I think he had a clearer sight of the essence of Christianity than half the popes in history.'

Here Hester put in a word, not at all sweetly uttered. 'Christianity can never perish. Christ said so.'

'And Zoroaster, Mohammed, Gautama, and Confucius have all said the same about their religions.'

'None of them happened to be God,' snapped the Dowager, as if reminding him of a fact he'd forgotten.

'And who knows that Christ was God?'

'I do for one.'

'Then you're fortunate. Considerably more than half the world has never for one moment, in two thousand years, believed him to be God.'

'Good God!' said the Dowager, appalled. That this was merely a statement of historic fact, didn't apparently lessen for her its blasphemy. She muttered, 'I call that blasphemous talk.'

'No, dear lady, it's not blasphemy to state a truth. It's more like blasphemy to suggest that it's wicked to think differently from you. That, I submit, is blasphemy against the free spirit of man. I'm not sure that it isn't the sin against the Holy Ghost.'

'Oh, I'm blasphemous, am I, because I refuse to tolerate talk against God.'

'Precisely, madam.'

An uncompromising bomb in the midst of one's powder magazine can deprive anyone of words; and only the Dowager's lips moved with impotent anger; it was Hester who said sullenly, 'I don't know where we're getting to, at this rate.'

'To the truth,' Prenders suggested.

But Jimmy, while still walking in front, turned a little way round and said, 'I quite agree with Mrs. Brakewaite. Quite. Either we believe our religion is God's word or we don't. I do. I emphatically do.'

It was noticeable that she kept her language restrained in the presence of Bishop and Dowager. No 'Like hell I do, bugger it,' or other jolly defiant shock for their ears. Rather did she now, un-consciously, swing her leather bag like a censer in our direction, as if we needed purification after defilement by Mr. Prender. Indeed, all through our journeyings I had observed that she liked to play jackal to these two big lions and only act the free, independent, slangy laywoman before lesser creatures like Clem and myself.

But Jimmy's censer didn't trouble Mr. Prender—or cleanse him. He merely proceeded, for the edification of us all, to quote Horace Walpole. If the Bishop had excerpts from sermons available, Prenders as a lecturer could summon much similar aid from past lectures. 'Remember Horace Walpole? "At last some curious traveller from Lima will visit our England and give a description of St. Paul's like those of Baalbek and Palmyra." And Macaulay. Don't forget Macaulay. "Some traveller from New Zealand shall, in the midst of a vast solitude, take his stand on a broken arch of London Bridge to sketch the ruins of St. Paul's".'

Here the Bishop, trying to say something apt, or to say something at any rate, introduced a quotation from *Paradise Lost*. Looking up at the double ranks of pillars through which we were passing, he said, 'It all reminds me of Milton's "With grave aspect he rose, and in his rising seemed a pillar of state, majestic though in ruin" ' whereupon Prenders instantly and unnecessarily and unhelpfully reminded him that this referred to Beelzebub; at which the Bishop laughed, 'Oh does it? I'd forgotten,' while Prenders must needs press on further with, 'Or there's Goldsmith. You remember: "The sorrowful traveller wanders over the awful ruins of others. Here stood their citadel, now grown over with weeds, there their senate house, but now the haunt of every noxious reptile. . . ."'

While he was talking Clem and I had come up behind the Dowager, whose anger had driven her several paces ahead of the blasphemer, and we overheard her impatient question to her daughter, Maureen, 'What's he saying now? What did he say, child, what did he say? Can't you tell me what he said? You know how deaf I am.'

'I didn't rightly hear,' Maureen answered, bored and dull.

'But of course you heard. Your hearing is excellent. Don't just put me off like that. I want to know.'

'I . . . didn't . . . rightly . . . hear,' Maureen repeated, enunciating

61

every word louder and more clearly, after this claim to deafness, 'because . . . I wasn't . . . interested.'

But even so Lady Lampiter didn't catch this explanation—not because of the deafness but because she seldom listened to anything she didn't want to hear, or when she wanted to speak herself. 'You may be deaf yourself one day. Then you'll understand what it is to miss what people are saying. He said something about London Bridge, didn't he?'

'I think he said St. Paul's would be nothing but ruins one day. Or very soon. Or something like that.' And, very ready to shovel the fuel on to her mother's indignation, she added, 'He was certainly arguing that Christianity would go the same way as everything the Romans believed.'

'What a wicked thing to say. In front of Alexander too.'

Since Alexander had long been dragging on his mother's hand to break free and study a train of camels padding along between the village and the river in the valley, I couldn't think Prenders' remarks had done much to deflower him. Meanwhile his grandmother was continuing, in the loud voice of the slightly deaf, so that we heard all, 'I thought we were a group of Christian people under the guidance of our dear Bishop. But now he tells me that this Mr. Palmer doubts half the things that are the very essence of our faith, and that Mr. Oslow half agrees with him. Where are we? Personally I've no sympathy with these half-hearted Christians. I have more respect for a whole-hogging atheist any day. What use are waverers to anyone? As for this awful Mr. Prender, I can't make him out at all. The Bishop says he used to be one of the most devout and dedicated Christians— and listen to him now! What's happened to him? What's *he* doing in our midst?'

Yes, what? Prenders had caught up with us two, and, aware of the indignation smouldering among the women, he asked in the most innocent way, 'But what did I say? What upset the silly cows?'

'It's arguable,' I suggested, 'that you served up some dishes very ill-suited to a company which includes two bishops and several saintly ladies.'

'Nonsense. One must treat people as adults, ready to listen to any

62

and every opinion. I intended it all as a bracer for the ladies—and for the old Dowager especially. Do the old relic good. A real tonic. She ought to be grateful to me for it.'

'Very few women are adult,' Clem averred. 'And not many men.'

'I've hardly yet begun to be,' I offered, as a contribution to peace and goodwill, while Clem continued, 'She probably agrees with St. Louis of France who once said that a layman should only argue with an unbeliever by driving his sword into his bowels as far as it would go.'

'And those are your Christian saints!' Prenders spluttered the words. ' "Saintly women"! My hat! God, I could have given 'em much stronger medicine. I could have quoted W. K. Clifford's remark that Christian beliefs were the slender remnant of a system that had left its red mark on history and still endured to threaten mankind. That'd have shaken the Lampiter and the other saints. Or there was Miall, a pious congregationalist, on Lady Lampiter's beloved C. of E.: "The whole thing is a stupendous money scheme carried on under false pretences; a bundle of vested rights stamped with the sacred name of Christianity." I think I'll quote them that at the first opportunity. Do 'em good. Make 'em think.'

'Please don't,' I begged.

'Well . . . I don't know . . . People ought to be helped to grow up at about sixty.'

There we left it, and it was in the ensuing silence that I placed the members of our company into their various pigeon-holes. Five I imagined were quite untroubled in their faith, and thus could all be put into the same pigeon-hole: the two bishops and three of the women, Hester, Lady Lampiter, and Millicent Hilder, who, by the way, had now become for me, with my taste for easy and pleasant enshrining titles, The Springing Jimmy. A separate hole would be needed for Clem and me who were well and truly troubled but both hungry for a faith that was calm and wide; and yet another for Maureen who had no interest in religion at all. Alexander, I felt, could go in with his mother for he clearly had no great interest in it either. As for Prenders, an assertive and aggressive unbeliever, he seemed

to require, not so much a different pigeon-hole as a distant cupboard
to himself.

§

'Come, children,' said the Bishop in the happiest of moods, pleased
to be loving us all and leading us. '*En voiture.*' We had reached the
end of the long columned street where it debouched into the circular
Forum and were looking down at its heavy paving blocks which still
bore the marks of chariot wheels. 'We've a long way to go. Sixty
miles to Jericho. Get into your chariots.'

'Jericho!' exclaimed Jimmy Hilder, springing up and down with
enthusiasm.

'Yes, Jimmy, as far as I'm concerned you can go to Jericho—ha,
ha—' the *ha, ha* added lest she should misunderstand.

She didn't. She just said, '*Oh, Bishop!*' in coy reproach and with
an extra spring to show that she was jolly too.

'We go down and down, and down and down, all the way,' the
Bishop continued, joyously informative. 'We're on mountainous
heights here, several thousand feet, and we go down to the lowest
place on the surface of the earth.'

'What? Where?' Jimmy in her excited interest leaned her head
forward with its mouth slightly open as if like a fish she was eager to
snap at and engorge the appetizing news.

'The Dead Sea. There's nothing else on the earth's face like the
rift through which the Jordan runs to the Dead Sea. It runs down and
down, working its way through the world's deepest canyon. It's
already about seven hundred feet below sea-level at the Lake of
Galilee—that's right isn't it, Freddy?'— this to Bishop Parrett of the
Solomon Islands—'and it reaches more than twice that depth when
it empties into the Dead Sea.'

'Right enough,' said Solomon Islands. 'Thirteen hundred feet
down at the Dead Sea. The lowest spot in the world.'

'The Dead Sea!' Jimmy clasped excited hands in front of her
breast as she might have done in her high-school days if told that she
was going to meet Rudolph Valentino or Douglas Fairbanks. 'The
Dead Sea!'

'Yes, so come on, all,' enjoined the Bishop. 'To the lowest place on earth. But geographically only, my dear Jimmy. Not morally.'

'Oh, *Bishop*!' Reproach. As though one should say, 'Naughty! Naughty!'

'And then—after the Dead Sea—Jerusalem. Jerusalem the Golden, the place where we really want to be.'

' "With milk and honey blest",' offered Jimmy.

But here Prenders must intervene with one of his unhelpful comments, which was inconsiderate of him, I thought, when the Bishop—and Jimmy—were in such good spirits. He said, 'Milk and honey! The odd thing about the sacred River Jordan, in which the best people like to be baptized, is that its waters are peculiarly turbid and foul. Coming all that way down that ghastly deep crack, which is hotter than hell, they bring all sorts of filth and poisonous stuff to deposit in the Dead Sea. And the water in Jerusalem, Jimmy, is pretty unfit for drinking.' Prenders was short, broad, with thick dark hair, and, truly, in this unfortunate moment, I thought of him as an earthy Sancho Panza among all us quixotic dreamers.

The Bishop after a disconcerted look at him tried to restore the general gaiety of all, which his contribution had depressed, by saying jovially, if not wittily, 'Well, come along to the Dead Sea, fouled or not, all of you. From a dead city to a dead sea.'

And Prenders, a little apologetic for his unsavoury contribution, admitted, 'The wines are quite good and the beer. And there's always Evian or Pepsi-Cola.'

'Yes, always Pepsi-Cola,' said the Bishop hurriedly and cheerfully, for the sake of all. 'Now come.'

We got into the cars again. I had intended to do a leap into a front seat next the driver so that Clem would have to share a bench with Maureen and her brat, but Clem, for all his talk of a buried Franciscan within him, had the same scheme and achieved it before me with a wink. So I was back with Maureen and Alexander, he seated between us this time.

I prayed she wouldn't talk at once because I wanted to look my last on this amazing, absorbing Jerash or Gerasa, and think my last thoughts about it. As we drew away I looked through the car's back window at those chains of broken columns looking like a dead city's cold and bony skeleton standing erect in a desert place. And remembering Prenders' quotations from Shelley and Macaulay I wondered with them if in some future century the cold skeleton of London would stand like this, with little but desert around it. And travellers come to it for a morning's excitement.

Then Jerash was behind us and we were on a road that wound over or around, but chiefly down and down between empty butter-coloured hills or high grey rocks crowding together like sheep. It crossed the River Jabbok, fringed with oleanders since the ground here in spring-time was watered and fertile. This was the place where Jacob wrestled with an angel till the breaking of the day—'I will not let thee go except thou bless me—' a good precedent, perhaps, for some of us on this pilgrimage. When we passed the 'ford Jabbok', shepherds were thigh-deep in the stream between the oleanders, washing the sheep-skins and spreading them out on the banks to dry in a hot sun.

The Jabbok behind us, Clem turned round from that unworthy front seat and talked across Alexander to me in my corner. He talked about the things he believed and those he didn't believe—talk which must have made little appeal to Alexander, caught between us, and hardly more to Maureen on our flank. 'My hero and saint,' I remember his saying, 'has always been Erasmus, just as his hero was Socrates. What's so sad, Jon, is that, for a few years at the beginning of the sixteenth century the beautiful humaneness and tolerance and liberalism of Erasmus looked like winning the world, but Luther laid waste all that, and his hour has never come again. Nor, four hundred years later, does it look like coming. Less so than ever, I sometimes think. Still, just as he used to say, "St. Socrates, pray for us", so I say "St. Erasmus, pray for us." ' And what all this imported to Alexander—or Maureen—I can't imagine.

Driving rapidly on, we passed many a Bedouin astride his loaded donkey, and our Arab driver, a merry fellow who had no objection to repeating his jokes, pointed each time to the donkey, looking so small beneath its burden of man and cargo, and said only, 'Jordan's jeep.'

Sometimes when we topped a hill we could see, violet in the distance, the hills of the Syrian desert which rolled for hundreds of miles towards Euphrates and Tigris, a desert shut away from the sea by the fertile corridor of Lebanon and Israel. Then, as plunging ever deeper and deeper through clefts and chasms, we got nearer and nearer to the land that had once been Canaan and Judah I found myself thinking how strange it was that the little land of Judah, lying in the midst of that stormy corridor, a marching ground and battleground of far greater nations, should have held the future in its hands. Judah in its first days was little but a tribal encampment with a tribal god, and yet what happened as the years went by? This, that nothing written by its neighbouring Syrians, Assyrians, Phoenicians, Egyptians, has survived to trouble anyone's memory, while words written in that small, erring, often tortured kingdom still shake and shape the world. Job, Isaiah, the 'Second Isaiah', and the grandest of the Psalmists, still trouble and uplift the best of our human stock because they reached to spiritual heights unsurpassed in all centuries since.

We went on, down and down, towards the Dead Sea pit and the homeland of these Hebrews on its farther side.

7

Qumran

IF I was to learn nothing else on this pilgrimage I soon learned that Clem had far more charity than I had, and that I would do well to copy him. When we had been returning to our car, and despite his ignoble leap into the front seat afterwards, he had spoken charitably about my Springing Jimmy when I was making fun of her. He had talked about 'a fine determined courage in her resolute joviality and not least in her bar-parlour language', and when I objected, 'But Clem! That awful springing walk! It destroys me', he had called it 'a fine defiant marching through the world'. He had dealt most understandingly with her 'escape from lonely spinsterhood, and from that long nose and long thin figure, into Church work'. She was, he said, one of those restlessly active 'back-room girls' who were half the strength of the Church—never missing a meeting of the Church Council, ever available to the Vicar for work in the G.F.S. or the C. of E.'s Children's Society, or the Sunday School, where, no doubt, she taught the poor kids Heaven knew how many heresies. She was a hot Tory at election times, dashing from committee room to committee room, but never talked politics at any other time because her main and almost sole interest was in Church affairs. 'She forgets she's a Tory till an election comes along and then she's invaluable to the local association. You'd never believe the labours she's capable of then. Her little basement flat is almost a committee room.'

After he'd given me this outline study of Jimmy Hilder I was almost prepared to love the girl, as I imagined her at church bazaars, parish parties, and election meetings, springing about all over the place, nobly.

And now, back in the car, Clem displayed a like charity towards the brat, Alexander.

Almost as if he liked the cub.

Both our bishops had insisted that before leaving the Dead Sea we must visit the caves at Qumran where the Dead Sea scrolls had been discovered. But as our car went down and down, and round and round the mountain corners Alexander announced that he was going to be sick. And he was sitting next to me. And who knew what would materialize? I drew closer to my window and suggested, pretending solicitude, that he also should sit by a window. 'On your other side,' I said to his mother. In short, like the priest and the Levite, I chose to pass by on the other side.

But Clem turned round from that ignoble front seat and, like the Samaritan, comforted the boy, even healing his dangerous condition, by telling him with wonderful skill, making it an exciting story for a boy, the fantastic tale of the discovery of the Scrolls. He had studied it all before coming out East, and he made such a bedtime tale of it, that Alexander listened open-eyed, and at times open-mouthed, and forgot to be sick. I too was captivated. And Maureen hardly less.

'It ought to be exactly your cup of tea, Alexander,' he said, 'because it's the story of a treasure-hunt, quite the most famous for many a year, and all started by a boy; an Arab boy. It's better than Aladdin, better than Ali Baba, better than *Treasure Island*. Listen, Alexander. One summer day, and only a few years ago, Muhammad, a little goat-herd, was pasturing his flock among such scrub as they could find in the wilderness by the side of the Dead Sea. And suddenly he saw he'd lost one of his goats. Now it's certain he'd never read the New Testament but he did exactly what Christ said any good shepherd would do: he left the ninety-and-nine goats safely feeding and went after that which was lost. He came to a big cliff and was surprised to see a big black hole in it like an entrance to a cave. The hole was too high and difficult to reach, so he did what any boy would do, he aimed a stone through it. He was a good shot and the stone went nicely through the hole. And what do you think? There was a noise like a stone crashing on pottery. Funny! Extremely odd! So, as you can bet, he threw another stone, and again that sound of a crashing or cracking among pottery. He pulled himself up and looked into the darkness of the cave. He couldn't hold himself there long, but he was there long enough to see tall earthenware jars arranged in rows.

'Next day he told all this to a boy friend who, being older, declared it was "all my eye", but went back with him to the place, nonetheless. Together they climbed up and into the cave, and—not a doubt of it—there were the rows of tall, pinkish jars. They looked into them and saw what looked like useless rags and bundles of brown leather. They took one of these strange messy bundles home to their Bedouin camp and when they unrolled it—good heavens!—it stretched the whole width of a wide black Bedouin tent. They didn't know that this was a manuscript of the Book of Isaiah, a thousand years older than any other manuscript so far found, and that the news of its discovery would set the world alight.'

Alexander's eyes were alight.

'Soon all the papers in the world were describing this and the finding of other fragments as the greatest archaeological discovery ever made in the ancient East, which as you've already seen, my dear Alexander, is simply littered with history. And now, as you can also imagine, all the Bedouin fathers, leaving their women and boys to pasture their flocks, set about pasturing themselves far more profitably by ransacking every cave near-by and finding more and more of these fragmentary scrolls, which were now literally and exactly worth their weight in gold. Literally and exactly, Alexander, because people were paying for them a pound per square half-inch.'

'But how did the scrolls get into the caves?' Alexander asked, which I thought was intelligent of him.

'Well, just near all these caves you'll find the ruins of a monastery where a stern religious sect called Essenes had made their home in the Dead Sea wilderness that they might prepare themselves there to be among the Elect in the great and terrible Day of the Lord. This they expected soon, a Day of Visitation when all the world should be purged, the dominion of Belial come to an end, and the Saints reign in power and glory—'

'Dominion of who?' asked Maureen.

'Belial. The Prince of Darkness who's got hold of us now. As you must feel. Well, the great and terrible day came in a fashion they didn't suspect—the sacking of Jerusalem and its razing to the ground by the Roman Emperor Titus in A.D. 70. It seems likely the Essenes saw what was coming, hid their library of scrolls in caves, and ran, hoping, no doubt, to return to them. But they never did, Alexander. Their monastery was used as a barracks by the Roman Legions, since it was a good strategic position commanding the desert and the Dead Sea. Later, perhaps with the same idea, it was used by Jews in revolt. But neither Roman Legions nor rebellious Jews ever knew what was in the caves behind them. Nor did anybody till little Muhammad, nearly two thousand years later, uncovered the secret. The Romans left, the Jews left, and the desert swept in again to occupy the monastery and make it part and parcel of itself. While the scrolls, comfortably clothed in their earthen jars, just slept at peace in their caves.'

'Thank you, Clem,' I said. 'You're a poet.'

And 'There's a nice story, Alexander,' said Maureen.

§

After this it was exciting to see that we were at the junction of the Jericho and the Dead Sea roads. There was excitement too in the bishops' car, it seemed, for Brakewaite stopped our caravan and, visiting the drivers, instructed them to go first to Qumran. Qumran was only a few miles distant, and all our eyes were at the windows when our driver with a grin said, 'Khirbet Qumran', as if it was one of the more humorous incidents in our journey, and we saw before us heat-parched hills, cracked and crumbled and rain-combed. By the car's bumping we knew that the good tarmac road had yielded to a rough track of stones. The car stopped and I saw with one of the great thrills of my life that it had stopped right against a rough stone wall of the ruined monastery.

We got out, looked around, and knew that we were really standing in the 'waste howling wilderness' of Judaea.

In the car a draught had cooled us a little, but now we stood beneath the dead weight of the sun in our Earth's only basin thirteen-hundred feet below the sea. Yonder was the flat and vast grey shield of the Dead Sea, still and silent as death and backed by the high grey mountains of Moab, its spread of water giving off no coolness for us but rather a heat like that from an oven door. We could understand in this moment that its fifty-mile expanse of salted water has no outlet, and needs no outlet, except upwards as invisible vapour into the broiling sun.

But my eyes did not stay on the Dead Sea, for I saw across a dry and sinister little wady, its sides a pale and dank unwholesome green, three salt-whitened and rounded headlands, stratified and striated, with black holes in them looking like entrances to caves. And the one on the left, the Bishop told us, was the most famous cave of all where the findings had been so many and wonderful as to disable belief.

I was so enchanted and lured by it all that I wandered off alone, forgetting the existence of Clem and Maureen and Alexander. I had got myself on to a level plateau above those white rounded capes with the idea of looking through some of the black holes into dark caves beneath. At one place, walking on a low hillock like a white cap crowning one of the headlands, I was staring up at a dark cave entrance above me, with my mind two thousand years in the past, when I stumbled heavily over an unobserved obstacle as high as my shins. Because I am so tall it was out of my view. But it clearly belonged to the present day, for it yelled loudly and proved to be Alexander crawling out of a hole on hands and knees. Had he been a foot or two nearer the cliff's edge my collision with him might have shot him, rolling and hurtling, for some hundred feet down into that grim little wady.

I snatched at him and held him tightly. In talk with his mother I might have thought that it would be a good idea to burn him, but now I was distressed at having so nearly killed him.

'Oh, my dearest boy!' I said (and fancy calling him that, but then I *had* nearly killed him). 'I'm so sorry. I never saw you.'

'I was coming out of the hole,' he explained unnecessarily, adding with more justification, 'You hurt me' and rubbing arm and shoulder.

All of him from face to foot was whiter than any miller with the parched and powdery dust. And all of his face was making it clear that he didn't at all appreciate being fallen over.

'I had no idea you were in that—' but then of course the truth broke upon me: he was in that hole because, like the Bedouins, he wanted to find scroll fragments and sell them at a pound per square half-inch.

His mother had now rushed towards us and was holding him upright and brushing him down. Clouds of salt-white dust came smoking off him. Sweating in his eagerness to find a scroll, he had turned the dust on his temples into clay. His sun hat which had impeded a satisfying search in this hole he held crumpled in his hand.

'I'm so sorry,' I said again to her. 'But I really had no idea he was going to issue from a mountain.' Trying to laugh things off, I added, 'I was looking up and he was a long way down. And he's so small.'

'And you're too big,' said the boy, rudely.

Intolerable little beast, I thought at first, but then, with a beginning of Clem's charity, wondered why, if it wasn't rude for an adult to call a child 'so small', it was damnably rude of a child to call an adult 'too big'.

'I didn't know he was anywhere near, and it was an unavoidable collision,' I offered in further apology. 'But I do hope I haven't hurt him.'

'Not at all; he's—' Upon my soul I still think she was about to say 'Not at all; he's pleased,' but one look at perhaps the sulkiest face a desert has ever seen, showed her that this would be impossible today, and she altered it to 'Not at all; he's perfectly all right.'

Hearing this, the boy pulled himself violently away from her and rubbed his elbow as a demonstration that she lied.

'What were you doing in that hole anyway?' she asked of him, and since he was obviously in no mood to answer anyone, I provided the solution. 'He was looking for scrolls. Very sensibly. He was hoping to find a fortune. But I'm afraid I did crash into him rather heavily. It was rotten luck for him.'

'Not at all; he quite understands,' she said, drawing him back to continue cleaning him.

Never was there a face less disposed to understand. Which was of some comfort to me because I could now feel less charitable towards an unforgiving little pig. And I thought it would do him no harm to learn that he'd been engaged in crime.

'I suppose you know,' I said, feigning a smile, 'that if you'd found even a fragment of a scroll and kept it, you'd have been committing a serious crime.'

'Why?' he demanded impatiently, as if nothing could be more unreasonable.

'Because any and all archaeological findings are by law the sole property of the Government.'

'But the Bedouins did it,' he said very truly. 'And made thousands of pounds.'

'Certainly they did—unhappily—but the Jordan Government has all that properly in hand now.' I wasn't at all sure that this was the truth, but I thought it good for an erring boy to think so. 'No one must do it now. On pain of the-Lord-knows-what.'

'Would they be put in prison if caught?'

'Oh, yes,' I said cheerfully. 'Even if they were only caught *trying* to do it. And for all I know, in this primitive country of Jordan the punishment for trying to commit a felony is death. Probably a hanging in public as an example to others.'

'*Death?*' The child's face showed such alarm that I had to pat him comfortingly on the shoulder and say, 'Well, you needn't worry, Alexander. You haven't been caught and can still stay alive. We won't tell. And anyhow it's possible I was exaggerating a little.'

'Mr. Palmer was being funny,' explained Maureen, to soothe him. 'He likes a joke.'

That underlip of Alexander's showed plainly that he was not amused. And, really, I saw no reason why he should be.

So much for Alexander. As for Maureen, I began to think that with her readiness always to forgive me and her instant desire for my peace of mind ('Not at all; he's pleased') and her motherly soothing of Alexander, I had been doing her less than justice. Clem's charity towards all was rebuking me again.

§

Thinking of Clem and our long talks together, about his inadequate faith or my lost faith, I turned to look again, before we got back into the cars, at the heaving empty wilderness which stretched through the sun's glare, over arid humps, shreds of wiry scrub, hot gritty desert floors and salted flats to the great, still, silent surface of the Dead Sea. Beyond, high in the eastern skies, loomed grey ghostly shadows, the mountains of Moab.

One's heart with a church one had loved, and one's head in a wilderness.

8

The Name of Names

JUST where the road from Jericho to Jerusalem, not far from Bethany, swings round the southern shoulder of the Mount of Olives, the bishops' car which was in front stopped us all again, and Hester came to our doors and asked us to come to her husband for a general parley. We all got out and joined the bishops at the door of their car.

'Listen, everybody,' said Bishop Brakewaite, 'Freddy has an idea.' (Freddy? Oh, yes, of course: Freddy Parrett of the Solomon Islands, the spare bishop.) 'Freddy's idea—and it ought to have occurred to me too, but he's a much better man than I am—I had fully intended to stay comfortably in my car—but his idea is this. When the road turns the next corner, you will have your first sight of Jerusalem—of the Old City, I mean—the Holy City. I think none of us except myself and old Prenders have seen it before, and I'm sure you'll agree with Freddy that this will be too tremendous a moment to be spent in a hurrying car. These boys—' he winked at the Arab driver of his car—'like to go at ninety miles an hour and wake the dead with their horns. So Freddy suggests that we all walk to the point where the great vision is granted us.'

'Oh, yes!' said all. Jimmy sprang up and down in an excess of agreement. 'Jerusalem! Jerusalem!' she cried and clasped her hands before her breast (as she had done when given the prospect of seeing the Dead Sea). She held them there till the agitation was at rest.

'And further, children, since it's only a mile or so down the road

76

and up to St. Stephen's gate where we enter the city, I suggest we go on foot all the rest of the way—you are all young.'

Suitable laughter from the Dowager and Hester. Loud from the Dowager.

'The road goes down under the Mount of Olives and passes the garden of Gethsemane. I'm sure you'd rather walk on foot over such holy ground.'

Here all said, 'Yes' softly or just nodded, and the Bishop proceeded, 'Yes, we'll go through St. Stephen's Gate on foot. You'll remember how General Allenby after capturing Jerusalem, refused to ride into a city where our Lord had walked on foot.'

Those of us who remembered this nodded, Jimmy repeated, 'Oh, *Jerusalem*!', and he just said with a light laugh, 'Well, come along then, my dears. "Happy band of pilgrims If onward ye will tread...." Literal words for once. Follow me.'

And we all walked on to the corner of the white road. Quietly.

The two bishops led. As ever, the women segregated themselves, Hester and the Dowager talking so incessantly that it seemed they had not stopped their gossip since they started it at the Air Terminal four days ago. Maureen was being dragged along by Alexander who, to my surprise and to his credit, had been inspired by the Bishop's words. Or, at any rate, he wanted to see a Holy City. Thus I, though in fact as excited as he, was able to walk towards the great moment with Prenders and Clem.

Jerusalem. Name of names. Jerusalem and Rome, the two greatest names under heaven, and was not Jerusalem the greater? Both had conquered the world in their different ways but Jerusalem still held its conquest, for what was the Vatican City but Jerusalem sitting enthroned on the seat of the Caesars in Rome? There was a third mighty name, as I had remembered on the road to Damascus: Athens. Athens whose intellectual conquest of the world Rome, its happy captive, had carried and distributed over the whole Hellenistic empire. Jerusalem, Athens, Rome. 'This title then read many of the Jews, for the place where Jesus was crucified was nigh to the city, and it was written in Hebrew and Greek and Latin. Then said the chief priests to Pilate, "Write not The King of the Jews, but that he said, I am King of the Jews." Pilate answered, "What I have written I have written." '

True enough, and he had written more than he knew.

So far from hurrying my pace like Alexander, I found myself wanting to go slower so as not to arrive at the great vision too soon and unprepared.

But . . . here it was. We had come to it, an ancient city across the Valley of the Kidron, its long square crenellated walls cream-coloured and a dulled yellow, but washed now in the evening light with rose and apricot tints. And behind the battlemented walls the Golden Dome of the Rock, the domes of the Holy Sepulchre, and the minarets and towers. With a splendour of evening sky about it all.

We stood still. And there was silence among us. I was glad that silence possessed us. In my thoughts there was a kind of glowing wordlessness, for there are moments in life that have an exaltation above the reach of words.

Jerusalem. . . .

As we walked down the road under the Mount of Olives with the dusty, steep, untidy Valley of the Kidron between us and the long city wall, we lapsed back into talk, but not easily, rather quietly, as if that silence had not yet done with us. I looked often down into that haunted valley. Bestrewn with listing tombs it was otherwise empty except for some terraced olives struggling for life in the white stony soil, a ribbon of vines on its flanks, a black Bedouin tent at one end of it, and much litter in its dry stream-bed. I was still walking with Prenders and Clem, and after a while, as we got farther down the road, and away from that silence, Prenders became fluent and was particularly good on the Valley of Jehoshaphat as he called this Valley of the Brook Kidron.

So ardent a theologian as I had been in my youth still knew parts of the Bible well, and words were running in my thoughts, 'When Jesus had spoken these words he went forth with his disciples over the Brook Cedron where was a garden into which he entered with his disciples.' I could see the olive trees and cypresses of the garden a few hundred yards ahead of us. Gethsemane. But my thoughts went further back; back a thousand years before Gethsemane's pain. I saw

King David, after that heart-shattering revolt of his beloved son Absalom, crossing the Brook Kidron with all his loyal and loving followers that he might quit the city and go over Olivet into the desert. 'And all the country wept with a loud voice, and all the people passed over; the King also himself passed over the Brook Kidron, and all the people passed over towards the way of the wilderness.' Here was Olivet and I could see the King climbing it with his head covered, and all his good loyal people covering every man his head too, in their great sympathy. 'And they went up weeping as they went up.'

But Prenders dispersed all these memories by calling it, not the Kidron Valley but the Valley of Jehoshaphat. Neither Clem nor I was wise to this title, and he poured out before us his exposition. He was in his top form.

The traditional Valley of Jehoshaphat, this deep and tumbling depression into which we were looking, was to be, he said, the place of the Last Judgement, so it should have its personal interest for us. God would need a deep valley for the Judgement of all the nations, and the Moslems just as much as the Jews held that this was to be his Valley of Decision. They called it the *Wady en Nar*, or Valley of Fire, and it was, or it used to be, the ambition of all good Moslems as well as of pious Jews to be buried here so as to be handy for the Judgement. 'They like to go ahead of the queue, you see. In case there proves to be a shortage of places in Heaven. Notice the tombs.' Of course there was another conception of this great day. It was the 'Day of the Threshing' when God would gather all the *goyim*— 'and that's us, we gentiles' into this valley for judgement after their abominable treatment of his chosen people throughout the centuries. 'And right richly, on the whole, will the *goyim* deserve their judgement.' Either because he'd once been, like me, an Anglo-Catholic or because he was an expert on Eastern religions he could leave me nowhere with his Bible quotations. Splendidly now he delivered, with all the platform-skill of an old lecturer, in a dropped voice, Joel's magnificent prophecy, ' "Let the heathen be wakened and come up to the Valley of Jehoshaphat for there will I sit to judge all the heathen round about. Put ye in the sickle for the harvest is ripe; the press

79

is full, the fats overflow—" God, how these boys could write!—
"Multitudes, multitudes in the Valley of Decision, for the day of the
Lord is near—" but unfortunately it goes on, Jonny and Clem,
"Then shall Jerusalem be holy and there shall no strangers pass
through her any more." ' He looked up the opposite hill to St.
Stephen's battlemented Gate. 'Bear that in mind as you go through
St. Stephen's Gate, though this part of the prophecy would appear
to be temporarily abrogated now that strangers bring such good
shekels into the sanctuary.'

§

We were in Jerusalem, the city that haunts the world. Not Rome,
not Athens, can do to one's heart what the narrow streets of this, the
Holy City, can do, for here, long centuries before Athens awoke to
win the mind of the world or Rome to win its body, this little walled
and gated city had begun its slow work upon the world's spirit,
delving deeper than they, since spirit lies deeper than mind or body.

Near St. Stephen's Gate, in a garden, is the crusaders' Church of
St. Anne, large, simple, austere, unornamented and yet abundantly
satisfying. Prenders stood between Clem and me as we gazed up at
its high, square western front, and I conceive that his thoughts of the
crusaders burst the floodgates of his mind, for he poured forth
plenty.

This was the substance of his lecture that evening. 'Ever consider,
Jonny, how subtly the popes recruited for the crusades? They just
set about sublimating the natural belligerence and savagery of the
faithful by telling them that, instead of hacking one another to
pieces which would merit hell, they could fight their way to Heaven
through the hacked bodies of infidels. They could thus enjoy the
best of both worlds: much glorious slaughter here on earth and eternal life hereafter. "Let all of you observe a Truce of God at home,"
Pope Urban II ordered when he loosed the First Crusade, "and let
your swords find only the bodies of his enemies who are profaning
his holy places." This would be accepted by him, God's Vicar on
Earth, he said, as a complete and justifying penance. At the same
time, no less successfully, he consecrated a few other vices. His dear

children-in-God were men of greed as well as of ferocity, so he nicely harmonized financial profit with spiritual merit. Not only did he promise a full remission of their sins but also of their debts and their taxes. No wonder that when Jerusalem fell to them at last after a day of such butchery that its gutters streamed with blood, and the conquerors, whether on horseback or on foot, had to splash through it to the Holy Sepulchre, their eyes dripped with tears of joy even as their swords dripped with heathen blood. Imagine it: all their sins forgiven, and they sure of Heaven! Hours of lovely fighting, Jerusalem theirs, and they free of their taxes and debts and sins. But there's one thing I can't help admiring them for, Jonny: it was a day in mid-July and must have been as hot as hell, but they came along, butchering their way to the Sepulchre, in full armour—breast-plates, chain mail, vizored helmets, to say nothing of huge shields and swords. And real good fighting is a warm game, I imagine, even in winter. How the poor fellows must have dripped with sweat as well as with tears and other chaps' blood.'

Inevitably we went from the crusaders' Church of St. Anne along the Via Dolorosa to the most famous of all crusader churches, the Church of the Holy Sepulchre, and my thoughts as we crossed over its forecourt and entered through its Norman door were with those blood-splashed Norman knights from the West, bringing their tears of triumph and their shouts of joy along with their dripping swords. They seemed to symbolize the hunger of our poor human race for something in Christ and at the same time the enduring blindness in most of us to all that he was and meant.

Hardly any other feeling came to me at first in that dim and crowded church, heart of a holy city, because the garish and tawdry place hurt and irritated me. The endless sanctuary lamps, the giant candlesticks and painted candles, the Christmas-tree globes and baubles, the mosaics and icons of beaten brass—or was it beaten gold? It seemed yet again to express a vulgar blindness in men's loyalty to the Vision born here—but then I decided more happily that it was a matter of taste, no more; who was I who had once so loved ornament and soaring incense, rich vestments and pageantry, and was now seeking to work my way back to them, to object to all

81

this gleaming and multiplied splendour? Nevertheless I found myself longing to escape to some quiet and empty place where I could be alone and think, and all the time my mind was seeing the slope of Olivet beneath which we had come walking towards Gethsemane and St. Stephen's Gate. I felt I would like to sit alone there, thinking my own thoughts while I looked down again upon Jerusalem across the Kidron Valley.

But then as I drifted among the led crowds and the guide instructors, passing by Coptic priests, Greek priests, young Armenian seminarists, a Franciscan friar, a cowled monk; as I strove for the fact of 'where I was' to fill me, I did, now and then, shutting my eyes to think and think, manage to know and feel some of it. Once or twice it caught my heart with thoughts that were nearly adequate. And nearly unbearable.

I had lost the others and was now alone. I was away from the tireless voices of the Dowager and Hester. Quiet voices speaking other languages were but a distant rumour around me. And I *thought*.

If—*if* these crusader walls did indeed enclose the low hill and the garden beneath it with its rock-hewn tomb; if, up above those stairs, was the actual soil on which the cross had been lifted; if it was on this stone (as they said) that Joseph of Arimathea laid the limp body of a dead young man that he might anoint it and wrap it in fine linen and wind a napkin around its thorn-pierced head; if yonder was the rocky shelf on which the wrapped body was laid before—before it disappeared; if so, if so, then think of this place in the midnight darkness when the shuffling crowds were gone and all the tawdry display was invisible, and the two places, hill and tomb, watersheds of the world's history, stayed silent and unvisited—then what ghosts might not come here to brood. A centurion. A penitent thief who had also died here. A good man who in love had given up his private tomb, of which he was doubtless proud, that it might house the poor wrecked body of an executed criminal—and did he, by the way, since the tomb was now empty and forsaken, sleep in it himself at the last? A woman remembering how the first light of day had come over the crown of Olivet and begun to light up the garden so that she saw —oh, God!—that the tomb was empty—'as it began to dawn', says

82

Matthew, 'at the rising of the sun', says Mark. Even perhaps the greatest ghost of all who had appeared here when it was still a garden and the dawn was brightening—but enough; perhaps such thoughts were getting near to blasphemy. Or were but foolish dreams.

More and more I longed to escape and be alone on Olivet's arid slope where I could ask myself again and again, *Who* was that young man who in this place said 'Father, forgive them' and, three hours later, a few paces further away, loosed a magnificent cry of triumph, '*Tetelestai!* It is finished. It is done. It is achieved.'

Because I did not know. I still did not begin to know.

9

Metamorphosis of Mr. Prender

It looked as though I should have opportunities next day to be alone. Temporarily I was deserted by the faithful Maureen and deprived of the presence of Alexander. Alexander, who missed little of what was said in his hearing, had been impressed by Prenders' statement that the water of Jordan, even though princes had it brought from Palestine for the christening of their young, was in fact foul and sometimes poisonous, because of the deep hot trench of the Ghor through which it ran. And now, after Maureen had coyly asked me at the hotel, 'May I sit at table with you, Mr. Palmer? That'd be divine,' and after Clem had said, 'Yes, you'll have to guide and support your girl-friend now, Jon. Love has its duties as well as its joys; and there's real love there; after I had myself heard her telling Jimmy Hilder, "I adore Mr. Palmer"'—after these alarms, Maureen arrives at the breakfast table to tell me that Alexander was persuaded he'd been poisoned by Jordan's stream, and that he had, in fact, what he called a tempera chewer.

She said he was feverish but only mildly.

'How much?' I confess I asked this in the hope that the child would require her all day.

'Between ninety-nine and a hundred.'

'Oh, that's nothing,' I said, and quickly corrected myself lest the hope should be taken from me. I hastened to explain that she must certainly keep him in bed till he'd had a whole day without a tempera chewer.

'Oh, but it's so sad,' she bewailed. 'There's so much that I want to go and see with you all.'

I had my own interpretation of that 'you all' so I repeated, trying at least to sound sympathetic, 'Still I'm afraid the rule is he mustn't get up while there's a trace of fever.'

'Perhaps I could get him books to read and toys to play with, while I—'

I discouraged this. 'It might be all right, I imagine, if you feel he can be trusted to stay warmly in bed when you're not there.' But then I felt ashamed and really sorry for the poor girl who'd paid just as much as I had (and even more because of the brat) for this pilgrimage so I comforted her, 'But don't worry, dear—' yes, I said 'dear' in my pity— 'he'll get well quickly,' and I even went so far as to offer, 'Perhaps I could stay with him for a few hours and enable you to get out—' though there was not really any credit to me in this because I was confident Alexander would raise a fine scene rather than have Mr. Palmer as his nurse. I went further, I went so far as to give her hand an encouraging pat and to say again, 'There's seldom much to worry about when children of his age run tempera chewers.'

'I suppose not,' she grieved. 'I suppose I must stay with or near him, today at least.'

But it was not on that day, or the next, or for many days, that I had my session with silent thought on the Mount of Olives. The Bishop had set his heart on taking us all to Bethlehem on this first day, and thence to Jericho which we'd passed by in favour of the Dead Sea Scrolls, and he was so beamingly happy with his plan that, as Prenders put it, 'we simply mustn't disappoint His Beatitude.'

There could be no Maureen and Alexander with us on this Bethlehem journey, and I felt such a pity for her over this that I told her *I* would take her to Bethlehem one day. There are not many acts in my life of whose merit I have little doubt, but this is one of them. It would involve taking Alexander too.

'Would you really?' she asked, adding '*Really?*' as if I'd promised the ineffable. 'Oh, you *are* an absolute angel. I shall keep you to that promise. Bethlehem! That'd be bliss.' I'm not certain after this lapse of time that the word wasn't 'blissikins', a favourite word of hers, but I don't stand out for it.

'Of course I would,' I said. What else could one say? I said it with suitable masculine smiles that indicated a delighted willingness to guide and protect a 'little woman'.

'Oh, it's so sweet of you. Absolutely adorable.'

'Not at all,' I protested, adding grimly to myself, 'He's pleased.'

This very decent offer waited for me and seized upon me on our return that afternoon from Jericho. She ran up to me in the hotel lounge and said in her best girlish manner, head inclined to one shoulder, 'Oh, Mr. Palmer, you did say you'd take me somewhere nice when I got free. Would it be too much to take me somewhere nice now? Or are you much too tired? Yes, of course you are. But I've been tied here all day with Alexander who's being rather peevish and rude while you've been just enjoying yourself.' ('Just enjoying oneself' of Bethlehem!) 'My mother says she'll look in on him now and then and play with him sometimes. He's sitting up and doing a jig-saw puzzle of Jerusalem.'

'But what's Alexander's view of visitations by Granny? I hope you'll lock up your hair-brushes.'

This was lost on her, and I had to remind her how the Dowager considered her departed husband should have used the back of a hair-brush on Alexander whenever suitable, which would be frequently. And probably urgent now. 'He's an intelligent child—' flattery—'and even if you lock up your hair-brushes he'll probably suspect that she's capable of going back to her room and getting one of her own. And it could be that he'd be right.'

More than likely, I thought. Whensoever he was being peevish and rude.

'Oh, you're so naughty,' she said, chiding me archly, demurely. 'And so unkind about people. You *are* a dreadful man, aren't you? Mummy can be quite sweet at times.'

Well, possibly. Once, behold, there was honey found in the carcase of a lion.

'Darling Bishop Brakewaite even offered to come and play with him for an hour or two. Wasn't that rather lovely of him? A bishop!

And Hester Brakewaite too. And Jimmy Hilder said she'd help. Oh, I do think people are sweet. So *take* me,' she begged, hands now joined behind her like a schoolgirl, eyes asking help from mine, the very picture of a weak and dependent maiden pleading for a strong man's support. 'Anywhere you like. Absolutely anywhere. I don't mind.' Which seemed to imply that her interest was less with Jerusalem than with Mr. Palmer. 'Just a weeny little walk, somewhere.'

'All right,' I agreed, perceiving that I must be sweet like the others. 'Come along, my dear.' Her whole manner required that 'my dear' so I gave it to her. 'Let's wander out.'

But not on to Olivet. I was not going to let my hour on Olivet be profaned by this nonsense. Olivet with Jerusalem across the valley would mean little to her. Her thoughts would be far from it. And I could but suspect where they would be. By now, as a fruit of these frustrations, I was beginning to indulge a presentiment that some knowledge would be granted me when I was alone on Olivet; I would learn there something of what I longed to know.

Well, we wandered together through the streets of Jerusalem and beyond, but to this day I don't know what were the roads we took. I had turned our faces northward so as to avoid the Mount of Olives, and I conjecture we must have gone out through Herod's Gate and through the northern suburbs till we were past the Tomb of the Kings and on a shoulder of Mount Scopus. After about half an hour she slid her arm into mine, affectionately. After less than a full hour she leaned her weight against me as we walked, leaned it heavily as with love. That we finished up on Mount Scopus, believe me I know, because I searched a map later to learn what had been the site of a terrible incident—'terrible' used in its natural sense of 'striking terror'.

We were on a steep slope, hardly to be called green, because its rocks and soil were bone-white beneath the thistles, purple and yellow, the scant grass burned to straw, and the white stones spattered everywhere. In truth it was an earth that brought forth thorns and thistles, as the Lord promised to Adam and his descendants in punishment for his sin. A few lean and black-bearded goats gleaned for some herbage among the thistles and stones. But the unfriendly hill rose to a ridge, and there were buildings along it, which this map was to tell me later were those of the Hebrew University and the Hadassah hospital.

Mount Scopus.

A steep unlovely slope and, tiring of it, we sat down under a twisted and tormented hedge of cactus. In the still and empty air, and from the edges of Jerusalem, we heard the song of an Arab chanting on the radio and the voices of children in the streets. For one of us it seemed the place was romantic enough.

'You're a wonderful guide,' she said, when we had been seated two minutes, side by side. 'You know everything.' Which was nonsense because I didn't even know where we were or much of what we had passed. I had merely made conversation by talking tritely about the Holy Places.

But I did my best now to be worthy of this praise by exhibiting all I knew about the Jericho from which we had come, and the Inn of the Good Samaritan, and the days when Palestine was a territory mandated to Britain, who kept peace—or tried to—between Trans-Jordan and Israel. She made a show of listening but again and again I guessed that her thoughts were engaged with a different matter. And it was not long before my guessing was justified.

We were both leaning back, I on one elbow, she with both her hands pressing the stony ground behind her, and suddenly she swung herself sideways and said, 'Oh, I'm tired after my day with Alexander, but it's so lovely here, so restful,' whereupon she lay back pillowing her head on one of my outstretched legs and asking, 'Do you mind this? It's so comfy. You don't mind, do you?'

'Not at all,' I was obliged to answer, adding in thought the inevitable corollary, 'He's pleased.'

So she remained there, only pushing her head further into my lap that her eyes might look up into my face, mischievously.

Obviously this was a continuing invitation to kiss her. And for a minute or two I thought 'I suppose I mustn't disappoint her.' At one stage I even reflected that since she had some prettiness this kindness on my part wouldn't be wholly unpleasant. But at once I remembered

Alethea, and the memory was a blow on the heart. As in the car climbing Mount Lebanon I said to myself, 'How can the poor girl know that just now I have no heart for her or anyone else in the world? Were you Cleopatra or Helen of Troy, dear girl, I'd have nothing in me for you—nothing at all.'

Still, just to please her, could I not give her one chaste kiss and leave it at that? No, no, a kiss might fling doors too wide and imply a willingness to set out for Heaven-knew-where. No, the risks of such behaviour were too many. So at first I left her head lying where she had placed it. I talked down to it but as far as possible avoided direct glances at it, because of that mischief in her eyes. And all the time I could imagine her thinking something like, 'Of all the dull heavy sillies! Has he no red blood in him?' 'Yes, Maureen dear, plenty of it; all too much, perhaps. But not for you, bless you, dear. Nor—oh, if only I could tell you this to save you from hurt—nor for anyone else on earth. There was a girl, Alethea. . . . And all around her is ruin and ashes. . . . Just now, and for a while. Perhaps for a long time. She married a man twenty years younger than me, only a little while ago, and . . . well, there it is. . . . Let it pass. . . .'

But then I thought of Clem's charity and my wish to copy it, and again I found myself musing, 'Oh, come! Have a heart. Take the risks for her sake. Why not? Give the poor child what she wants.'

And I did at length bend my head and give her a kiss, risking all.

In the first moment of its application it was quite pleasant but that moment was instantly overtaken by terror because I had not lifted my face eight inches from hers before her free arms were around my neck that she might pull my mouth down again and kiss it —kiss it not only with hard pressures but with a rough rubbing of her lips along mine, this way and that, between the pressures. I have told you that the avidity in it was terrifying. The prospects were terrifying. My heart thumped its trepidation, like drums in Africa beating an alarm.

And yet I hadn't the heart to hurt her by pulling away my exploited mouth and bringing it back to a place of safety. I waited till she was finished, or had wearied of love, and thereafter I talked merrily rather than let her guess that I was now filled with terror.

We rose to return, but before we took one step away, she asked, 'Where are we? What is this place? Do tell me, because I shall remember what happened here all my life. I see it's somewhere outside the walls of Jerusalem, but has it a name? If so, I want to know it. I want to remember it all my life.'

Gracious, gracious! Where had we got to? Was she thinking of me as a new possession, and a lasting possession?

'Oh, darling Jonny—I may call you that, mayn't I?—I've been wanting to for days—oh, my dearest, it was so lovely, being given a little love. Tell me the name of this place, as you love me. Has it a name like Mount Zion or something?'

'I don't think it's Mount Zion,' I said in some desperation. 'Mount Zion's in the City of David, isn't it?'

'Is it?'

'Yes, I think so. Far away on the other side of Jerusalem.' And I was pleased that it was so well away. Indeed as I spoke of the City of David and Mount Zion my thoughts ran far from her and gave themselves again to a tiny insignificant nation living on its burnt Judaean hills, with David's city for its capital and Solomon's temple for its heart, and thinking thoughts and writing words that would enlarge the soul of Man for all generations to come. 'Mount Zion is over there by that church,' I said at last. 'The Church of St. Peter-in-Gallicantu, where Peter heard the cock crowing.'

But she wasn't interested in that forlorn bird-call, the most famous in all history, which broke the heart and built the soul of Peter. And so laid the rock on which the church would be built.

And yet it was here, within calling distance of us now, that the cock stood forlornly crying. In its ignorance and innocence.

'Well, what is this then?' was all she asked. 'Tell me it's a Mount of some sort. I want it to be a famous Mount.'

'I don't know, but I fancy it must be Mount Scopus—because of those buildings up there.'

'Mount *what?*'

'Scopus,' I said with increasing despair.

'Darling Mount Scopus. I shall love it all my life. And Jerusalem too, of course,' she allowed, glancing towards the white suburb outside the city wall. 'Yes, darling Jerusalem. I shall always love it now. And Mount Scopus.'

Oh, dear, oh dear. It was as if she'd found in Mr. Palmer precisely that for which she'd come to these holy places.

'I'm happy, I'm happy. Let's go home.'

To what? To what? For all the way home she kept her arm in mine, often pulling me against her side in a new upsurging of love.

And all the next day, whenever possible (the Dowager, confined to the hotel by internal troubles, was sitting with Alexander) as we visited the Temple Area, the Wailing Wall, the El Aska Mosque, the Pool of Siloam, and other unsuitable places for necking, Maureen kept beside me or linked arms with me, pressing me close, or looked up into my eyes mischievously. She even leaned against me, saying, 'I like someone nice and tall,' and never knew that this blandishment, so like the words of another, pierced my heart and turned a blade there. Alethea.

The attack was in being and the whole day was in ruins for me, because I now believed, with some umbrage against Heaven, that I had ruined all the rest of this holiday by an act in imitation of Clem's charity.

§

But that evening, when we were back in the hotel and Maureen had hurried upstairs to Alexander, Prenders beckoned me mysteriously with one crook'd finger to follow him into a corner of the Lounge. There, far away from all listeners, I found he had installed Clem Oslow, after capturing him. 'Sit, sit,' he ordered; and his first words, once we were all seated, he in the middle, were as mysterious as that beckoning finger. They were, 'Are you prepared to do a bunk? Tomorrow?'

'A bunk? Bunk where?' At first I thought he had perceived my hapless misappropriation by Maureen and was suggesting flight. But it was nothing to do with that.

'Clemmy is ready to bunk.' There was indeed something pathetic about the way this embittered and often soured man seemed to find relief in calling those he liked by these friendly diminutives. There was more than a hungry goodwill in these endearments today, however. Arrival in Jordan seemed to have worked a metamorphosis in Prenders. He was alight with some private gaiety. 'I've settled it all with Clemmy. He'll do a guy with us. Clemmy agrees.'

'Agrees to what?'

He continued to speak in riddles. 'Let's be done with the springs of Christianity for a few days, I've been saying to Clemmy, and go ever so much further back.' He pointed east towards the desert.

'What do you mean? To the sources of Islam?' In my bewilderment I was forgetting that Islam arose in the world six hundred years after Christianity.

'Islam! Heavens, no. Islam is modern stuff. God, it's only thirteen hundred years since Mohammed started that nuisance. I mean twelve centuries before him. Back to the sixth century B.C. That's where the springs are.'

'In Iraq?'

'In Iraq, certainly. In Babylon. I propose taking you both to Babylon.'

Clem spoke. 'We've got to repeat the Exile. He's taking us captive from Jerusalem to Babylon. His other name is Nebuchadnezzar.'

'Yes, Babylon and thereabouts,' said Prenders, 'but only for a day or two; not for fifty years. And on the quiet, please, or others'll want to come. Maureen, for instance. And Alexander. Alexander'll certainly want to come.'

Clem submitted, 'I don't fancy that Alexander's interested in the springs of his religion.'

'But then there's James Hilder. Think of that. God save us from James. Or, worse still, the Dowager. *She* might want to come. The Dowager who thinks we ought to flog everybody and, when possible, hang 'em. What *she's* doing on this jaunt I don't know. Though I believe she says just the same about me. She knows nothing whatever about Christianity.' A strangely indignant sentence from one who called himself an infidel. It was passionately indignant.

'All right, Prenders. Babylon,' I said. 'But how do we get there?'

'Quite simple. Seats on an aeroplane tomorrow. To Bah'g-dah'd.' Like other Orientalists Prenders always spoke of this fairy-tale city as Bah'g-dah'd. Which sounded ridiculous to me. 'It only takes about three hours. That's why I told you both to get visas for Iraq and Iran.'

'Iran? Oh no, not Iran too. You're not taking us into Persia?'

'Just a little way. Only a little way,' he admitted apologetically. 'There's something I want to show you there. Something that'll make your eyes pop out of your head. Something that'll really start you thinking.'

Clem spoke: 'Mr. Prenders, sir. How, please, do we get from Baghdad into Persia?'

'That's not going to be difficult. I have a friend, Davy Sellars, in Bah'g-dah'd. He's one of the second secretaries in our embassy. A nice fellow and quite mad. He'll work everything for us. He'll handle the hotel and restaurant keepers when we pay our bills. That should be worth watching. Not but what I'm quite good at the game myself. There are several consecutive steps in it. They need understanding. But if the worst came to the worst I couldn't bring the diplomatic pressure to bear as Davy can. His house in Bah'g-dah'd belongs to the embassy, and he's an awful liar, so he's able to work all sorts of diplomatic immunity for those he loves. I wouldn't put it past him to suggest that His Excellency himself, the Ambassador Extraordinary and Plenipotentiary, might come and determine the correct bill, on his return from taking tea with the President. Or, more likely, he'll say you're the Ambassador's brother and Clemmy his first cousin—if he doesn't say Clemmy's a cousin of the Queen— a distant cousin, of course. Like all good liars he likes his lies to be credible. Alternatively he might say you're in Oil. Oil opens all doors in Iraq. Yes, I think—at the hotel, at any rate—he'll say you're Oil.'

'Why have you only just sprung this amazing idea on us?' I asked, my fingers beating a song of resignation on the table. A few bars from the Eroica symphony.

'Because I gave Davy this hotel address and got a letter from him this morning. He's mad for us to come. At once.'

'Yes, but wait,' Clem interrupted. 'We've only got about two more weeks. How long is it going to last, this joy-ride into the sixth century B.C.?'

He scoffed again. 'Pooh. Two nights in Bah'g-dah'd, one in Persia, one more in Bah'g-dah'd, and so back again. It's quite possible Davy'd motor us all the way back, right across the Great Syrian desert, which'd be something worth doing. He's quite capable of it; it's only about five hundred miles, and he's as crazy as a coot.'

The Great Syrian Desert! Then perhaps, after all, God was on my side because I'd tried to do a charity in the fashion of Clem. I could fly at once from Maureen's arms. Across the Great Syrian Desert. Across five hundred miles of it. Across the centuries.

Act of God or not, I'd seize the advantage of it. But first I must feign some doubt. 'But look, Prenders. We can't just "do a guy", as you put it. We'll have to tell the Bishop at least.'

'Yes, I suppose we must,' he agreed unwillingly. 'But the Bishop only. And then go quickly. Before the women get talking.'

So it happened. Less than forty hours later, at Amman airport in the morning, seats being available, we three were primed into a huge silver bullet and fired across the Great Syrian Desert to Baghdad.

10

Ozymandias is Everywhere

THIS Davy Sellars, Prenders' friend, who stood awaiting us at the
Baghdad airport, fitted well enough Prenders' description of him.
A man under forty and a fellow of Balliol he yet had none of the
obvious but properly reticent awareness of his natural superiority
which is traditionally—and maybe slanderously—attributed to the
Balliol man: his talk and manner were rather those of an impish
undergraduate or of an over-lively medical student before a practice
and a surgery have sobered him. He was an earl's younger son, but
there was nothing aristocratic about his figure or face. In figure he
was less than medium height and a little fat; his face with its bulging
cheeks, eyes wide apart, and small nose resembled, I thought, that
of an intelligent, amiable, and laughing cat. Though a dozen years
younger than Prenders he greeted him with a hand on each shoulder
and exaggerated words. 'My very dear fellow, this is quite magnificent. I've everything arranged for you and your friends. Absolutely
the best hotel, the place all the big business pots go to. A fine place:
bedrooms and balconies overlooking the Tigris.' I was beginning to
worry about the costs, less for myself than for Prenders, when he
went on, 'It won't dare to overcharge you now it knows that you're
buddies of mine. Sorry I can't be with you tomorrow but His
Excellency is perturbed as usual about something, so we've all got to
work. But I've fixed up a hired car for you, a Chevvy. With a decent
Iraqi driver who's another old pal of mine. Ibrahim. He'll take you
anywhere you want. At about a hundred miles an hour. Meantime

I've got my old bus waiting outside to take you to the hotel. Come along, come along, come along.'

It was only later, when I'd learned more about Prenders, that I wondered if Davy's good heart and native compassion had put this over-stressed friendliness into his welcome.

His old bus, when we were outside the airport, showed itself as a shining Cadillac almost twice as long as most British cars and as wide (or so it seemed) as half a roadway. When we were in it he drove it through streets where, apparently, no Highway Code troubled motorists or donkey-riders or camel leaders or pedestrians. Similar vast American cars and occasionally an English Land Rover, raced hooting through ox-drawn carts, camel trains, little donkeys laden with bales or men, old blind beggars with bowls, and streaming pedestrian Arabs, the men in anything from long Bedouin robes to neat-washed European suits that laboured, without success, to look like the products of Savile Row, the women either in yashmak veils showing only their interested eyes or in loose western dresses and open head-scarves, unashamed.

Next morning a big Chevrolet, red and white, and spreading its wings as if it longed to 'take off', stood before the hotel doors under a Mesopotamian sun that, kindly so far, seemed to be offering its benediction on whatever journeys we had in mind. Prenders talked fluently to the brown Iraqi driver, but neither Clem nor I could understand what he was saying or whether it was good idiomatic Arabic; we could only marvel at its fluency. Turning to us he relapsed into English. 'Down the Tigris first. Only twenty miles or so. No distance. No distance at all. Something you've *got* to see.'

'What's that?' asked Clem.

'Never mind. My God, you'll see it when you see it. Get aboard.' Prenders, metamorphosed, had shed all bitterness and was as merry and mischievous as a child pulling on your hand because he's delighted with some surprise he's prepared.

'Babylon?'

'*Hell*, no! Babylon? No, no, *mon vieux*. What are you talking about? Babylon's on the Euphrates. Didn't I say Tigris? Tigris, *Tigris*. We're in the Land of the Twin Rivers. Come on. Get in.'

As soon as we were clear of the fine Baghdad mansions and the mud huts of its last fringes we were on what seemed a desert road; its sunbaked and impacted earth flung up a wake of hot dust behind us that drifted away under the sun. Now, apart from the low rolling sandhills, nothing was in sight but the distant palm-trees marching along by the river. Soon the road itself ran by the river, but with no palm-trees near it; under the glaring sky there was only the muddy-brown Tigris twisting and turning through a dun-brown desert.

Then—suddenly—a huge, a giant arch. Standing there before us. Of yellow brick it seemed in the blazing sun; a vast, elliptical, ruined vault with one high wall extending at right angles from it towards the river. One mighty vault, a stretch of proud lofty wall, and the desert sand with its scrub. The river racing beside it. That was all.

The car stopped abruptly. 'Ctesiphon,' said Prenders.

'I beg your pardon?' Clem queried. To him this word—or name— had conveyed nothing. He had devoted much homework to the Holy Land but never a half-hour to these places we'd got to now. I kept quiet because my ignorance was no less than his but needn't be deployed. Here was no name like Babylon or Nineveh or Palmyra.

Doubtless delighted by our ignorance, Prenders pronounced again, 'Ctesiphon'. He even spelt it for us, and thereafter was splendidly informative and happy. When is a man happier than when he's doing what he knows he does splendidly? 'Ctesiphon. For seven centuries the proud capital of the Parthian and Persian Empires. Seven centuries I said. And there's all that's left of it. Here was the golden throne of the Great King, the King of Kings. Surely the most royal city in the world after Rome. Why, it shared the world with Rome. I can't remember how many Roman emperors fought to capture and subdue Ctesiphon. Certainly Trajan, Hadrian, Severus, Valerian— and, yes, Julian the Apostate. Its population must have been enormous because it yielded up a hundred thousand prisoners of war to one of these emperors—Septimus Severus, I think. And now look around.' And now, at last, Ozymandias appeared. He came on that low, musical, platform-voice of Prenders. Prenders' voice when he used it expertly like this was really beautiful. One could believe that, as the Bishop said, he had, in his time held audiences staring and spell-bound:

> ' "My name is Ozymandias, King of Kings:
> Look on my works, ye Mighty, and despair!"
> Nothing beside remains. Round the decay
> Of that colossal wreck, boundless and bare,
> The lone and level sands stretch far away.

Ozymandias, Clem, is everywhere in the deserts of the East. I'm going to show you a greater one than this; the greatest of all, I think. Let's get out.'

We had been looking at the back of this astonishing arch, but now our driver had taken us a little way past it along the roadway between that single high wall and the river. Here he had stopped again.

Prenders leapt from the car as if eager to be first out. His eagerness was still like that of a happy boy—happy with his surprises for us and his superior knowledge; eager to disclose the first and display the second. 'Come. Come along,' he ordered, and led us into the open sandy space under the awful dreamlike over-arching of this tremendous vault. Eighty feet wide, I have learnt since, and a hundred feet high to the arch's crown. The greatest span of bricks ever laid by the hands of men.

'Taht-i-Kesra. The Throne of Chosroes.' Prenders murmured the words in a kind of low reverence. 'This was Chosroes' central hall, marvellously decorated in its great days.' He kicked at the sand beneath him. 'I imagine there was a magnificently tessellated pavement here—but now only the desert sand and the scrub. Read Gibbon on the sacking of Ctesiphon by the Moslems. According to him the ferocious followers of the Prophet rushed in yelling "This is the white palace of Chosroes. This is the promise of the Prophet of God." And the booty they grabbed was so enormous that their general was able to reward all of his sixty thousand soldiers with the equivalent of three hundred pounds apiece.' He looked up at the high walls, which bent, soaring, to make this enormous elliptical curve above us. 'Yellow bricks', he said. 'Baked in the sun. But once covered with marbles and mosaics, which showed all the constellations of the Zodiac worked in golden stars. The palace of Chosroes with his luxurious capital spread around it; and what now? Only silence. Silence.'

Little doubt but that one of us, unless his memory was remarkable, had deliberately done some homework before luring us here.

After staring up, he wandered from under the arch, sadly, as if in a dream. We followed him to the banks of the river which ran so near to the palace's one high lateral wall. Standing there, he, and we, copying him, looked down at the mud-thick waters of the Tigris hurrying by, like a somewhat soiled bride, to find and mingle with her lover, the Persian Gulf, three hundred miles away. 'Tigris and Euphrates,' he said. 'They rolled like this for all of seven hundred years as the frontier between those two mighty empires.' Swinging round, he looked eastward across the desert to where, perhaps a hundred miles away, there ran along the horizon an endless, grey-blue, swaying shadow, the Zagros and Pusht-i-Kuh mountains. On their backs lay the tableland of Persia.

His eyes stayed fixed on that long grey panorama. 'The Pusht-i-Kuh,' he said, 'And Persia.' Then, turning to look again at the arch, he repeated, 'Sun-baked bricks. Bricks baked in the sun. Standing here, you can grasp a thousand years of history. Given an undrying river that can turn a desert into a garden all round it, and a fierce sun, that'll make fine solid bricks of clay in an hour, and you can see why these famous cities rose here by the rivers' banks—Babylon and Seleucia and Ctesiphon. But always the hardier and fighting hillmen come down from the mountains and have the relaxed and softened plainsmen at their mercy. A plain under high mountains is asking for history to visit it. These Mesopotamian cities disappear easily because the country has neither stone nor timber. Only sun-baked bricks. Come back into the car. I'm going to show you the perfect, the classic, demonstration of all this, the coming of the men from the mountains and another great city gone back into the desert.'

'Babylon?' asked Clem.

'Yes. Babylon.' But he could not yet abandon that great arch. He had to look at it again, bestriding the empty sands, and sigh, 'How often in history a great empire reaches the zenith of its power and wealth just before the end comes. Chosroes built that haughty palace somewhere about A.D. 550 and in less than a century the all-conquering Moslems came, and that was more or less the end of Ctesiphon. And the end of the Graeco-Roman East. The end of the centuries-old rivalry between Persia and Rome for the dominion of the Levant and Western Asia. The new Semites out of Arabia came flooding over it all and brought the desert back with them. As you see. The desert is home again in Ctesiphon, claiming its own. Oh, come. Let's get into the car, and go back a thousand years. To Babylon.'

Without waiting for our assent to this journey through a millennium, he went to the driver of the car who, on his instructions, turned it to face the way we had come. Prenders got in, saying nothing more to us, still thinking, perhaps, of Ctesiphon in its great days. And now the car was speeding back to Baghdad, and I could only look out of the rear window at that colossal arch, straddling the desert, till I could see it no more. I was sorry to think I would never see it again.

Perhaps Clem was thinking the same because he spoke no word till we were in the suburbs of Baghdad. It was then that he asked, 'How many miles to Babylon?'

Prenders took him up at once. ' "How many miles to Babylon? Three score miles and ten. Can I get there by candle-light? Yes, there and back again." Oddly enough, it's just about seventy miles from here to Babylon. So we'd better hurry if we don't want to come back by candle-light. But this boy'll get us there in an hour or so. We'll have time enough to sit by the waters of Babylon and weep.'

Our driver took some secondary road to Babylon instead of the fine main-road to Basra. It ran along by the tortuous twistings of the Tigris, and at its beginning seemed to be all desert on the right hand and fields on the left, where the river watered them. Then it was desert only except for solitary palms down there by the river. After about an hour we came to a junction where a sign-post pointed one way to 'Basra' and the other to 'Babylon', as if in its view, as in God's, a thousand years were as nothing—no more than an evening gone. The Babylon road, branching right, left Tigris behind, making, said Prenders, 'for its sister, Euphrates'. A forlorn country it was that our twentieth-century car now crossed, drawing its wake of travelling dust behind it.

But at length—yes—we began to see the many mounds of Babylon. Relics very different from the Ctesiphon arch standing alone and monarch of all it surveyed—which was illimitable sand and scrub. Here were hillocks and long heaps and embankments and dykes spread over a great area. Fifty square miles, Prenders said, at which we whistled and wondered, but supposed he knew what he was talking about. 'But these were clay-lands again, and it was a clay-brick city, and it's gone, it's gone.'

Our driver stopped the car at a small rest-house advertising Coca-Cola and American cigarettes, whence an ancient Iraqi guide in a red tarbush and flowing robe emerged and offered, with ingratiating smiles and an American accent, to be 'your guide, father, your guide.'

'No, no, *imshi iggri*,' said Prenders. 'I guide, cock. I know it all. *Saïda*, Abdel.' And he waved a friendly hail-and-farewell to the old gentleman who retired, doubtfully approving this arrangement, into his canteen.

An admirable guide Prenders made, leading us from one earthy hillock to another. The largest of these, deeply excavated, might have been a close collocation of First War trenches all assembled together in the heart of a hill. Ruined walls, steps, terraces, platforms—all of them contiguous and some of the walls still bearing in low relief the figures of bulls, or of the lion and dragon of Babylon. At one point, Prenders explained, we were among the ruins of the Castle whose hundred rooms, he said, had doors of cedar and bronze and walls adorned with gold and silver and precious stones. He showed us what he believed to be the remains of Nebuchadnezzar's throne room.

So we wandered on hardly able, as is always the way, to digest all these wonders and extract the fullness of emotion from them. 'I am not realizing it. I'm not realizing it,' I had to tell myself again and again. We came to a river, lined by a string of palm-trees. 'Not the Euphrates,' Prenders said at once. 'Lord, no. The Euphrates used to run through the midst of Babylon but it long ago changed its course.

This is a tributary of it, naturally: the Shatt-al-Hilla. But it's one of the waters of Babylon, so let us sit down and weep.'

We sat above the water, I struggling hard to be worthy of where we were. It was now the full heat of mid-day, and the sun blazed down upon a dead city and this sheet of water. I tried to imagine the water as Euphrates and to see reflected in it the resplendent palaces, the hanging gardens, and the towering ziggurat temples piled up towards Heaven in pyramidal shape, ever smaller storeys above those beneath. Prenders broke in upon my thoughts by murmuring, ' "Babylon is fallen, is fallen, that great city . . . the great whore that sitteth upon many waters. . . . And upon her forehead was a name written, Mystery, Babylon the Great, the Mother of Harlots and Abominations of the Earth. . . ." '

From now onward he was a fount of Biblical quotations, so much so that I wondered if he had not come prepared with this array of excerpts. To my surprise last night I had seen in his hotel bedroom a little worn Bible on the bedside table. There it was, worn and torn with use, by the bed of a professed unbeliever. Presumably it had belonged to the days of his faith and he had brought it along with him since we were visiting Bible lands. But at his bedside and open! Still, the possibility that he had prepared his speeches for today didn't mar their effect on me; they were too apt, too stirring, and too helpful to one who wanted to be worthy of where he sat.

There were silences between these quotations while he gazed before him. And when he spoke them they were delivered in that clear but lowered voice of the lecturer who knows how to hypnotize an audience.

First, ' "And Babylon shall become heaps, an astonishment and a hissing. . . . Therefore the wild beasts of the desert shall dwell there . . . and it shall no more be inhabited for ever." Jeremiah, as I'm sure you recognize.'

We did not.

Then, ' "And Babylon, the glory of kingdoms, the beauty of the Chaldees' excellency, shall be as when God overthrew Sodom and Gomorrah. It shall never be inhabited, neither shall it be dwelt in from generation to generation. . . ." Isaiah,' he explained, and looking round upon these mounds and heaps of desolation, he reminded us how Isaiah had foretold one certain truth: that the Arabs would always believe, as they did today, that the whole place was haunted. Never would the Arab pitch his tent there, or the shepherd fold his sheep.

Lastly he came of course to words we all knew. ' "Daughter of Babylon, wasted with misery . . ." '

But it was when he had forgotten all desire to display learning, and probably all desire to hear his own voice reciting great words; it was when he had lost himself in thoughts which stirred the depths of him that he really had Clem and me rapt with interest.

'Can you tell me,' he asked as we lolled there, 'the date when Cyrus the Great, having conquered more or less the whole of Persia, up yonder on that tableland, came down from the mountains, laid siege to Babylon, and captured it with monumental ease?'

Naturally we could not.

'Well, it was in 538 B.C. And that, you may remember, was the end of Belshazzar. *Mene, mene, tekel upharsin.* Cyrus entered the city on a day in October and it may be that he passed by just where we're sitting now. Or perhaps sat here. Five-thirty-eight. And B.C. Now have you ever thought that the sixth century before Christ saw the most extraordinary light breaking upon the minds of men all over the world—and in places quite out of touch with each other? It was, I always say, the first great lift of the mind of Man towards—' he shrugged as if half-ashamed of what he was going to say—'towards what I suppose we must call "spiritual vision". The first Enlightenment.'

'How do you mean?' I asked, for I could not perceive of what he was speaking.

'Well, look. How's your history of the sixth century, B.C.? Say from 590 to 520.'

'Mostly forgotten. If it ever existed.'

'You, Clemmy?'

'Faded beyond recovery, my dear chap. Faded as though it had never been. And indeed it probably never was.'

'All right. Then listen. Leave it to me.'

11

The Infidel Prophet

'ALL right. Then listen. Leave it to me. It's now five hundred years before Christ and we're ever so far from Jerusalem or this Babylon; we're in North India, and there's a young prince there who suddenly leaves his home and rides away into the mountains that he may be alone to think and think till he learns what's wrong with the ways of societies and in the lives of individual men. He lives a hermit's life in the mountains, and so terrible are his penances that his fame echoes, so we're told, all over the Ganges country like a great bell hung in the sky. But none of these austerities helped. All ascetism and mortification left him just as dissatisfied as he'd been in his old days of luxury and pleasure. So though it shocked his disciples, and no doubt muffled that great bell, he decided to eat and drink. He went on wandering alone, till one day he sat himself down to meditate by the bank of a river, just like us now.' A powerful gift of narrative was Prenders', when something was really inspiring him. 'But, unlike us, he was sitting under a tree—a kind of fig which has ever since been called the Bo Tree—and the whole truth began to shine upon him. Any idea yet of whom I'm talking?'

'I had none whatever till you mentioned the Bo Tree,' Clem confessed. 'But it's Buddha, of course.'

'Even so. Gautama the Buddha. And for him the truth, which he called the Way, or the Path, was something like this. Self is the keyword to suffering. Only with the elimination of self goes victory over pain. All desires—bodily desires, worldly desires, even spiritual desires—must be sloughed off like the skin of a snake if the soul is to attain Serenity. Maybe he went too far in demanding the destruction of *all* desire—but go on listening. In the same century, on the other side of the Himalayas, far away in China, there arose a great teacher, Lao Tse. He was the royal librarian in a Chinese city, but he too was dissatisfied and decided to withdraw from men that he might think and discover the True Way, as he too called it, the "Tao". He wrote a book which because of its high nobility is one of the sacred books of China. The ways of men, he says, their works and their service, must be free from all selfish purposes. He counsels, "Look at the grass and the hedgerows, how they spring up without a word spoken or any display of pride. It is the way of Tao, not to act from any personal motive; to conduct affairs without feeling the trouble of them; to account the great as small, and the small as great; and to recompense injury with kindness." That's Lao Tse at his best, five centuries before Christ. I won't trouble you with Confucius—' here for a second the self-display peeped out again, because he explained learnedly, 'Confucius or K'ung fu-tsze, to be accurate. But kindly note that he was almost an exact contemporary of Lao Tse, and if his doctrine is not as spiritual as that of Gautama and Lao, it is ethically noble with its picture of the Ideal Man—the "Superior Man" as he calls him, rather uncomfortably for us westerners who've had some experience of Nietzsche's "Superman". But the Superior man of Confucius has nothing in common with that conceited bully. He's a fine suave creature of elegant and considerate manners. You can see the stamp of Confucius on any Chinaman in Limehouse today—'

Clem nodded as if he'd certainly noticed it, but Prenders held up a finger to stop him speaking.

'At precisely the same time as Buddha and Confucius there was an extraordinary uprising of spiritual awareness among the Hindus, which produced the *Upanishads, their* sacred books. And above all, above all—' he touched me on the shoulder—'don't forget the Greeks, miles away from India and China, who suddenly, and from no apparent cause whatever, flung open the windows of Man's mind for the first time to the dawn of philosophy and science, of physics and metaphysics, Thales, Anaximander, the Eleatics, Pythagoras—' learned names dropping again—'but leave them, leave them, they were intellectual rather than spiritual; I want to come to the one who means most to us sitting here.'

He paused. We waited. He looked behind him again at the earth mounds which were so many barrows holding the bones and dust of Babylon. He looked again at the water before our feet. And resumed, 'Have you any idea to whom I'm coming now? He arose here. Here in Babylon. It was in 586, the beginning of this sixth century, that Jerusalem fell to Nebuchadnezzar who carried all the flower of its population captive to Babylon, leaving only the poorest in the land to act as vine-dressers and husbandmen. And for nearly fifty years the captives sat here by the waters of Babylon and wept. Saying "Sing us one of the songs of Zion." And then, "But how can we sing the Lord's song in a strange land?" And after some fifty years of it, at about 540, suddenly, the great poet of the Exile spoke. No one knows his name. We can only call him the Second Isaiah because his songs, almost unbearably beautiful, are found in the last chapters of Isaiah. But *what* an Unknown! He really sang them a song of Zion. He had been watching the career of Cyrus the Great, up among those mountains, how he'd conquered Astyages, the King of the Medes, and Croesus, King of Lydia, and he was confident he would come down from the Persian mountains and capture Babylon and, being a man of magnanimous temper, set the people of Jehovah free. How they must have thrilled to his words! "Comfort ye, comfort ye my people, saith your God. Speak ye comfortably to Jerusalem and cry unto her that her warfare is accomplished. . . . Get thee up into the high mountain; lift up thy voice, lift it up, be not afraid; say unto the cities of Judah, Behold your God. . . . He shall feed his flock like a shepherd; he shall gather the lambs in his arms and carry them in his bosom, and gently lead those that are with young." Is *that* poetry? Remember he was thinking of Cyrus coming from the mountains, a thought which gave him what my old teacher used to call the loveliest sentence in our language: "How beautiful upon the mountains are the feet of him that bringeth good tidings, that publisheth peace." '

Prenders' voice broke as he spoke this sentence; he seemed to be swallowing back tears, so did it move him. He may have been back among splendid quotations, but no longer with any thought of self-display. He was too far lost in admiration and exultation for that.

After another great sentence, 'Come down and sit in the dust, O virgin daughter of Babylon,' and demanding, 'What do you say to *that*, mate?' he went on, 'And not only is he a mighty poet, he's also perhaps the Hebrew prophet with the loftiest vision. His Jehovah is no petty God of a little tribe, fighting other gods, but the one and only God, creator and sustainer of the universe, who "stretched out the heavens between the span of his finger and thumb and can hold all the seas in the palm of his hand." "Behold the nations are as a drop in a bucket and are accounted as the small dust in a balance; behold, he taketh up the isles as a very little thing." Fine, would you say? And Cyrus *did* come down and set them free?'

Here he snatched from an inside breast-pocket that little worn Bible which must have been waiting there all the time and, wetting his finger, whipped over its pages to find more that he wanted to read. As he turned the pages, he said, 'And this God is the God and Saviour of all the Gentiles as well as of the Jews. Yes of all us poor *goyim*. Here we are, here we are. "Look unto me and be ye saved, all the ends of the earth; for I am God and there is none else." The monotheism that was sounding in the Hindus' *Upanishads* ever so far away, is ringing loudly here, on the voice of a nameless Jew, captive in Babylon. But that isn't all. Not only is his Jehovah a universal God but he's a God of righteousness. He *is* Righteousness. Listen: "Is not this the fast that I have chosen? To loose the bands of wickedness and to let the oppressed go free, and that ye break every yoke? Is it not to deal thy bread to the hungry, and that thou bring the poor that are cast out into thy house; when thou seest the naked that thou cover him? ... Then shall thy light break forth as the morning. ..."'

Eyes alight with enthusiasm, his voice possessed and fired by every great word he was uttering, Prenders struck me as surely the most remarkable case I was ever likely to encounter of an Infidel Prophet, inspired as he expounded the loftiest of creeds. I suspected a childish delight in his new rebellion and vagabondage, which were both denied by this inescapable obsession with the great religions of the world. He went expounding on, 'In his view, you see, Israel's task is to spread this righteousness all over the earth, and it's here that he achieves his sublime conception of an Israel which is the Suffering Servant of Humanity, who must honour its world-saving mission, even though persecuted, despised and rejected. This true Israel— whom we may think of, not as a little suffering nation, but as all those of whom the world is not worthy—must suffer in loneliness of soul till its task is consummated and its name is vindicated by God before the eyes of all. It's the voice of this Unknown which declares the meaning of all that went before him in Judaism and all that was to come in Christianity. I'm not saying what many have said, that he actually foretold the coming of a carpenter and joiner's son in Judaea five hundred years later, but that he stated the everlasting truth which that young man would enact—I think this Second Isaiah thought of his *nation* as the Suffering Servant—but at least it was out of his nation that the young man came. Anyhow, this is probably the noblest vision, not only in the Hebrew writings, but in all the sacred books of humanity. ... He beats them all. ... Oh, well ... but that's enough. I talk too much.'

Clem said, 'No, no,' smiling. 'You've treated us to a marvellous lecture. By the waters of Babylon.'

'That's the trouble. I was a lecturer once, and we're creatures of habit. Come.' He rose. 'We must be getting back. We've done with Babylon. "Babylon is finished, is finished, that great city."'

I attempted a jest. 'Do we now go back to Jerusalem? Is our Captivity over?'

'Oh, no. Not yet. Not at all. Not going back to Jerusalem yet Going further ... further.'

'Oh, dear! But where? Where now?' I pretended dismay.

'Never mind. It's not too far. And I've got it all fixed up with Davy. Eastward, not westward.'

'Eastward? Persia?'

'Yes. Didn't I tell you? Just a little way into Iran. Don't worry. Just a one-night stand. And in parts it's very beautiful. Up on the tableland.'

'You mean we'll have to spend a night in Persia?'

'Just one. Yes. Just one. A strange and lovely country . . . in parts.'

'But are there hotels in Persia?' I asked in my ignorance.

'Of course there are. And they're good and they're cheap. If you know how to bargain and refuse to be anyone's sap. But we shan't need a hotel, except perhaps for a meal.'

'Why? What do you mean?'

'You'll see. And you can leave all the bargaining to me.'

'Oh, dear! Clem, what is he up to now? Still, if it's anything like as interesting as today, Prenders, I'll buy.'

'Me too,' said Clem.

'It'll be interesting enough,' he promised us. 'And the staff-work is all done by Davy and me.'

'Such as?' I inquired, not wholly at ease about 'staff-work' by Davy and Prenders.

'You'll see.'

§

So impressive had he been with his scholarship, his eloquence, and his clear spiritual insight that I had now forgotten there was some dubious shadow surrounding him, but my head and my heart were startled into recollection of this before we'd been five minutes back in the hotel.

Davy stood in the hotel vestibule, having come to learn how we'd fared. He was talking with a big swarthy gentleman in a red fez, but, as he saw Clem and me he called, 'Ah, there you are! But where's old—' and he stopped. Abruptly. He stuttered, 'Old . . .' and changed the form of his question. 'Where's Number Three?'

'Prenders?' Clem answered. 'I think he's out there practising his Arabic on the driver.'

'Oh, well, let's leave him at it. For the Lord's sake come and drink. I want to hear everything, and I'm sure you want a Christian drink.' He turned towards a passing waiter. 'Ali, tell Mr. . . . that we're all in the Bar. He knows of old that—excuse me—' his fist to his lips covered a slight eructation—'that's the usual place to find me.'

I didn't catch the name he'd mentioned; it was no name I knew;

and I couldn't understand why he should want this stranger to join us. But so benevolent was his manner, and so unstable his utterance, that I guessed he'd already had a few Christian drinks in advance of our return, and was possibly a trifle confused. His eyes were moist, and certainly not with tears. As we followed him, he said, 'I told old —excuse me—I told your Prenders that we'd assemble in the Bar. And thank God—or perhaps I should say "thank Allah" here—that the writ of his good Prophet doesn't run in this saloon. You can get any drink you bloody well like here. And thank your stars, both of you, that you're not over the border in Kuwait. No drinking there. Worse than Glasgow on a Sunday. Bad enough in Glasgow, but hell in these broiling bone-dry countries where life and thirst are almost the same thing. I last without a thirst for ten minutes. No more.'

The bar of the River Palace Hotel was little different from any American bar in a western hotel. In this pre-dinner hour it was nearly full and loud with voices. Americans and British—mainly business-men, I supposed—sat along the counter or at tables in conversation with one another or with Iraqis in smart European suits that paid no regard to the room's heavy, lifeless heat. Davy having ordered what he called 'the only possible drink in this God-forsaken and over-heated country—Bourbon on the rocks', we found a table at the back of the room. A white-coated waiter brought the drinks, and Davy said 'Cheerioh, you two bastards,' drank, wiped his lips with a knuckle, and began, 'Well, come on, chaps. Spill it all. You did Ctesiphon—'

But before he could get further Clem asked what the many Moslems at the counter or the tables were drinking.

'Much the same as this, probably. Scotch on the rocks. It's the favourite.'

'But—pardon my ignorance—I thought Mohammed forbade all alcohol.'

'He certainly did. But there you are, it's all rather like Christians keeping Lent. One has to break one's fast occasionally in the interests of business. Or out of courtesy. We Arabs are the most courteous race on earth. A bit homicidal sometimes. But courteous. Always cour-teous. And, my God, hospitable. Arab hospitality is a religion with us and a lot nearer our hearts, I suspect, than some of the injunctions of the Prophet. Rather like cricket in England. Playing the game and being sportsmanlike and behaving like a gentleman and so on. We really believe in that ever so much more than in Queen Elizabeth's C. of E. and the jolly old Athanasian Creed—wouldn't you say? If Mr. Athanasius was right, I shall perish everlastingly. Which would be a pity in some ways. You did Ctesiphon and Babylon? Dear old Babylon. She was a whore, wasn't she: the Whore of Babylon. What the Prots used to call the Church of Rome, and the Church of Rome call the Prots. Here's to Babylon. *And* Bourbon. And here's to us, dammit. Fine types, and may there soon be more like us.' He wiped his mouth again. 'Have some more? Say when you want it. Excuse me—Babylon is quite a dump to go and see, isn't it? And you couldn't have a more wonderful guide than old Garron.'

'*Garron?*' I asked, bewildered.

'Yes, there's nothing the poor old boy doesn't know. Here's to old Ctesiphon.'

Garron? Had I heard it aright? Against the noise of many voices and that loud clap of laughter in a distant corner? Who was Garron? Prenders he must have meant; the words 'guide' and 'nothing the poor old boy doesn't know' showed this.

Poor?

Had the name and the 'poor' slipped out because Davy's tongue was loosed with drink? Or was he, here in this bar, like Hester Brakewaite in her drawing-room, pressed by a desire to speak of some dark but heady story that hung around the figure of Prenders? He was suddenly silent now. Was it that he had only just, in the midst of a jubilant mood, remembered that he had promised Prenders to 'say nothing' and was now doing battle with his scruples rather like Hester Brakewaite that first time I met her?

'Garron?' I said, presenting the name as a question.

No answer. Clearly a paralysis of indecision had hold of him.

Clem, whose eyes had also opened in surprise at the name, spoke my question more fearlessly. 'By Garron you mean Prenders?'

'Yes, that's it. . . . Prenders. . . . Old Prenders.'

'But wait,' Clem objected. 'We don't know Prenders as Garron.

Garron, did you say? We've never heard him called anything but Prenders.'

A drawing-in of Davy's lower lip that his upper teeth might close on it. And a further silence. 'You . . . er . . . you don't know all about him?'

This time I answered. 'We know nothing about him except what our leader, the Bishop, has told us. That he is—or was—a lecturer in oriental philosophies. An oriental scholar of great distinction, he said. Speaking Arabic and Persian and half the languages of the East.'

'Oh . . . is that what he said? . . . Oh yes, that's all true. He was a lecturer all right. . . . And a very fine one too. . . .' Six words to gain time. . . . 'Yes, quite a genius at the game, I believe. Especially with young students, I've always heard. Able to draw them in crowds.'

'But doesn't he still lecture?'

'Still? . . . I don't know. . . . I really don't know.'

Plain that the battle within him was continuing.

Since I now longed more than ever to know what was the shadowy secret around our Prenders (or Garron) I was unscrupulous enough to hope that Davy would defeat *his* scruples and pour it all forth, with the usual conscience-placating request, 'But keep it to yourselves, there's good chaps. This is all in the strictest confidence, mind you.' I even spoke words that might help him towards this disloyalty; I said, 'I very much wish we did know. We all wish we did.'

But Davy's scruples won. And perhaps his diplomatic training played its part in this victory. 'Oh, well . . . Prenders is Prenders, a strange chap and very mad—' just what Prenders had said of him. 'He's always been called Prenders. It's one of his names all right: Prender Garron. Mum's name, very likely. But there it all is: I don't really know how much he wants known or doesn't want known. I'm fond of old Prenders. We all were.' He changed the subject quickly. Awareness that his tongue had slipped sobered him a little— but only a little. 'So you did Ctesiphon? You must tell me all about it. But first what about some refills? No, no. On me, on me: Arab hospitality.' And he clapped his hands to attract the eye of a waiter. He repeated, 'No, no,' as we contested this excess of hospitality, and mentioned British hospitality. 'Unthinkable. Unthinkable. This is good old Arabia'; and while he was still looking for the waiter, and there was as yet no drink in our glasses, he anticipated its happy arrival by toasting us with misty eyes and no glass in his hand. 'Well, here's to you, cockies. Cheers abounding. Happy days to you all.' And he clapped his hands again and signalled to the waiter. 'Hi! *You.*'

Prenders arrived at this moment, and the clap drew his attention as well as the waiter's. He came bright-eyed and grinning towards us, well pleased with the day's work and his part in it. He had plenty to say, and jokes to make, and when the new drinks had come he mischievously disclosed to Clem and me, while Davy sat smiling at us all with a kind of liquefied benevolence, some of his designs for the morrow, which shook us not a little. And at times horrified us.

12

The Great Road

PRENDERS had not disclosed all his designs: he was still holding some behind riddles. We knew we had to start very early in the morning for the journey into Persia, but the goal of the journey, its end and aim, remained a mystery. The same car stood before the hotel doors at six in the morning with the same driver, whom Prenders now called Hosein, after one of Islam's greatest saints and martyrs. Hosein (his name was Ibrahim) was a big fat laughing Arab, in slacks and open shirt like ourselves but wearing a white Arab headcloth with a red circlet. When Clem and I arrived, yawning, he was rearranging some equipment in the car's wide boot, and, to our alarm, this included groundsheets, sleeping bags, two folding camp-beds (why only two?), tropic lanterns, Primus stoves, a camp kettle and a supply of eating utensils. Whether Prenders meant us to see so early all this paraphernalia I do not know.

Clem asked, 'What's all that in aid of?'

Which drew only a grin from Hosein and the words, 'Food. Sleep, no?'

'Sleep! Oh, lord!' I exclaimed, 'Wherever do you suppose he's taking us now?'

But just as Clem answered, 'Oh, well, leave him to it. He enjoys his game,' Prenders appeared.

I demanded of him, 'How far are you really taking us? Prenders, answer please.'

'Well ... about ... about three hundred miles, all told. Lovely country.' He tried to smile, but a guilty look behind the smile raised in my mind some distrust of that 'about'.

'Three hundred miles in a day?'

'Good gracious, yes. What's wrong with that? It's only about the distance from London to Carlisle, and these boys drive. Like hell they do. And it's flat going for the first hundred miles.'

'Yes, and then mountains.'

'Mountains, certainly. But mountains go down as well as up. And much of Persia's a plateau. Do it in seven hours . . . or so.'

'I agree with that "or so",' said Clem.

'Well, say eight. I'll be generous and give you eight. That means, if we stop at a place I have in mind for lunch—interesting place— we'll be there by four . . . or so. In the beauty of the evening.'

'And where's "there"?'

'You'll see. And what's more you'll think it worth it. You'll thank me. So get in the bus, for pity's sake.'

Shrugging our acceptance, we got into the car, Clem and I in the back, Prenders by the driver because he could speak his language. The car went off at no gentle speed through the empty morning, and when it was clear of the Baghdad streets, it shot ahead like a guided missile in space. With the last mud house and the last palm grove behind us we were able to glimpse, away to our left, the twin golden domes and the four golden minarets of Al Kadhimain's holy mosque, each of them caught, like the Sultan's turret, in a noose of early sunlight. I begged that we should stop and visit this most famous place.

'*Visit it!*' scoffed Prenders. 'Unbelieving giaours like us? We wouldn't be allowed across its threshold. If we so much as asked to do so we'd raise an uproar from everyone standing by. Including the blind beggars.'

'Why?'

'Because it's a holy of holies to the Shi'ite Moslems. Two of the Prophets rightful successors, according to the Shi'ites, are buried there. If you want to know their names, they are Musa Ibn Ja'far Kazim and Ibn Ali el Jaward.' Real good name-dropping, this.

'I see,' I said. 'Thank you. Now I know all.'

By this time the golden domes and minarets were fading into the morning haze and we were speeding over country so flat and empty that Hosein was able to lean back in his seat and leave only one hand on his wheel while he drove at some monstrous rate, smoking a cigarette. Ninety-odd miles were devoured in some ninety minutes and we were at Khanaqin, the last town on this side of the Persian frontier. Only a little way farther and we reached the foothills of the Persian highlands and began to climb. To climb towards a high heaving tableland which, as Prenders informed us proudly, was one of the loftiest countries in the world, marvellously placed between the low, level sands of Iraq and the low, level steppes of Russia. Was there anywhere, he asked, a more abrupt change from the sands of the desert to a land of high mountains and high uplifted vales—anywhere a more sudden change from palm to poplar and pine?

'I'm sure I don't know,' I said.

But after he'd said this, and as we went higher and higher, I began to feel superior to the Bishop and his party, not forgetting Maureen, all so far away and low down, across the Syrian desert.

No highland poplars were visible to us yet as we climbed up and up, or down and up again, towards the ridges of the passes in the Zagros mountains—and towards whatever remarkable sight Prenders was carrying us.

'How much further?' I asked as we went grinding up a slope with a cloud of dusty white earth following.

'Only about another hundred miles . . . or so,' he said in his guilty and apologetic voice, 'but just think—' and, turning round to speak at more length and lay balm on any impatience behind him, he urged us, 'Just think: what do a hundred miles matter when you're now on the most interesting road in the world? Why, the more of it, the better.'

'Interesting?' I queried the word because we seemed to be driving through a mountain emptiness, first along a mountain's foot, then along a shelf with a precipice at our side, and then through a narrow infolded canyon, or across wide hill-bound valleys, a few of which, in contrast with the arid hills around, were lush and green. 'Spectacular, yes. Even melodramatic. But why interesting? Wouldn't boring be a better word? Don't you think so, Clem?'

'What I'm thinking all the time,' answered Clem, 'is that he's got us wherever we are now and that it's he who'll have to get us out.'

'Great God above,' Prenders complained. 'The ignorance of you two is overpowering. Don't you realize that there's no more famous highway than this in the whole wide world?'

'Why?' I demanded, almost indignantly, because it was difficult to get excited about a road that at times was hardly recognizable as a road at all. Though metalled in some fashion, and maybe tarmac'd, it seemed in places little more than a wide track of compressed earth and dust; so often had the neighbouring desert swept in and swamped the handiwork of men. A temperamental track, it needed the springing of our broad American car to deal with its occasional tantrums. Just now there was an ancient lorry in front of us which Hosein was eager to overtake, but it was rattling and jumping and dancing on at a ludicrous speed for any old lady so battered and worn. It infuriated Hosein by throwing up behind it a wake of windblown dust, tall as a travelling fog, which not only obscured our vision but covered our bonnet and wings with a powder like that on some old harridan's face.

'Why? *Why?*' Prenders echoed. 'God save and help me! Didn't someone call the Thames "liquid history"? Well, this road is the very dust of history. It's just about the oldest road in history. It's still the one great road from off the Persian tableland to Baghdad and all the rest of the Middle East, but twenty-five centuries and more ago it was the single highway from Ecbatana, the capital of Media, and the old name for Hamadan, down from the mountains to the Babylonian plains. History was marching up and down it ages before it had so much as discovered the Thames. At this very moment we're going through the heart of the old Median Empire, a country which belongs to a time centuries before Islam, centuries before Christ, centuries before Nebuchadnezzar, and a century and a half before Cyrus the Great himself. Cyrus, having polished off the Medes, came storming down it with his Persians to overthrow Babylon and set the Jews free. Darius must have accounted it his greatest road, as we shall see—'

'What do you mean: "we shall see"?'

But Prenders in spate was not to be arrested or diverted. 'And don't forget Darius had an empire stretching from the Balkans to the Hindu Kush, the greatest power ever seen up till then on the face of the earth. And this was his royal post-road, the road for the King of Kings. His couriers and satraps and dispatch-riders came galloping down it to the ends of the earth. It's the immemorial trade-route for the caravans, and the pilgrim's route to the holy places of Islam—especially for the dead pilgrims—oh yes, it's the historic road of the dead pilgrims.'

'*Dead* pilgrims? Come again,' was Clem's request.

And Prenders elucidated this bizarre remark at length, which of course was what he had wanted to do. He explained that it was a desire of pious Persians to be carried down from their mountains and buried at Kerbela in Iraq, as near as possible to the tomb of Hosein the Martyr. 'The caravans of the dead used to bring these pious corpses down, wrapped up like bales and slung on each side of a pack-mule, with all the mourners following behind. For the Arabs the custom duties on these imports—at Khanaqin which we passed just now—or should we say these invisible exports?—and their burial fees at Kerbela have always been a most satisfying business, pleasantly helpful to their trade-balance.' He swung a thumb towards all the country on our left. 'Roughly speaking, everything north of this road is Kurdistan, and we'd better keep our eyes skinned for Kurds; they are in a permanent state of angry rebellion against the Arabs and make excellent highwaymen. "When your camel falls, out comes a knife" is one of our prettier proverbs in the East. I think on the whole we'll ask Hosein to remove that Arab head-dress.'

This was all he said for a while but just as he had stirred my imagination as we sat among the ruins of Babylon, so now he had changed the whole character of the landscape at which I had been looking with uncomprehending eyes. Everything was exciting that had been desolate. He had flung it all back, except for the dead pilgrims and the Kurds, into the world of twenty-five centuries ago, so that when we passed a village of mud houses, a water tower, a derelict caravanserai, or met the oldest motor-bus I'd ever seen still functioning—its roof piled with rugs, carpets and bales so that its lashed freight measured the height of the bus itself—all these things offended me like anachronisms long centuries out of place.

§

The heat of the morning raised a luminous and shimmering haze from the dusty road. Miles of switchbacking road through this lifting haze brought us to the saddle of the Pai-taq Pass, and we went downward towards the large straggling town of Kermanshah, spread over a wide plain. It was strange after miles of mountain desolation to come upon a fertile and flowering plain only framed by mountains far away. Tall poplars and cypresses, oaks and firs, rose from it, flocks of sheep roamed over it, and this city of a hundred thousand people, one of Persia's greatest, lay sprawling beside the immemorial trade-route and pilgrim's way. It was in this moment that I understood how Persia was but a sprinkling of large and beautiful oases on a vast upland desert. Over this oasis today the sky was blue and rainless, the light brilliant beneath the sun's glare, and the air a hot breath on the cheek. Though barely summer the grass and wheat were brown beneath the fire of the sun.

I asked of Prenders, 'Have we arrived? Are we there? Is this what you are dragging us to?'

'Not quite,' he said, somewhat guiltily. 'No ... not quite yet.' And he added encouragingly, 'Very nearly. Very nearly.'

'Precisely what,' asked Clem suspiciously, 'does "very nearly" mean?'

'It'll only be another—' he hesitated—'another twenty miles ... or so.'

'But we're getting used to your "or so's". For my part I interpret each "or so" as a good third added to your first estimate. I am, you may remember, an accountant. So shall we say another thirty miles?'

'Well ... about that,' he admitted. 'Yes, just about that.'

'Good God.'

'But then you'll really see something. In an hour, an hour. And you'll bless me abundantly for having brought you. We'll get some lunch here,' he said, turning to a less ambiguous subject. 'Take us to food, Hosein. Take us to some reasonable hotel where we shan't be ruined. We're but poor men, all of us.'

We were now in the populous city, a town of narrow twisting streets and broad straight avenues; of mean mud-hutments and fine mansions within walled gardens. More and more as we drove honking and blaring through the crowded streets I got the impression of a city which History had left behind. Dilapidation drooped in tatters from most of its buildings, whether small and humble or large and grandiose. The walls of all, whether wattle and mud or of beautiful brickwork were powdered white with the traffic's dust. Little belonged to Time's present hour, except the American cars like ours and, more rarely, a large American lorry. For the rest, it was a traffic of overburdened donkeys and mules, their packs almost touching the ground while their bells tinkled with an inappropriate happiness; camels yet more heavily freighted and sustaining sourly but obediently their destined lot in life; old hooded carriages, and here a droshky, like a horse-drawn bath-chair for two, which reminded me that the Russians used to come this way. Of the pedestrians the westernized men in lounge suits and trilby hats walked among Kurds in big black turbans and baggy trousers sashed with cummerbunds, while eastern women slunk against walls and hid their faces for a brief purdah as our untrustworthy male eyes went by.

The hotel before which Hosein stopped our car was no palace though calling itself Grand Hotel Taq-e-Bostam. We brushed past the beggars at its door—'Baksheesh, captain? Baksheesh?'—and went rattling through a bead curtain into the restaurant. It was hardly two o'clock and there were still men at the tables drinking tea from glasses or, when the tea was too hot, from the saucers on which the glasses stood. Some were playing chess. Apart from the tables and chairs and the magnificent rugs and carpets covering all the floor or hanging from the walls, the large room had little furnishing.

The *maître d'hôtel*, who was the hotelier himself, could not have been more courteous and smiling. He was a small browned man with a huge, heavy nose leaning over a black moustache so thin and a black beard so furry that one guessed his face, in all his forty years, had never known a razor. He greeted us proudly in English, ' 'Alloa? Allo! How . . . do . . . you . . . do? You are very well, I hope?'

'Yes, we are well,' Prenders reassured him. 'And you? You are in good health, I hope?'

'But yes. Thanks be to Allah.'

'Thanks be to Allah,' Prenders agreed.

The hotelier, nodding, either in appreciation of this thanks to Allah for his state of health or in gratitude to the same Source for our good condition, bowed us to seats around a table. Prenders now submitted his requests in what I supposed was Persian, but our host waved this aside, saying, 'I speak English very good.'

'You certainly do,' Prenders flattered him. 'Marvellously.'

'Yes, I have terribly all-right English. You are Americans?' He asked it, smiling to suggest a delight at the idea. 'In Kermanshah we have plenty American guys.'

'You do?'

'Oh, sure. Okay. Tourist guys,' he explained. 'They come to go to Taq-e-Bostam to see—'

Prenders held up quickly a silencing hand. 'Yes, of course, they would.'

'You are going there?'

'No, no. Not to Taq-e-Bostam.'

'But you are Americans too?' he said again, though doubtfully this time as if not to go to Taq-e-Bostam (wherever or whatever that might be) was not to be American.

Prenders shook his head. 'English. English.'

'But your car? It is American.'

'It belongs to our Embassy in Bah'g-dah'd,' said Prenders, clearly thinking that this lie would answer as well as any other and might impress this gentleman and produce good food. After all, the car was, so to speak, an in-law relative of the Embassy through its hirer, Davy.

'You have been advised to my hotel by a tourist agency, no?'

'Dear me, no.' The idea that in Persia he needed a tourist agency obviously aggrieved the *amour propre* of Prenders. 'I know Persia well.'

Our host had not heard this because he was wanting to make a point. 'The tourist agencies recommend me because of my eats.'

If there was truth in this, it was good to hear. I was hungry and Prenders had told me that Persian meals were good, though monotonous.

Prenders played up to him. 'Well then, show us your eats. This'll be the first meal my friends have had in Persia. So the honour of your great country is in your hands.'

'I shall do it very proud,' he promised, and, bowing, he hurried away through a service door to his kitchens where he began shouting, apparently in a fury, to his servants there.

'And he'll do *us* proud when the time comes to pay,' said Prenders.

'Pity we've no longer got Davy to deal with him,' said Clem; and this was tactless of Clem with so sensitive an *amour propre* as that of Prenders. It hurt Prenders that we should think him less skilled than Davy in the art of bargaining with Persian salesmen, which was, we gathered, a matter of declining, now smilingly, now bluntly, now with delicacy, and anon with fire, to be swindled. 'You can safely leave all that to me.' It was, he explained, a recognized sport in Persia, with the salesman in one court, his customer in the other, and between them a net—the suggested price—which went up and down, enlarging and shrinking, according to the skills of the two opponents. 'Unfortunately, if played properly, it takes time, perhaps an hour or so, and we've no time to lose if we're to get to—to where we're going to. But I'll do my best.'

Whatever the price would be, the meal was certainly good. First a fat boy-waiter, probably one of the best patrons of the cookhouse, brought us an iced soup which seemed to be made of cucumber and nuts. Then came plates of broiled lamb which Prenders called *chelau kebab* and said was a staple dish. A large dish of pilau rice, saffron tinted, accompanied the lamb and a basin of vegetables. For dessert there was a bowl piled with peaches, nectarines, oranges, figs, grapes, pistachio nuts and pomegranates, all encompassing a huge melon which is the monarch of fruits in Persia. 'Bread' came in the form of thin, flat, unleavened discs like the chupatties of India.

It was a pity we had so little time to spend with these delicacies, but we finished quickly—and now the moment of settlement was upon us. 'Now for it,' said Prenders, and we all rose for it, and our little bearded host came towards it, bowing, and holding his bill in his hand. He came smiling—an amiable, wide smile stretched between the thin black moustache and square black fluffy beard.

'I don't like that smile,' said Prenders.

My own thought was that this browned man approaching us looked more like a Turk than a Persian, one of our cousins.

'How much?' asked Prenders, taking the bill.

Our host left the bill to answer this, merely saying with his pleased and ingratiating smile, 'That will be all.'

What the 'all' was I did not learn at first because, after one blasphemous exclamation from Prenders, the loud, warm, rapid interlocution that ensued was conducted in Persian, American, and English, often with both parties talking at once. I gathered only that the opening sum was, in Prenders' view, outrageous, a shock, a disappointment, a source of sorrow and even of despair. Despair of humanity as at present constituted and a new doubt as to its future. He began his display by expressing no more than this shock, this sorrow.

'Oh, no, Ahmed,' he submitted in a tone of great, even sweet, reasonableness. He must have got the name, Ahmed, from the bill head and was offering it as a token of a friendliness unspoiled, despite the shock, the sadness, and the need to summon up all his powers of forgiveness. 'No, no, Ahmed, you mistake us. It was only your excellent meal that we bought; not your hotel.'

'But that is the price for the meal. It is not big. It is okay.'

'Big? Big, Ahmed? It's on a level with your mountains around. Look: Kermanshah is on a plain. Could not the price come down on to the plain?'

But to Ahmed these first shots in the game were serious; it was no moment as yet to introduce a joke. 'It is the fair price. Everything is very dear in Persia.'

'You're telling *me*.'

'I do not alter it. I have to live.'

'But, Ahmed, we have to live too. We cannot be ruined. We must have some money left to get back to England.'

Ahmed was ready to allow a brief joke here, so he laughed loudly—and long—at this one. When he could speak again, he protested, 'You. You have much dough. Persians are poor. English and Americans rich.'

'Whether we are rich or poor, Ahmed, in England we do not think that the price of an article depends on the income of the buyer. It depends only on what it is worth. Whether we are American millionaires or penurious English, the value of your meal stays the same. Doesn't it? Or is it, perhaps, that Persian hotels levy income tax on behalf of the Government?'

'That I do not understand.'

By this time all the men in the room had risen from their tables and were standing round the four of us to watch and enjoy the play. Chess was deserted for a game more immediately interesting. The fat boy-waiter who had been refilling tea-glasses at a counter left his samovar and joined the audience that he might miss nothing. One young man even came in from the kitchens, a sweating dishwasher or assistant cook in an apron, to learn what it was all about and now stood by the others. All in this gratifying 'gate' were in western dress except two obvious Kurds in high turbans and high cummerbunds. No Americans were in sight; one guessed that the plenty American guys only came here when the better hotels were full. None here but were lifelong students of this local pastime.

Prenders tried a new shot, an effective one down on to his base-line. 'Or is it perhaps, Communism: "from each according to his wealth; to each according to his needs"? But we are not men of wealth, and you are no man in need. You are a man of substance, Comrade Ahmed. Look at your splendid hotel.'

'I am no Communist.'

'No, no, of course not. I thought not. No Communist.'

'But my eats are very good, and worth all I ask for them.'

'They are worth a fair price, certainly, and we will give it to you. I thought the saffron rice was excellent.' But he turned to us to mutter—not for Ahmed to hear, 'Four hundred rials each! Twice too much—three times—in a flea-bitten hotel like this. Listen now, Ahmed.' Never did sweet reasonableness sound more appealingly in a disputant's voice. 'We know that God is great and that there is no god but Allah and Mohammed is his prophet, but we know also that the followers of the Prophet are honesty itself, as they are instructed to be in the Quran. Or have I got it wrong? Is that only so down in Bah'g-dah'd? No, I can't believe it. You are strictly honest, I know.'

'I am very honest. Of course I am honest.' He turned to the on-lookers all round this centre court, and asked them with a look of grievous hurt, 'I am okay, am I not?'

Not one of them said anything in response to this appeal, either because they did not think it was required of them or because they could not, as honest men themselves, reply with a 'Yes'. One man nodded, but more in loyalty, I felt, than in conviction.

So, since no voice rang with attestations to his honesty, Ahmed lifted his own to affirm it again and loudly. 'I am very honest. I know my business, and I know you will thank me for selling you this very lovely meal at such a price. I am a fine business-man.'

'You are indeed. The best.'

'I have to make a living, that is all. I am a guy that has to live. So I think we stay at this very nice price.'

'I think we do not. Okay?'

I turned to Clem at my side and asked in a low voice, 'Are you clear yet whether these exchanges are expressions of mutual affection or amount to a free fight?'

'A free fight beyond question,' Clem declared. 'Mr. Ahmed is very angry indeed. Ready to explode.'

Prenders, who had heard this, turned to us and said, 'Not at all; he's pleased'; and turned back to Ahmed. 'Certainly you are a fine business-man; we are all agreed on that. But we are fine business-men too and extremely anxious to pay the right price for everything. Have a cigarette.'

'Ah, no.' This was not said in any mood of disaffection but merely in adherence to the Persian custom which ordains that you must always refuse any offer once—or, better, twice and thrice—before accepting it, which you'd intended to do from the first.

Prenders, well acquainted with this mannerly custom, kept the cigarette case in position beneath Ahmed's eyes. 'Now come along. English cigarette. Very good. Very popular in Persia.'

'Ah, no. . . . No, no. . . .'

'Not?' The cigarette case stayed up there in place, held between Prenders' finger and thumb. 'Ahmed, you will please me if you'll take one.'

'No, no.'

'It will please me. Very much.'

'Well . . . well . . . if that is so . . . perhaps . . .' Ahmed bowed and took out a cigarette.

One of the standers-by lit it for him.

For a second Prenders looked around these standers-by as if he'd an idea of offering cigarettes to one and all, but discretion overthrew this generous idea. There must have been a dozen or more in the assembly, and if each in turn declined two or three times before the acceptance which had been certain all along, too much time would be devoted to this courtliness, and we had to hurry on.

So he resumed the contention (or whatever one might call it) and attacked suddenly on a new flank. 'Oh, I see. Yes, I see. I've got it. I've got the point of it. It is a joke. A little joke. That's right, isn't it, Ahmed?' And he smiled brilliantly at all the humour in this joke. Surprisingly Ahmed smiled brilliantly too, and so did all the spectators, rather as when a man yawns in a room all watchers reproduce his yawn. But after Ahmed had carried his smile to a completion by throwing back his head and laughing richly, he said, 'It is not a joke.'

'Not?' Prenders' face expressed the utmost surprise. 'Oh—but it must be.'

'No. There is nothing funny about it.'

I was fascinated by the difference between these two arguers: one from our cold western island, hands fiddling before him but using no part of his body for emphasis except lips and eyes; the other from a hot Eastern plateau arguing with arms, shoulders, palms, head, and the whole body from waist upward. Shoulders especially when despair, frustration, indignation accompanied his upturned eyes; they even played a part in what I assumed were ejaculatory prayers to Allah.

'Then if it's not a little joke,' said Prenders, 'it's simply—yes, of course: it's just that there are a few mistakes in it. Some unwitting miscalculations. Of course. Stupid of me. Take it dish by dish. Soup. . . . The *chelau kebab*—it was excellent. I always enjoy it. . . . Vegetables. . . . Fruits. Of which we partook little because we had no time. But they were good to look at. The sight of them was worth something, perhaps. As I add it all up—oh, chupatties, yes—we owe you just about half of what you ask.' For friendliness' sake he dropped into broken English. 'You see, I live in Persia long time. Tehran. Isfahan. That's why I speak your language so good, and learn the exact price of all things.'

Perceiving the first signs of surrender on Ahmed's face, he drove home his advantage by a yet more effective statement. That he had lived in Tehran and Isfahan was true enough, but this next statement was a powerful lie, stirred by memories of Davy and the Embassy down on the plains. He said, 'In Tehran I had many friends in our British Embassy there, who used to take me sometimes to meet the Shah. Yes, at the Gulestan Palace. A beautiful place. Lovely garden. Look, Ahmed, we give you a little over half and add—naturally—a commission. A handsome commission.'

As this offer was perhaps larger than Ahmed had hoped to receive when play ended, and as Prenders' access to the Shah might—possibly—be true, he took the bill from Prenders' hand. He frowned over it. He went through it a second time—soup, *chelau kebab*, vegetables, fruit. He twisted his mouth over it and allowed at last, 'But wait . . .' We waited. Everyone waited. They smoked as they waited. 'Yes, do you know, there is a slight mistake there. You are so okay. But only slight one.'

'And there.' Prenders pointed to the fruits. 'We ate hardly any of those. No time. But we were glad to see them, Ahmed. We enjoyed looking at them.'

Ahmed thought deeply. 'Ah, but that is yes so. I agree that is yes so. You did not eat. I think it's possible we've got a little wrong. Here and there. Perhaps because you were in such a hurry for it. You ask for bill. I hurry over it.'

'Could be that. Could well be that,' Prenders encouraged. 'Yes, we didn't give you much time. In that I admit we were wrong, Ahmed. *I* can never get accounts right if I'm hurried.'

'Yes. . . .' Ahmed mused over the bill. . . . 'I think . . . I think now you point it out . . .'

But before he could finish his thoughts Prenders had produced an unmistakable thousand rials, and was thrusting them into the host's already opening hand. The hand closed on them with smiles. Smiles all round. From Prenders, from us, from the audience.

Close of play.

The audience went back to their tea or their chess, the fat boy-waiter to his samovar, the assistant cook to his hot kitchen, and we three went from the hotel after amiable good-byes from our host.

'You come back to see me, I think I am sure,' were his last words.

'If Allah wills it,' Prenders conceded, with a smile for him and a grimace for us.

Nearly thirty more miles to where Prenders would be; and the road was still up and down amid the Zagros mountains, so it was an hour before, abruptly, with no word spoken, Hosein, evidently obeying secret orders, swung the car round the rough bases of a high mountain and, having completed this right-angled turn, stopped.

'Thanks, Hosein,' Prenders said. 'Exactly right.' And he alighted from the seat beside him. To us through our window he said without a smile, without expression of any kind, 'We're there.'

13

Under Bisitun

BUT where? After alighting too and looking round at the general desolation I could see nothing but this precipitous mountain on one side of us, and on the other an empty plain stretching to distant hills.

'Look better,' said Prenders.

I looked at the jagged mountain. At the plain. The mountain at first glance was no more than a towering pile of stormy rock, every aspect of it fissured and cracked and crinkled. It rose hugely, and as it were angrily, from smoother foothills to a skyline of rocky, conical peaks. On this plain, at some distance from the foothills, was a large caravanserai, but plainly it was derelict. It followed the universal Persian pattern: four long sides embracing a spacious courtyard; the side—or front—facing us a long arcade of twelve vaulted chambers open to the plain. In the midst of the twelve rose the high arched entrance.

'Well? Notice anything?' asked Prenders.

'Is it the caravanserai?' Clem ventured.

'Lord, no. That's only of yesterday. Doubt if it's two hundred years old. And, anyhow, it's dead. Possibly tribesmen shelter in it sometimes and leave their messes there.'

I sighed. 'Well, what *have* we come to see, please? Now that we're here.'

'Try again.' Hands patiently behind him, he waited. 'And bear in mind that, as I told you, this was the great highway of the world. The Royal Road of the King of Kings.'

I looked again at the broad white dusty road running by the mountain's foot. I looked at the far-spread plain. I looked up again at the mountain beside us; it stared out violently at the plain. The sun was now falling low in the sky and it flung an amber glow on all those piled and angry rocks. And I saw.

Hundreds of feet above us a large area of the vertical and wrinkled face had been smoothed flat as a stone wall. And carved on this wall was a procession of nearly life-sized figures, facing one unnaturally taller than they. Straining to see better, I perceived that nine of the figures were roped together, neck to neck, sorry captives in single file. The giant figure, facing these, had his foot on another captive who lay supine, but with arms upraised in a plea for mercy. Above this file of luckless captives floated a strange bearded figure with sun rays for his skirts and lightnings flying from his waist. Incised on panels beneath and beside these sculptured figures were inscriptions in characters like the footprints of birds. At least I knew enough to know that this was cuneiform writing.

I let loose a 'Good God!'

Prenders said, 'Yes, you're right. The good god Ahura Mazda. He's the boy sitting in the sky, clothed in sun rays.'

'But . . .' I began.

'This is the holy Mount Behistun. Or Bisitun, as we usually call it now.

'Again?' Clem begged.

'Bissi-toon.' He enunciated it carefully, proudly. 'Bissi-toon. A dwelling of the gods.'

'But what's all that about?' I pointed to the sculptured figures and the crowded inscriptions. 'And why, please, have you brought us here?'

'Because it's the greatest inscription in the world. Because it belongs to that astounding sixth century before Christ. The tall boy is Darius the Great, and he had it cut here soon after the capture of Babylon. Because it makes me think. The god flying above Darius is Ahura Mazda—'

'Who exactly?'

'Ahura Mazda, the Lord of Wisdom, Zoroaster's god, the spirit of light and truth.'

'Thank you. I see.'

'Yes, Ahura Mazda, the everlasting opponent of Angramainyu, the spirit of evil and darkness and lies.'

A small light began to glimmer before me. 'Are these two fellows by any chance the same as Ormuzd and Ahrimam?' I asked, climbing to meet him on his own level of learning.

'Of course. But those are mere popular corruptions of Ahura Mazda and Angramainyu.'

I bowed in acknowledgement of this correction, while thinking, in this Prenders of ours there's always a pedant using only the most scholarly names in a scrupulously accurate pronunciation. Consider 'Bah'g-dah'd.'

'And this was an obvious halting place,' he pointed out, 'for all travellers on the great road—'

'Obvious to you, but not to me. Why should they halt here?'

'Because of springs that come from this mountain. Look at that old caravanserai. Darius, like Ozymandias, supposed that his triumph and his mastery of the world would endure for ages and he placed his record of it here for the generations to see as they passed by. In fact Alexander the Great laid his empire waste in less than two hundred years.'

'What do those cuneiform inscriptions say?' I was pleased to sound my one real note of culture.

Prenders gazed up at the inscriptions as if he were translating them from these hundreds of feet below. ' "I am Darius the Great King, the King of Kings, King of Persia, King of the Provinces, the son of Hystaspes . . ." ' Prenders' eyes were still turned upwards. ' "Thus saith Darius the King. That which I have done I have done only by the grace of Ahura Mazda. For this reason did Ahura Mazda bring aid to me because I was not a liar nor a wrong-doer but according to rectitude have I lived—" and a whole lot more of that kind of cock. There follow the names of all the conquered nations, stretching from the Indus to the Euphrates and the Jordan and the Nile—and even the Danube—roughly all the world that mattered.' Now, by lowering his eyes, he allowed that he was speaking only from memory. 'Somewhere there's a nice piece about his triumph over a Median pretender, Phraortes. "I seized Phraortes and led him forth. I cut off his nose and his ears and put out one eye, and later I hanged him on a cross in Ecbatana." And yet he imagined he was a devoted follower of Ahura Mazda, the spirit of all goodness. He says charmingly, "Ahura Mazda has granted me this empire. By the grace of Ahura Mazda I hold it. Within these lands whoever was a friend I have protected, and whoever was hostile I have destroyed." Those captives are nine of the hostile waiting to be destroyed. Ten with the one under his foot. But the future wasn't with him and his enormous, world-wide empire. It was with two small countries hardly bigger than English counties.'

'You mean?'

'Little Judaea. Little Greece. His sculptures have lasted for ever but not the glory. They're almost as good as ever after twenty-five centuries of storms and rains and blistering suns. You can still read the records. They are written in old Persian, neo-Elamite and neo-Babylonian.'

'Are they?' we said. Rather as if we knew what he was talking about.

'Yes, and it was because there were three languages that we were able to break the secrets of cuneiform. Here,' he said, going to the car's boot and opening it, 'we camp. As a few million others must have done during two or three thousand years. Under Bisitun.'

'What? Here in the open?' Clem asked this without enthusiasm.

'Of course. Why not? That's what Darius expected us to do. He foresaw travellers halting here for centuries, and—if I may be coarse —he probably saw them straddling before the mountain and relieving themselves. That's why he wrote his graffiti on their lavatory wall.'

We looked up again at the graffiti, while Prenders drew out of the boot the quilted sleeping-bags, the two camp-beds, a hurricane lantern, and several aluminium food containers.

Clem still objected. 'I thought you said the nights could be as cold as the day was hot.'

'Sure. That's right. And that's why I don't believe in camp-beds. The cold blows up through the canvas under you. I shall sleep on the ground. You do as you like.'

'Why not sleep in the car?'

'Hell, no. Four of us, *no*. Not only uncomfortable but worse—dull. It's quite a proper custom in Persia to sleep out of doors on a summer night. In the old days a Persian gentleman would sleep on his flat roof with that night's selection from his seraglio.'

'Well, unfortunately,' said Clem, 'we haven't our seraglios with us'; and he looked towards the caravanserai with its twelve pointed arches, each admitting to an open chamber. 'Why not shelter in that thing?'

'The serai?'

'Yes. Then we could each have a bedroom to ourselves.'

Prenders stared at Clem—a stare that included some hidden jocularity. Grimly he said, 'Let's go and see.'

We went towards the serai, and while we were all of twenty or thirty yards from those vaulted chambers, its breath came forth to meet us. A fetid breath. We shut our lips tight to hold it out. I saw Clem's mouth pressing upward towards unhappy nostrils, and Prenders' mouth pressing upward in a grin.

We walked through the stench into the first chamber. And there, amid a litter of discarded tins, cartons, bottles, and rags was the carcase of a dog lately dead and now putrescent. A cloud of insects danced above it like a ballet of dust-motes in a sun's ray. Also visited by a ballet of insects were the recent 'stools' of squatting cameleers or migrating tribesmen. We looked into the next chamber and the next. In some were plats of dried camel-dung intended, so Prenders told us, for fuel.

'We'll sleep in the open,' said Clem.

A range of foothills lay tossed beneath the mountain's rearing face, and we chose the crown of one of these for our camp. From here we could look down upon the ancient highway, so far as it could be distinguished beneath its dusty bed-spread blown from the dusty plain.

The sun was still above the horizon, the day still hot, and we enjoyed drinking coffee from our vacuum flasks. A rest, and we began preparations for dinner.

The Baghdad hotel, perhaps tutored by Prenders or Davy, had

catered lavishly. In the food containers were hot soup, caviar, portions of grilled chicken, vegetables, salads and fruits. In carton tubs was yoghourt, and in bottles a local mint drink called sekanjebeen. For those who didn't fancy this there were bottles of white wine and red.

Prenders filled a petrol stove from a gallon picnic can and lit it. Then, lying supine, hands linked behind his neck, head pillowed on a rock, he said of a sudden, 'Yes. Ahura Mazda.'

To hear him uttering this name was to see at once the god flying above us on the rock-face with the sun's rays and the lightnings for his skirts. But Prenders was now looking down upon the road below.

Musing, he went on, 'Cyrus came down that road to conquer Babylon, and he brought Zoroastrianism in his baggage train. Bringing it to the Jews in their exile. It may seem a long-forgotten religion but its spirit lives for ever in all that the exilic and post-exilic Jews learned in Babylon, and all that Christianity took from them. Ahura Mazda shines brightly, for those who can glimpse him, in the Hebrews' Jehovah. See? I've brought you a long way behind the old Bishop's Jerusalem, and even behind Babylon.'

Clem, now listening with a fixed interest, asked how exactly Zoroastrianism affected Judaism and Christianity.

'Because,' our lecturer answered, 'Zoroastrianism at its pristine best, before power-hungry priests and disciples of inferior minds corrupted and adulterated it, as happens with every religion, was—at that strange hour in history—the purest and noblest religion in the world.'

It was almost angrily that Clem demanded, 'Why?'

'Because for the first time—east of India, at any rate—it proclaimed not only a perfect monotheism but also the highest morality. Ahura Mazda—up there—was not only the god of all the world, he was also Light and Goodness and Truth. He was all that could be described as Truth, just as his opponent, Angramainyu, was The Lie. The Truth. The Lie. Zoroaster's favourite words. No religion before had ever insisted so firmly that morality was as eternal as God himself, and that's why it seems so clear to me that he partly inspired that grand, incredible poet of the Exile, the Second Isaiah. You can hear an echo of his voice again and again in the Second Isaiah. Why, Zoroaster even taught goodness towards all animals, an ultimate reach of goodness which the East has never learned yet.'

For me at this time Zoroastrianism was no more than the name of some eastern religion that survived only, I supposed, among a few Parsees in India. The sole thing I recalled about it, and that but dimly, was the little faded flower of knowledge which I'd already displayed—that it declared the world to be a battlefield between Ormuzd, the power of good, and Ahriman, the power of evil. Evidently Clem had also culled this flower for he now asked, 'But where's the pure monotheism in a universal combat between Ormuzd and Ahriman? I should have thought that if anything was pure dualism, this was it.'

'No.' The word snapped out. 'Not in the Master's religion at its best. Not at all. A popular degradation of it. That very great soul saw the victory of Ormuzd over Ahriman as assured in the end, when all that's evil will be somehow caught up in the arms of good and Ahriman reconciled to Ormuzd.'

'So even the Devil will be saved?'

'I know nothing about the Devil,' said Prenders irritably. 'But I believe Zoroaster was in sight of a tremendous truth which one day, perhaps, we shall be able to see. But it's too difficult for most eyes to see. So let's leave it that Truth and Goodness triumph over everything in the end.'

'Wait,' Clem commanded. 'Listen.'

His eyes had turned towards the great shoulder of the mountain round which we had come.

The sun was now behind the grey shapes of the Zagros mountains, and the first cold wind of evening touched us as we lolled there, waiting—Prenders having asserted that no gentleman dined before seven.

'Listen.'

Bells. A jingle of bells threading through the quiet of the evening. And voices. Voices often loud and shouting.

And here it came with its bells and its voices: a long camel train round the bend of the mountain and along the road beneath us.

The plods of the camels' feet beat a soft accompaniment to the bells.

On and on it came in Indian file: forty or fifty camels, one or two with their calves, half their size, padding unladen beside them. Most of the drivers walked by their beasts, but some sat perched on high among the slung masses of bales and sacks and rugs. From these bulking loads the looped necks of the camels protruded like the curved necks of dinosaurs.

If not Prenders, then Clem and I, unfamiliar with the East and its camels, were fascinated to watch this circus-procession as it padded by, all its animals ruminating sullenly as they came. Doubtless, they'd been chewing their cuds, sideways in their long mouths, through all the hours and all the miles of the day's march. A sour smell from their dribbling lips came towards us even on our high place. Their elongated nostrils, lifted so high above their munching mouths, suggested, as always, that since there was no escape from their life-long servitude to men, they accepted it with a sneer.

'The camel,' said Prenders, who had risen on an elbow to watch, 'is about the most stupid of all man's domesticated animals but he assumes an expression of the utmost aristocratic hauteur—in which, you'll agree, he resembles so many of our aristocrats at home. Think of the old Dowager.'

Yes, but it was rather fine, I thought, that in the fell clutch of circumstance they kept their heads unbowed and maintained along their nostrils that splendid permanent sneer.

While I watched, one of them turned his eyes towards us and, whether or not the sight of us lazing in comfort there was the last straw, he gave us a look of total misanthropy and with a muted rumbling in his throat, which was manifestly pejorative, knelt down on nobbled knees, prayed perhaps, for a judgement on mankind, and sat down—if the couching of a camel amounts to sitting. He was disposed to call it a day.

(Lo, I have borne my burden, said Hippolytus. This is death.)

His session, with rest and peace in mind, brought the whole string of animals to a halt. They all stood quietly where they'd been stopped, their faces expressing nothing but a philosophic, if soured, acceptance of anything that could happen in life—whether continuation or change, endless motion or unexpected rest, a day-long monotony or a pleasing moment of variety.

The driver of the now recumbent camel beat it and kicked it with loud execrations. Others of his colleagues whose beasts had been halted by this member's insufferable behaviour came and added their kicks on flank and buttock, and their shouted denunciations.

Clem and I rose in fury. 'Stop that! *Stop* it!' we called and shouted execrations too, but at the men, not at a tired animal staging a token strike, well justified. 'Stop it. Swine! Dirty cads. Filthy cowards, you.' And other such observations.

The men only looked up at us with the friendliest smiles, imagining we were on their side and calling down *our* maledictions on a mutinous animal.

'Their English is limited,' said Prenders who had now sunk his head back on his stone pillow. 'And, anyhow, what's the good? Man's oldest domesticated animal, and they've treated it like that since long before Abraham came out of Ur.'

'I care nothing about Abraham,' said Clem. 'Let them know that *someone* disapproves.'

'But they don't know, my dear Clemmy. They probably think you're trying to help them in their righteous treatment of an undisciplined brute.'

'I don't care *what* they think,' said Clem, and went on shouting at them, till at last one or two looked up as if wondering, in a sudden surprise, whether his shouted comments carried some element of unjustified criticism.

Well, the camel, after enough kicks and pulls, took up the burden of his days again. Inelegantly he got to his feet and all the other camels, who had waited for their erring brother, resumed their elegant walking, with noses in the air, long swinging strides, and unconsciously dainty padding down of their feet. Some were now opening their slit nostrils to sniff, as if they divined water in the distance or, better, some dried and prickly brushwood for a tasty evening meal.

Their passing left clouds of grey dust afloat upon the evening wind, and Prenders, hands still behind his head on his stone pillow, murmured softly, 'He sped; but the dust he cast yet hangeth there. . . .'

As this was plainly a quotation we asked, more out of politeness than interest, whence the line came and what it meant; which launched him on to an enthusiastic discourse about the excellence of Persian poetry, especially that of the Sufis. Not once as he spoke did he lift his head from the pillow.

'Sufis?'

'Yes, Sufis, the wonderful succession of mystics that Islam, of all unlikely religions, gave to the world. They were chiefly Persians, for the Indo-European is more ready to soar into mysticism than the Arab. The Persian mind at its loveliest rebels against the harsh monotheism and commonsense worldliness of the Prophet. I wonder sometimes if this divergence is partly accounted for by the harsh sands and cruel suns of the Arabian desert compared with the gentler airs and frequent green loveliness to be found up here among these Persian mountains. Be that so or not, the Persian mystical poets are among the most spiritual, joyous, and exciting in all literature.'

This from our infidel.

He soon had us in his power again, caught in tight bands of interest.

The greatest of the Sufis was Rumi, he said. Rumi had lived in Khorassan at the beginning of the thirteenth century till he was twelve years old when his family fled from Persia before the terror of the advancing Mongols. 'So think of it, six centuries ago a boy of twelve came along this road beneath us on the way to Bah'g-dah'd and Mecca, and he was to be Rumi—Rumi, saint and mystic, and a glory of Persian literature. That was Rumi's line: "The heavenly rider passed. . . . He sped; but the dust he cast Yet hangeth there." You see, to all mystics God is the great Illimitable Alone, but to the Sufis he is also somehow immanent in any and every creation of his. And was this ever better expressed or in smaller words: "He sped; but the dust yet hangeth there. . . . Gaze not left or right; Only his dust is here And he in the Infinite." A superb translation by—' here Prenders hesitated and stumbled—'a brother professor. It's getting cold, as I promised you it would. Let's have a fire in our dining-room.'

'How, please?' asked Clem. 'Round the petrol stove?'

'No. There's brushwood somewhere. Those camels were smelling it, I'm sure. They can scent water or their dinner miles away. Let's go and look. Hosein will help.'

Hosein was sitting in the car with an Arab newspaper; we joined him and we all walked eastward in the tracks of the camels. And, sure enough, after no great distance we came upon a shallow ditch with a thin stream dribbling along it; it had wandered down the sides of Bisitun from one of that mountain's springs which had made this a halting-place for the contemplation of Darius's glory, and created the serai. Stunted shrubs, long dried in hot winds and brittle, fringed the meandering ditch.

The four of us heaved up masses of these, dragging them up by the roots, as advised by Hosein who said that the dry stalks would burn too quickly but the damped roots slowly. As we came back past the serai he left us and visited some of its abandoned chambers which, with their pointed arches, looked so like the deserted chapels of a dead religion. He emerged from one of these chapels with a splintered packing-case that must have come off the back of some migrant's pack-mule or donkey, and now with this under his arm he started visiting other of the chapels. When he rejoined us with a grin we learned that he'd filled his case with slabs of dried camel-dung.

'Fine,' said Prenders. 'Allah reward you. You must come and enjoy this fire with us, oh Hosein, my friend and father. But, as you love us, remove that head-dress, lest the Kurds come.'

Hosein, pleased with praise, said, 'I get more. I get many things' and he went to his car from whose boot he drew shards of broken wood and other odds and ends that would burn.

Then he and Prenders, who was not less enthusiastic now, laid the fire while Clem and I spread the meal. Darkness thickened around us, so we lit the hurricane lanterns and placed them on either side of our table, which was the tilted ground.

When the meal was over—it had tasted well by firelight and lantern light, and now by the light of a million stars—Hosein returned to his bedroom, which was the back of the car, leaving us on our hill. It was eerie to remember, as all too quickly the fire crackled down and died, and only the lanterns broke the darkness, the figure of Darius, King of Kings, brooding high above us while the great god Ahura Mazda brooded over *him.*

Prenders, thinking of them too—as who could do other in this silence?—said after a while, 'Jonny—and Clem—we shall sleep beneath the pride of Darius and the infinite benevolence of Ahura Mazda.'

Which carried him back—I don't quite remember how—to Rumi, and there on the low hill, hardly seen by me in the dark, a voice from a shadow yonder, he was reciting more quatrains from this well-loved poet, one of which, for the first time in these journeyings of ours, seemed to flash an answer to the doubter or dim believer in me.

I must always believe that the power with which it struck me owed much to those instant modulations of Prenders' voice, when with deep feeling and an actor's skill he drew out of any verse he was quoting the fullness of its music. His poem now, spoken in that low-pitched voice, was a flash, no more, in this strange, high, empty place and a starlit darkness. But it played in my mind all the rest of our pilgrimage, and does to this day.

'Yes,' he was saying, 'Rumi has other wonderful quatrains, my dear Jonny, that ought to say something to you and Clemmy. In one he asks "Who lifteth up the spirit? Say who is he?" And the answer comes:

> He who gave in the beginning
> This life to me.
> Who hoodeth like a falcon's
> Awhile mine eyes,
> But presently shall loose me
> To hunt my prize.

'But then comes the greatest of all the stanzas:

> As salt resolved in the ocean
> I was swallowed in God's sea,
> Past faith, past unbelieving,
> Past doubt, past certainty.'

Something leapt in me. Something good. I didn't see clearly what these words meant; I do not see now; but I felt they had opened a frontier to some country where a doubter could live at rest; where— but I do not know—doubt and faith were the same. They seemed to enclose some final truth beyond the grasp of reason.

And I knew too, first from Clem's silence, and then from his musing words, 'You must tell me that again in the morning,' that his hidden response was like mine.

Then, almost at once, while we were still in this mood, Prenders said, 'Far away in India the Kena-Upanishad says something very similar, but in cold prose.'

'And what's that?' asked the voice of Clem.

'It's cold after Rumi, but I suspect it means much the same. It says, "Who says that Spirit is not known, knows. Who claims that he knows, knows nothing."'

Plain from our silence that this didn't warm the heart like Rumi's poetry, but that we were meditating upon it and perhaps finding truth in it. For my part I was associating it with Clem's favourite aphorism, concerning the state of his beliefs, 'I do not know, Said the Great Bell of Bow.'

When Prenders spoke again, it was to repeat, 'It's cold,' but referring now to the night. 'I purpose getting into my sleeping-bag, with only the ground beneath me.'

Since it was now cold enough for us to wonder if there could be frost on the wind, we were quick to follow him. We unrolled the bags from their containers. Six foot long, robustly filled with duck down and quilted, they could be fastened around us up to our necks. The very look of them promised warmth and invited sleep. The camp-beds which Hosein had opened out for us we folded up again and laid aside. Like Prenders we laid ourselves on the ground.

And there we lay, looking at the stars for a while, Prenders on the farther side of Clem, I filling with astonishment—and amusement—that we should be lying here on this desolate hill, with King Darius up there in the darkness, and the ancient road of the King of Kings wandering along below. As often happens, Prenders broke the silence with words that were like a telepathic echo of my

own thoughts. In his present high poetic mood he said, 'It's silent . . .
silent . . . but we ought to hear the tread of a thousand ghostly
armies.'

In a similar mood, perhaps, Clem, after a further silence, said,
'Tell us some more about your Sufis, Pren. Or about Rumi. Give us
another of his poems.'

'There are over four thousand of them, my dear chap, and I only
know a few of them. Even then, I only remember the easy quatrains.
But I'll give you the gist of one of the most remarkable, if you
like.'

'Go on with it,' said Clem's voice from his bag.

'It's about the man who looked back on his way to hell.'

'Sounds a good bedtime story. Go on.'

'Well, it's the Day of Judgement and some angels are prodding
and goading, very rightly, a thoroughgoing sinner like me towards
his proper place in hell. They urge him, "Begone, dog, to thy kennel."
But the poor chap, with tears in his eyes, looks round at the Holy
Presence which is still there in the light. His tears fall like autumn
rain, Rumi says. The Holy Presence, however, only commands the
angels, "Say ye to him: 'Oh, ne'er-do-well, destitute of merit, thou
hast seen the black scroll of thy misdeeds. What dost thou expect?
Why art thou tarrying in vain?' " To which the unfortunate man,
so like me, answers, "Lord, I am a hundred times worse than thou
hast declared, but beyond good and evil, and beyond living right-
eously or behaving disobediently, I had a great hope of thy loving-
kindness." Then comes the poor old sinner's wonderful line: "Thou
gavest me this my being as a robe of honour. I rely on that munifi-
cence." ' Prenders, skilled orator as he was, paused to give full effect
to his last words and spoke them in a lower tone. 'And God said to
the angels, "Bring him back, for he never lost hope in me." '

Apart from a few commonplace words after his story ended, and
after our silence as a tribute to it, that was the last I heard from
Prenders. But as I lay waiting for sleep, and sometimes opening my
eyes to look at the great dome of stars above us, all so brilliant and
some of them diamond-sparkling in the still Eastern night, I was
thinking, 'Let him mock as he likes the Church and its God, and the

creeds and the parsons, I can see where his hunger lies. It lies where mine lies, and Clem's.'

§

He was soon asleep, as I could tell from his regular breathing. So quickly had he found sleep while I, on this strange bed, was far from reaching it, out of sight of it. And this sleep of his was plainly easy and happy. Was it, I began to wonder, that sleep had come quickly to him here because never was a room more open than that in which we lay tonight? It had no walls from one side of the world to the other, and no ceiling but the infinite night. In our hotel both at Damascus and Jerusalem, I had noticed, passing along the bedroom corridor after he'd gone to bed, that his door was not quite closed; its latch was not home. And I had remembered his saying in the aeroplane, 'I rather hate being shut up in any place where there's no chance of opening the door and getting out. We're imprisoned here for six hours.' Was his hatred so strong that he was happier with a room door not even latched? Well, no walls or door or momentarily imprisoning latch here. Let his sleep be good.

My thoughts left his figure for one as far away as his was near. Three thousand miles away. The night was yet early in England, and she in her youth would probably be out at some gay entertainment with him. Possibly she was dancing happily somewhere. One can be any age, alone in one's bed, and I chose now to be a child imagining that by fixed and firmly directed thought, and by repeating 'Alethea, Alethea', I could project my image across deserts, seas and continents to her, and be remembered for a little.

But I decided at last to resume my real age, and I did manage to work my way to sleep on this outlandish and distant hill before I need think of her lying with him.

14

On Olivet

We found all our party gone when we were back in Jerusalem. Our foray into Iraq and Iran had required more days than the effervescing Prenders had suggested. We ought to have guessed this, there being few liars like an enthusiast. We'd had to endure a two-days delay before getting seats on a flight from Baghdad to Amman. And now, the hotel told us, our bishops and ladies were all gone from Jordan into Israel, and we should find them in a hospice near Tiberias in Galilee.

I was not sorry about this. They were gone. Maureen was gone. She was through the Mandelbaum Gate and across the frontier into Israel (whence no man returns to Jordan). I was free to do what I had wanted to do before; I could stand on Olivet alone and look down on Jerusalem, thinking my own thoughts undisturbed, pondering my everlasting question, 'Who *was* he? *What* was he?'

We'd had to take an early morning flight from Baghdad which got us into Amman by ten o'clock. The drive from Amman to Jerusalem had taken less than two hours and we had therefore a whole long afternoon and evening ahead of us. So, when the sun of mid-afternoon began to lose its heat, I left the hotel alone and toiled up the Mount of Olives towards Bethany, not by the swinging highroad that came round the mountain, but by the lane past the wall of Gethsemane's garden and that of the St. Mary Magdalene Church; then up the rough, rutted trackway, past the churches of Dominus Flevit, the Paternoster, and the Ascension, till I reached the ridge above Bethany, where I paused and turned around.

I had a poignant reason for coming this way.

It must have been down this rough, white, sun-bleached track, the short way over the hill, that Christ came with his disciples when, for the last time, he left his well-loved haven of rest, a family home in Bethany, and set his face towards Jerusalem, that he might meet his hour.

Standing here, with Bethany behind me, under the hill, and that stony white road before me, I prepared my mind like an empty stage for such thoughts as would come. And the first thought to occupy and fill the stage was one that for me, alike in my days of faith and my days of doubt, has always belonged to this age-old stretch of roadway or wheel-beaten track dropping down from Olivet's ridge to the Kidron valley; one that has never failed to charge itself with questions and drama and beauty.

It seems clear enough from all the stories that Jesus spent his last few days, before 'his hour' as he called it, with that dear family of two sisters and a brother, and that it was from the night of Wednesday in this Passover week to the morning of Thursday that he slept his last sleep on earth—unless, as some think, he lay for a few tossed hours in a prison cell beneath the palace of the High Priest.

Probably the sun was low over Jerusalem or almost setting behind it when he said good-bye—and with what sadness—to the three dear friends and came slowly over the hill to pass where I was standing now.

'In the evening,' Mark says, 'he cometh with the twelve.' With the *twelve*? Then Judas must have stolen back to them after concluding his deal with the chief priests and have walked this way with him and them, knowing what in a few hours he would do.

I stood there, waiting for the sun to fall lower, and then, like that little company of thirteen men, walked down to where, by the Paternoster Church, the whole city of Jerusalem, walls and gates, towers and domes, broke upon my view. When they saw it that Passover eve, it must have been gaily adorned for the feast, and with the tents of the crowding pilgrims everywhere around its walls—

down among the cypresses, the olives, and the tombs in the valley of the Kidron, and on the slopes of the hills that 'stand about Jerusalem'.

Always as I picture this moment, when, coming down the slope, Christ saw the city thus arrayed, I see him walking a pace or two ahead of the others because I remember Mark's words, so vivid, so pregnant, 'Jesus went before them, and they were amazed, and as they followed, they were afraid.' One can almost hear the hush as they looked towards him, and in silence walked behind. Perhaps one of them broke the silence at last—good, loving but doubting Thomas (my latest patron saint) who on a like occasion had exclaimed, 'Let us also go with him that we may die with him.'

All these words of bewilderment and fear and love went with me as I too walked down the road with Jerusalem ever before me, following, as it were, behind that little company of long ago, and feeling with them much of their bewilderment, some of their nameless fear, and undoubtedly some of their love. Who *was* he? *What* was he, this strange, strong, rather stormy, dedicated, loving young man, Jeshua ben Joseph, a country boy as is so plain from all his stories about birds, flowers, shepherds, seeds, and harvest?

Who? I walked on with the one-thousand-nine-hundred year question.

How could I believe, try as I would, that yonder young man, leading his little company, had laid the stars in place, set the evolutionary ages rolling, and was God Incarnate walking down the Bethany track with his friends; God Incarnate coming for his break into history?

But to fail in believing this had never been, for me any more than for Clem, to say, 'I disbelieve'; it was more like saying, 'I don't know, I don't know, I wonder.' And then, as the road went twisting on towards the crossing of the valley and St. Stephen's Gate, passing once more the garden wall and the cypresses and olives of Gethsemane I was thrown deep into this wonder again. My mind plunged into a question that I had always wondered about but never heard posed and, still less, answered. It was this: who told the disciples of those words, 'Abba, Father, take away this cup from me'? The only person who knew about them was the man who uttered them, and he could not have told his disciples because they were asleep, and 'immediately as he yet spake' his ironic rebuke, 'Sleep on now and take your rest, for the hour is come and he that betrayeth me is at hand,' Judas and his crowd were all about him with their swords and staves and lanterns. And never again in life had he a chance to tell the twelve of that prayer in the garden because, as we know, they forsook him and fled. Never another opportunity *unless he told them after death.*

And if this, where are we? Who was he?

Yet surely it was told by him somehow. And thank heaven it was told. For of all the gospel stories written of Christ there are two I can believe with more completeness than any others; they are this nearness to a failure of the will, a breaking, in the garden, overcome, however, by that 'Rise, let us be going'; and then the despairing cry from the cross on the edge of death, 'Eloi, Eloi! Forsaken me, as all my friends have done?' To Peter he had said, 'I have prayed for thee that thy faith fail not,' and *his* faith failed for some seconds on the cross—only to rise again in the grand 'Tetelestai'. Who among those somewhat naive story-tellers would have invented for their exalted hero these utterly human but apparently less than glorious cries? Yet how we honour them for faithfully writing them down. And how much they do for the doubter, these surely authentic words. They tell him that moments of doubt, dark annihilating doubt, are inevitable ingredients of any man's faith, even of *his*. They suggest that in the fullness of his manhood he enshrined not only the sinless and the faithful but also at moments the doubting, the despairing, the lost.

More than any other recorded words of Christ these two breaking cries angle for my faith and draw my heart close to him.

So I was thinking as I crossed the valley of the Kidron and turned towards the city.

15

Beth-muri

WHEN we had passed through the Mandelbaum Gate and stood in Israel we decided after a conference to hire a taxi at once and be driven the hundred-and-thirty miles or so, half the length of old Palestine, to our deserted friends in their hospice by the Sea of Galilee.

The first Israeli driver we approached was delighted to take us there. A small narrow man with large Hebraic features, black moustache, laughing brown eyes and a blued ill-shaven chin, he spoke a good English and floods of it. Trained as a guide for American and English visitors he would be well able, so he promised, to tell us everything about every place through which we passed. 'Yes. Leave it to me.'

'But I know most of it already,' said Prenders.

'Leave it to me,' our guide repeated, being one who talked rather than listened. 'I tell you everything. I know it all. My name is Moshe. Ask me anything you want to know. I tell you all.'

'Thank you, Moshe,' I said.

And Clem said 'Shalom', which we'd been told meant something friendly but had forgotten what. Prenders said nothing. He wasn't associating himself with this gratitude.

'Come in. I show you Israel. I show you Galilee.' And, once in the car, Moshe rattled on, saying, Of course he knew the Beth-muri Hospice; taken plenty of people there; a Franciscan hospice by the shore of Galilee in the Plain of Gennesaret; a few miles north of

Tiberias; between el Mejdel, which was where your Mary Magdalene came from, and the little el Tabgah churches where Jesus fed the five thousand and after his resurrection waited on the shore with a fire of coals to prepare a nice breakfast for his disciples. They'd been fishing all night and caught nothing, you see.

It was strange that so palpable a Jew—and a practising one as he told us—should talk thus about a Jesus risen from the dead, but either there was a faint sceptical teasing in his words or, more probably, he provided for Christians what they wanted to hear, in language that would please them.

Capernaum. That was what we would want to see. Capernaum where Jesus first preached and it all began. Well, its ruins were at Tell Hum. Where was Tell Hum? Why, only a little higher up the shore from el Tabgah. Some people wanted to site Capernaum at a place called Minieh in the Plain of Gennesaret, but he wasn't having any of this. Tell Hum, unlike Minieh, had all the ruins of a great city; they stretched for nearly a mile along the shore and the most magnificent was the ruin of a synagogue which might well be, our scholar assured us, the very synagogue in which Jesus first preached and worked his miracles—though he allowed, as a scholar should— but only with regret and after a pause—that there *were* people who thought this ruined synagogue a hundred years later than Jesus.

So he talked for the first forty miles or so, turning his head towards us and leaving—never mind the speed of the car—only one hand on his steering-wheel. Not only did he point out historic places as he tore us past them, but he boasted all the way about the achievements of Israel, 'my new little country'. Look how it had fertilized all the mountains of Judaea which in Jordan, on the other side of the Gate, were still more or less deserts of stones and scrub. Down on the seaward plains he bade us look and see, how the Plain of Sharon 'blossomed like the rose'. Look, a citrus orchard, orange orchards, a banana plantation, avocado pears, fig trees, vineyards, vineyards. 'Can you see how every inch of my country's soil has been set splendidly to work? And how nobly it works for us?'

He was right. When the car had gone tearing through the hills below Megiddo, the vital strategic passes whereabouts, at Armageddon—he reminded us in the very words of our Apocalypse—the last great battle of the world would be fought between the powers of good and evil 'in the great day of God Almighty'—when we were through the passes and the Plain of Jezreel was all around us, stretching as far as eyes could see, we looked out upon a single vast savanna, chequer-boarded and multi-coloured, with its corn-lands and orchards, plantations and forests.

But now that we were in Galilee and nearing its immortal inland sea, Moshe appeared to have wearied of a road that was all wonderful for us, but all too familiar for him; he had sunk his chin, shut his mouth tightly and looked to be half asleep, though driving perhaps faster than ever in a desire for arrival and rest. He woke up only four times, I think: to indicate, sadly enough, Nazareth on its hills; Endor, 'where the witch was'; Mount Tabor with the monastery on its crown; and the Horns of Hattim where Saladin did battle with the last of the Crusaders and brought their kingdom of Jerusalem to an end.

I thought, 'He loved us for a hundred miles but now no more.'

Moshe silent, I was free to linger upon my own thoughts, and I fell to thinking how within six days I should have travelled five hundred years from sixth-century Babylon, where the great spiritual lights broke upon the captive Jews, to this Lake of Galilee and Capernaum where, if the Christians had it right, all those lights enlarged 'when the fulness of the time was come' into the final revelation.

At Kinneret the Lake began its burst upon our sight, lying in stillness and beauty among its grey enclosing mountains.

'Oh ... heavens ... heavens. ...' Clem could not withold his exclamations of wonder and delight. 'God, it's beautiful.'

And in a moment we were racing at high speed along its shores, a little profanely, it seemed to me, towards Tiberias and Beth-muri.

§

'This is Beth-muri,' said our guide, wearily. 'Yes. Your hospice. In there.' He had stopped the car and was walking to its boot for our baggage.

All I saw at first was a garden with trees behind a loose wire fence, and a deep-bearded Franciscan father, in brown robe and white cord, standing by its gate.

Prenders approached him with a smile. '*Pax et bonum*, father,' he said, partly perhaps to show that he knew this favourite greeting of St. Francis, but more, I am sure, in a surge of goodwill. Because the old bearded friar made a pleasant picture there.

In answer the friar provided for us a shining smile from amid the forest of his beard, but he said no words at first.

Prenders followed up this success with another of Francis's celebrated greetings, this time in the father's own Italian. '*Il Signore vi dia pace*,' he said.

'And to you too,' the good man replied in excellent English, as so often happens when you are abroad and try to air your knowledge of the natives' tongue. 'You are most welcome to our hospice, father.' Father? No doubt he surmised that, since the only two men of our party already in the hospice were bishops, and since Prenders had spoken in Latin and knew all about their Seraphic Father Francis, he was either some worthy priest or even, perhaps, another illustrious prelate. 'You are the friends of the English bishops, is it not?'

'Yes,' said Prenders. 'But only commonplace laymen.'

'One of them is in the garden, the Bishop Brakewaite. He is sitting there. You will see him there.'

'Oh, thank you, father. *Mille grazie. Le sono molto obligato.*' Prenders was resolved to get *some* Italian in.

'*Prego*,' said the good old man with the faintest bow and smile. '*Nulla.*'

We walked past him into the garden—and I stopped still. I was stopped by surprise. Who would have imagined, beneath a hot eastern sun, such a garden as this? Its broad lawns, tilting down in waves towards the lakeside road, were nearly as green as English lawns. They were watered, we perceived, by piped sprays when the evenings were cool. Spaced about their fresh and wholesome grass rose tall eucalyptus trees, tall slim cypresses like swords uplifted, and squat date-palms with their pineapple barks. But more remarkable than grass and trees were the splashes of colour everywhere—the magnificent purple droop of the bougainvilias down the walls of grey buildings, the great nosegays of almost Cambridge blue which were the jacaranda trees, the pink and rose of the oleanders marching before the front of the grey mansion, and the scarlet of geraniums massed in high clumps as big as rhododendron bushes in England. Added to these, all the beds in the lawns had familiar English flowers, nasturtiums, polyanthus, marigolds, snap-dragons, pansies, pinks.

And in the heart of all this sat our Bishop Brakewaite, in grey flannel trousers, open brown shirt, and a wide straw hat with brims bound in blue. Reading a book, he did not see us until Clem at his side said, 'Bishop, that rim round your hat should be purple.'

This alerted him to our presence. 'Oh, excellent!' he exclaimed. 'You are alive, after all. We supposed you'd been killed by Kurds, or died in the mountains of Persia. Yes, we bought these sun-hats in Tiberias and I tried to get one with a purple rim for Freddy. So you're not dead?'

'I'm not sure.' Clem looked round upon this improbable garden, so furnished with beauty and peace. 'I begin to think perhaps we're dead and have found you in Paradise. Though since we have our Prenders here I don't see how that can be. *He'd* never get into Paradise.'

'Nor Alexander,' said the Bishop, always quick to take up a joke. 'And our Alexander's very much here.'

'Well, that settles it,' Clem agreed. 'We're still in the world of sin. But, softly, softly, here he is.'

For Alexander, having heard voices and seen us from a window, was now running towards us. He ran straight up to me and said, 'Oh, you're all right, are you?' Was there a note of disappointment in the question? 'Mummy's been frightfully worried about you. She thought you might have been killed by bandits in the mountains. She said the Curs shoot at sight.'

'Kurds,' I amended. 'I think she must have said Kurds.' To my surprise I found that after seven days away from him and my fellow-pilgrims I was quite liking this totally irrelevant child.

'Did any have a bash at you?'

'None, alas.'

'Granny said that some of them might be gorillas.'

'Guerrillas, my dear boy. Not gorillas. Alas, there are no gorillas up there.'

'She thought that if they were guerrillas they might torture you.'

'But, alas, Alexander, we met none.' I added these 'alases' because, remembering my own boyhood, I guessed how much more exciting it would have been for Alexander if we'd been killed by bandits, or eaten by gorillas, or, best of all, tortured. There was inevitably a touch of disappointment for him in our reappearance, laughing and sun-tanned and enjoying a fullness of health. I chaffed him about it, ruffling his hair. 'There's one thing I'm certain of— *you* didn't worry very much. Now, did you? On the whole, it'd have been much more thrilling if we'd died rather horribly.'

The child had the decency to lie about this. 'Oh I don't know about that. I think I'm glad you're all right, really.'

He meant well, but voice and manner lacked conviction.

'And where's Mummy now?' I asked, covering a quick apprehension with a natural voice.

'She's out somewhere. Miles away. I was doing again my jigsaw of Jerusalem.'

'Good,' I said, and he supposed I was speaking of the puzzle.

'Yes, I'm getting awfully good at it. I can do it ever so quickly now.'

'Good. That's fine.' And if only I could solve the Maureen jigsaw as quickly . . .

The Bishop explained. 'All the women have gone out under the guidance of King Solomon—' his current name for King Freddy of the Solomon Islands. 'They're doing what everyone wants to do when arriving here for the first time—wandering on and on by the shore of the world's most hallowed sea. It's so difficult to come away from it.'

Hearing this, Prenders said, 'Come along too, Clem and Jonny. Come along to the little Tabgah sanctuaries. It's only a few miles along the shore.' And to outshine our late driver—under whose lectures in the car he'd been patently restive—he spoke of this place as *Ain et Tabgah*, 'the dyer's spring', and of the little church with the rock on which Christ prepared a fire of coals and breakfast for his friends as 'Mensa Christi'—though this last name may have sprung from the deep poetry in him and the buried love, rather than from his need of self-display. A fire of coals. I need hardly say that it was Prenders who pointed out to me later, with a light in his eyes, how Peter had been warming himself by a fire of coals in the High Priest's hall when he denied his master, and that it was by another fire of coals, far away on the sea's shore at Mensa Christi—prepared by whom?—that he was warming himself (having leapt into the sea to meet his master) when Christ asked him, 'Lovest thou me?' and commissioned him to lead and feed his Church.

Far from desiring to come upon Maureen by the shore, I pleaded weariness after our drive, and Prenders and Clem went off together. I found another hammock chair and brought it to the Bishop's side. The boy had gone back to his puzzle. The old Franciscan father had disappeared, perhaps to his prayers. To his Vespers, perhaps, for it was an evening hour. The garden was there for us alone.

16

'When the Hidden Things are Told'

WE sat in a curiously protracted silence, the Bishop and I. And the longer it lasted, the more it hypnotized me into being unable to disturb it. He must speak first. I did not know if it was only my imagination but had a change come over him since I'd last seen him only seven days ago? He'd always been cordial and kindly to everyone, with a genial benevolence that approached affectionateness, but now was there not a new unusual calm, a serenity and happiness, on his face? Or was this, perhaps, only the spell cast by a tranquil evening and the beauty of a garden? . . . No . . . I thought it was more. The old goodwill and gaiety had softened and settled, for a while at least, into that so calm and convincing rest one sometimes saw in the faces of nuns and priests who'd reached a sanctity I'd never have attributed to this good bishop of mine.

He spoke at last. With a smile he asked what, if anything, I'd learned in Iraq and Persia, and in reply I talked chiefly of Prenders' surprising and thrilling discourses: first in Babylon on the Second Isaiah and the wonderful spiritual dawns that in the sixth century had broken all over the world; then in Persia, under Mount Bisitun, on the supreme moral vision of Zoroaster and the exquisite mystical poetry of the Persian Sufis which had risen, centuries later, from the heart of Islam.

'Yes . . . wonderful fellow, old Prenders . . . in his way. . . .' Why did there lurk a sadness in those words, 'in his way'?

Laughing, I nodded and answered that Prenders was the most unconvincing unbeliever I'd ever met. He pretended a bitter hostility to church and creeds, but—

'Leave him. Leave him,' the Bishop interrupted. 'He will come back. One day.' And he turned to me with a smile of gentle understanding. 'It's going to be too difficult for him to kick against the pricks.'

'I wonder. I wonder,' I said, doubtingly, thinking of myself as well as of Prenders, and thinking too that this summed up so much of our story.

'He will. He will. It's nearly always too difficult.'

'I hope so. I only hope so.'

'He's not back yet, and I can well understand why.' To what was he referring now? 'But he'll come. He's an *anima naturaliter Christiana.*'

I had been feeling a great liking for this kindly man, but, as he displayed this piece of Latin I found it 'showy' like the 'House of Lords' on his notepaper and the heraldic shield on his car. After all, 'a naturally Christian soul' was quite as good as '*anima naturaliter Christiana*' and shorter.

Thus did I judge him harshly in the very seconds before he was about to open my eyes. . . .

He asked, Did I find Zoroaster and the Sufis any great help in my search for a stronger faith; and I perceived that the question was only polite; that he was really wanting to talk of something else.

'Any great help?' Difficult to answer. 'Only this,' I said, 'that the best of them all seemed to have arrived at the same God, whatever their country or whatever their century. But that's not much help to me, because I've always dimly believed in that picture. To believe in such a God has never been my trouble; I should find it difficult not to. My trouble . . .' and I told him of my walk down the Bethany track with my ever-insoluble question, Who . . . *who* was he? And what? How *can* he be what they say?

Silence. The Bishop's fingers turned round and round on his lap the paperback book he'd been reading. Rather to my surprise, I saw (in my curiosity) that it was the *Imitatio Christi*. I had expected it to be an easy novel.

When he spoke, it was as if my words had opened the gate to all he wanted to say. 'Luckily for me,' he began, 'I've never had any difficulty in believing. Perhaps that's because I've never had the brains you chaps have got. Believing's never been my difficulty. Only *acting* on my beliefs. That is all.' This he covered with a sad smile. 'Do you know that when—may I tell you this, Jonny?—that when I arranged this pilgrimage I was doing it for my own sake almost more than for anyone who'd care to come with me. I knew only too well, you see, that, however successful I may have been in the Church, I was a spiritual failure really—'

'Oh, *no*, Bishop!'

'Oh *yes*, my dear boy.' That familiar, easy address 'my dear boy' had undoubtedly drawn into itself this evening some of the heightened affection one feels for a friend to whom one is revealing a failure or a sin. 'Quite a large humbug, I'm afraid. Towards the end of last year I was in Sweden as the guest of the Archbishop of Upsala. All very grand. I might have been Canterbury himself. I came home in a Swedish ship from Gothenburg to Tilbury—*persona grata*, at the Captain's table. But in the train from Tilbury Docks I sat looking out from the railway viaduct at those awful grey streets of East London—all cramped little houses and crowded tenements and factory chimneys, and I saw the shabby stucco churches rising everywhere among them. Mostly they are large pillared and pompous edifices, an honest attempt to do something for these teeming slums, but they never had much success, and now they are little but monuments to their own failure. Most of them are empty except for the few faithful women who are always there with you—as they were at Calvary. Well, Jonny, I have similar streets in the south of my diocese, and similar huge grey churches as imposing as they are empty. And as I was thinking of these, all of a sudden, it came home to me like the deepest possible stab of a knife, that all these thousands of my poorer people had only one father-in-God, and it was I. And what a gift to them! I, if you please, was the chief representative to them of the Christ in whom I do really believe—and, well, God pity them! I'm not boring you, am I?'

'Boring?' I stuttered. '*Boring?*'

'Well, there it was. If I was a fairly good administrator, it was largely because I enjoyed authority and power, and if I preached well at times, quite a lot of it was in pursuit of my own glory rather than his. And this was all these poor people had got. Oh, I realized in that lumbering train that I'd succeeded in every way except the only way that mattered—yes—and the knowledge was sharp as a sword. For days and nights the humiliation of it haunted me—I could feel almost sick with it. In the nights especially: that hour of the night when your fears and sorrows are all about you in the pitch dark, while the clock goes ticking on and on. In the daytimes I strained to do my job a little better. But I'm over fifty, dear boy, and worldliness after fifty isn't easily shaken off. It goes walking with you everywhere like a cloud all round you. Oh, well, it's good to be utterly humiliated.'

Humiliated? It was I who was humiliated now, as he confessed all this to me, I who had crudely seen him as an amiable, ambitious showman, and never for a moment imagined the contrition that could load his heart. And yet here he was, a prince of the Church, a power in the State, sitting in a garden like a defeated child and laying bare his failure to one of the least faithful in his flock.

I could not speak, and he continued. 'Then at last I got the idea, and it became a sort of craving, that I'd like to go back to the Holy Land where it all began—back to places where he'd come to suffer and die, and there think and think and think. I don't quite know why this idea seemed such an obvious thing to do—I suppose the truth is I'm a rather simple-minded person, not having brains like Prenders and you.'

'No, forgive me, Bishop, I must object. Without ample brains how could anyone make some of those speeches you've made in the Lords or elsewhere which have rung through the country?'

'Easy. Easy, my dear boy. Because it's something that in one's lust for admiration one longs to do well and gives hours of preparation and practice to—when one might well be slaving for other people instead of oneself. I think I half thought that a pilgrimage to the Holy Land would be something like a pilgrimage to Canossa, where the Emperor stood barefoot in the cold for days till his excommunication was revoked.' He pretended to laugh at this. 'Another notion, childish, perhaps, but absurdly strong, was a hope that in these holy places some miracle might happen to help me. Still, whether there was sense in these ideas or not, they wouldn't let me go, and at last I just assured myself that, whatever my motives, this visit must do us all more good than harm. And I wanted my old friend, Prenders, to come too—' but here he sharply changed his tone, as if his talking had slipped too easily, and his first meaning must be covered up—'I mean, I thought that with his unsurpassed knowledge of the East he'd be a marvellous chap to have with us.'

'And has there been a miracle?' I asked, providing a smile to keep us both at ease.

'No ... yes ... no, I don't know. ... Depends what a miracle is. ... Depends what you mean.'

Strange answer. I sat in a quickened silence, wondering what these strangled words implied and not daring to urge him on.

'There was only this, Jonny: that yesterday I was walking by the lake towards Capernaum, quite alone and trying to imagine those fishing boats and the sons of Zebedee with their torn nets and, of course, that amazing request, "Follow me, and I will make you fishers of men", and as I stood there, thinking what a hopelessly incompetent fisherman I'd been in my particular lake at home—I was standing quite still and looking across the sea at those Gergesene mountains because they were all floodlit and beautiful in the sun— and suddenly I knew I was in the grip of an overwhelming desire for nothing less than to be—if I must use the old Bible words—"to be reborn". Or, in other words, to be at last, and however late, what I ought to have been from the beginning. It was a real ache in the heart, a real bodily pain, and I can only think of it now as some kind of ache of growth.'

Before us, as he spoke, there was a long flower-bed bordering the green lawn, and it was stocked with a row of young oleanders at the back and a row of smaller hibiscus plants at their feet. Each hibiscus bore its single trumpet-flower, blood-red and majestic in its loneliness and the Bishop, looking at these, said, 'What a gentleman that hibiscus flower is, in his lonely grandeur.... It's funny, Jon, because I'm no poet, only a secretly uneasy preacher, but I've found myself wondering in this garden ever since, if flowers feel this ache of growth as they break their buds and open out into the light. An ache that is also pleasure. Delight. Perhaps they do. Wordsworth probably believed so. ... Well, of course I've had my "purposes of amendment" before, which didn't achieve much, but never an experience quite like this, never with an ache that was actual pain—and yet, in the heart of the pain, a rather glorious certainty that I was going to succeed this time ... and even finally succeed. Anyhow, it left me, I'm sure, a little different from what I was before.' He smiled as he turned to me. 'Was that a miracle? Another little miracle in the neighbourhood of Capernaum?'

All I could answer, in the same smiling mood, was, 'It sounds like the best part of one.'

'Yes ... maybe ... who knows? Perhaps I found what I came to find.'

'I think you did, sir,' I said, as quietly and respectfully as I could.

'Well, perhaps. But now let's talk about you. Tell me more. About everything.'

I felt now that I could tell him anything. Till this hour I'd have had small use for him as a spiritual director. Now, after this humble confession, I was happy, at ease and fully confident in him as a director. In this one brief lonely hour he had become a man after my own heart. And he said many things that evening which have been of comfort and help to me since. I remember, to this moment, almost word for word some of the things he said in that garden.

Of the need for *some* sort of religion I remember his saying, 'Man without God sinks into something less than man. This is inevitably true of most of us because of that grossly selfish animal that waits in us all.' I nodded agreement with this, and he went on, 'Only look at the ruthless, savage slaughtering, torturing jungles that the men who have no practical religion are making of their various domains. In a word, we are all so easily beastly.'

When we talked again (in Prenders' wake) of the correspondence between the lofty visions of the sixth-century Hindus in India, Zoroastrians in Persia, Taoists in China, and captive Jews in Babylon, and then, eighteen centuries later, of Moslem Sufis in Persia whose mysticism was almost identical with that in the West, I remember how, after a contemplative silence he said, 'Yes, yes, I often think the Universalists who preach an ultimate harmony, one day, of "all men in God" may have the truth. That *extra ecclesiam nulla salus* is a dreadful saying only to those who don't understand its real meaning. Good Pius XII—on whom be peace—set about defining its true meaning in one of his encyclicals—'

'And what was the true meaning?' I interposed, with a hungry interest, for I'd always hated and despised the phrase.

'It was in his encyclical, *Mystici Corpus Christi*—I forget when—but there he says that the ecclesia, the Church, is not only the Church of Rome but all the invisible parts of the Body of Christ as well. His words were, I think—I've preached on them often enough: "Our Saviour's purpose on the cross was that he might reconcile with God all men held asunder by nationality and race into one body. A true love of the Church requires that in other human beings not yet united with us in the visible Body of the Church we should see brethren of Christ called with us to the same salvation." '

'Did he really say that?' I asked, for this was new to me and good.

'Yes, and it's really no more than the old merciful Roman doctrine that a man can become, unaware, a child of the Invisible Church by the "baptism of desire". Many times in sermons I've suggested that you could sum it all up in four tiny words, "God knows his own". Do you remember the first Isaiah's words, all of a hundred years before the Babylonian Captivity and your Deutero-Isaiah's miraculous voice—words which must have been a shock and a stench in the nostrils to some of his more intolerant and exclusive Jews: "In that day shall Israel be third with Egypt and with Assyria, whom the Lord of Hosts shall bless, saying, Blessed be Egypt, my people, and Assyria, the work of my hands, and Israel mine inheritance." If that isn't a glimpse of universalism in the distance I don't know what is. And I don't see why we shouldn't turn it into "Blessed be India, my people, and Sufism, the work of my hands, and Christianity, mine inheritance.'' '

Of my stubborn and enduring inability to know what to think of the Master in whom he so easily believed, he said, 'I feel sure, dear boy, that this inability will slowly lessen—very slowly perhaps. God does nothing sudden or blatant with any of us. Funny things happen to us. That's about all. I don't believe that even St. Paul's revelation was as sudden a thing as it appears to us in the stories. Remember those pricks. How long did he kick against them, I wonder. I suspect they were there long before the magnificent death of St. Stephen drove them right home. Look, Jonny: God is infinitely patient and of this I feel you can be sure: he is no less near to those who want to but can't picture him at all than to those of us who don't feel any difficulties; and even in some cases nearer.'

'And that's precisely what, according to Prenders, the Hindus said two thousand five hundred years ago.'

'I did not know that,' he laughed, 'but I'm glad to hear it.'

With all of which, though only a step or two nearer to the desired convictions, I was not a little comforted.

§

When that evening I had to encounter Maureen I perceived at once that, while I now stood higher in the Bishop's affection and he in mine, which is always a happy fruit of shared confessions, so far as she was concerned I was in the doghouse.

She was hurt and huffed, and enjoying her huff, because I, after 'making love to her like that on Mount Something' had been conspicuously chilly with her all the next day, repulsing advances, even though I'd promised to take her to Bethlehem, and on the following day had shot off in an aeroplane, Heaven knew where, without a word of farewell—nay, without a word of any kind. Picking up a girl and then putting her down. Like a toy one's tired of. Taking advantage of her just for the fun of it, just for an hour of pleasure—promising to take her to Bethlehem and going off to Baghdad instead, with never a word of explanation or apology—she was simply not falling for this kind of treatment; she was not the sort of person to be taken advantage of; no, and she'd let me see it; she'd make it clear that she was not at all disposed to speak to me for quite a time—which suited me well.

But oh, the answering chill of her manner was freezing indeed whenever she passed me; I thought she resembled more than anything else a walking refrigerator with its door ajar. And to hell with this! Just as though the lovemaking and the kissing had not been ninety-nine-per-cent her effort, her handiwork and lipwork, while my share had been no more than a kiss given in pity, and some subsequent weakness in being too soft to resist or discourage, by word or act, her enthusiastic assault.

The paths of pity are dangerous ways.

I was advised of her present condition by the Springing Jimmy who, as a younger woman than those two inseparables, the Hanging Dowager and Hester, had been largely her companion in the absence of us men, and after a time her confidante—a vessel one evening for the reception of her wrong. Maureen had unloaded it all into that ready container as the two of them walked together by the lake. I could picture them on that walk: Maureen interested not at all in the loveliness of this inland sea or in its hallowed associations, but only in her hurt and her resentment, and Jimmy springing along at her side. Possibly swinging her handbag either in tune with her sympathies or in time with her upward springs. And almost certainly treating the very secular Maureen to much of that dashing slang and some of those daring oaths which she would display before us laymen but omit from her talk with the bishops and the two senior ladies. 'But, Maureen, is it really worth worrying about? I wouldn't give it another thought, bugger it. Certainly it's rather a strange way to behave on a pilgrimage, but there you are: that's men. Irreligious men anyway; he says he's lost most of his faith and can no longer believe a whole lot. I can't see the bishops behaving in that style. Honestly, I wouldn't give him the impression that you care a bloody old damn, one way or the other, what he does.'

I gathered that this interesting discussion about me must have taken place while Prenders, Clem and I were lying under Bisitun by our dying fire and Prenders was thrilling my heart and mind with the words of Rumi, 'As salt resolved in the ocean I was swallowed in God's sea, Past faith, past unbelieving, Past doubt, past certainty.'

So far apart in that hour were my poor little Maureen and her nice Mr. Palmer.

Since Jimmy had taken an early opportunity of revealing all this to me—'Strictly I suppose I oughtn't to tell you, but I thought you ought to know and to decide what to do, but don't say I told you, dammit'—I had little doubt that she had also discussed it with Hester and the Lampiter, so that I was now held by them to be not only a man of incomplete faith but one of light and frivolous behaviour—though, to tell the truth, I could well imagine our Dowager, so eager as a rule for the scourging or slaughter of criminals, laughing her loud deep-voiced laugh and saying, 'Perhaps there's nothing very dreadful in a kiss or two on a holiday, and I'm quite glad to think my little Maureen is so attractive to him—though, of course, he *is* a married man and ought to control his desires.'

'To decide what to do, dammit,' Jimmy had said.

Well, I was thoroughly angry with Maureen for having cast me for this frivolous part, when the truth remained that I had merely given her this kiss in pity and submitted weakly to what followed. I told myself again that the paths of pity were sometimes mined and I set about venting *my* indignation, for a change, in a variety of ways: by talking loudly, gaily, and easily whenever she was coldly around; by laughing louder than usual in her hearing and so pretending that I was quite impercipient of any chill emanating from her or of any cause for this drop in the temperature; by opening conversations with her and troubling not at all when she turned away but promptly addressing myself to someone else with the utmost merriment; and even—intolerable—starting jokes with her who was acting soreness at me.

But even so, annoyed and punitive though I felt, and even though I had laid the true facts before a laughing Clem and a cynical Prenders, I did not speak the word 'pity' to Jimmy, lest she should repeat it to Maureen. I could not so hurt my poor Maureen, though conscious that it would have finally and immediately and splendidly cut this silly and chafing rope that now hung between us.

It soon became clear, however, that no such cruel cut was needed. My wicked behaviour—'caring not at all for a girl's feelings'—'going off to Baghdad instead of to Bethlehem'—then, on return, laughing and being happy and either unaware of her wound or utterly indifferent to it—this latter course of mustard-plaster treatment, carried on for a few days, at last flung the girl's head high and decided her to punish me by having nothing more to do with me beyond such cold polite addresses as occasions might require—which suited me excellently.

§

I stood on Acre's old sea-wall by a gun-embrasure in its battlements. I looked down at the half-ruined port below, so desolate now, cheated of all its ancient grandeurs by the bright and prosperous young Haifa, so assertive and indifferent, lying under Mount Carmel a dozen miles down the bay. I tried to imagine this Acre in its great days when those waters, still and untroubled now, must have known half the ships of the world: Phœnician and Tyrian traders, coasters from Grecian isles, galleys from Rome, merchantmen out of Venice and Genoa, and, most famous and picturesque of all, the crusading ships of our Richard Cœur de Lion, come to capture Acre and crown it as the capital of the Kings of Jerusalem.

When I had done with trying to recreate these bustling and fateful scenes, down there on broken quays which slept undisturbed today either by their memories or by the fingering of slow and dilatory waves, I turned to look at Mount Carmel's long headland on the other side of the bay. And thence across a calm sea of many tints, pewter and shining steel and dove-grey, towards the horizon and an empty sky. For I was trying to imagine something else now: I was trying to picture a cloud coming out of the sea no bigger than a man's hand.

We had come to Acre by way of Carmel and Haifa, but among all the villas and mansions and hotels on Carmel it had been beyond any man's powers, I thought, to recreate the great occasions there. So let me think here in Acre of Elijah's servant sent by him to look out across this sea; who reported 'Nothing to be seen' and was told 'Go again seven times.' And at last at the seventh time he announced, 'Behold, there ariseth a little cloud out of the sea like a man's hand.' And Elijah ordered him instantly 'Go up, say unto Ahab, Prepare thy chariot and get thee down that the rain stop thee not.'

But I never did imagine properly that little cloud, or the sky gone 'black with clouds and wind and a great rain', because I was suddenly conscious of someone approaching me and of a figure leaning an elbow on the battlement at my side. The Bishop. He asked what I was dreaming about. When I told him he nodded and smiled, but formally and courteously as one who had hardly heard. And he opened a subject very different. He said, 'I was talking to Prenders yesterday.'

'Yes?' I encouraged.

'It seems he likes you and . . . '

'Yes . . . ?'

To avoid getting deeper into the subject too soon, he laughed and said, 'Incidentally he says you're a wonderful listener.'

'Only because he's a wonderful talker when he cares to be,' I explained.

'Well, be that as it may, he's grown to like you and—Jon, look: you must have guessed that he has an unhappy story behind him.'

'I suspected so.'

'It's a very unhappy story, but he says he'd like you to know it because he thinks you'd understand. I agreed with him. I assured him no one would be more understanding.'

I was touched that they should call me 'understanding', I who had so crudely misjudged the Bishop; and, thinking this, I kept silent.

And the Bishop continued, 'I suggested he'd much better tell it all himself but at first he insisted he wasn't equal to this, so I told him I had just recently had some experience of how sympathetic you could be, and he agreed at last, saying "Yes, perhaps I'd feel less ashamed if I told him myself; it'd be awkward meeting him after you'd told him" but he begged me—' the Bishop hesitated and looked out far across the sea—'he begged me to—as he put it—prepare you for something rather—he used an old-fashioned phrase I haven't heard for years—rather shame-making.'

Pity ran out from me to a man who'd felt obliged to speak like this, and I thought to myself, 'I don't know that I've learned much on these wanderings, but I do know that at least I've arrived abreast of "Condemn not, and ye shall not be condemned." ' Something of this I said aloud; I said, 'Let him know that, whatever other doubts I may have about Christ, I do know how terribly right he was, when he said, "Judge not." . . . One cannot *know*'.

'That's what he feels about you, I think,' said the Bishop.

§

And the very next morning, early, as if he were anxious to get it over quickly, Prenders came towards me, where I sat reading in the Hospice garden, on the same flower-framed lawn where I had heard the Bishop's story. His approach was awkward, nervous and guilty, rather like that of a sad schoolboy coming into a master's room to confess and risk the cane. And he began with a stuttering difficulty, 'What about a . . . let's go for a walk. Along the brink of the lake. Or perhaps not . . . perhaps you'd rather rest. Yes, it's supposed to be a day of rest after that wearisome journey to Caesarea and Carmel and Acre. But . . . it's a rather beautiful day. . . .'

'There's nothing I should like better,' I said as naturally as possible, and rising.

'Good . . . he murmured. And 'Well . . .' and 'Yes . . .' while I gathered up my straw sun-hat (like the Bishop's, bought at Tiberias) and my sun-glasses from the grass. The sun was already hot and aglare.

We walked southward towards el Mejdel, talking about anything— Ctesiphon, Babylon, Bisitun—rather than about that which both of us knew to be the real occasion for this walk. He made, uneasily, some jokes about Hosein, our Arab driver, and Ahmed, the hotelier in Kermanshah, and I tried a jest about Ahura Mazda, but he didn't seem to want to discuss Zoroastrianism; he skirted away from religions. And all the time the Sea of Galilee lay empty and peaceful at our side, seeming to enforce its own stillness on the surrounding world. Unlike the sea before Acre, which had been pewter and bright steel, it stretched, under a dominating sun, through a gradation of colours, grey and blue and aquamarine, to lemon-hued hills on the farther side. Except for the cars on the lake-side road, no one was about. We passed only one group of fishermen, barefoot on the stones and in the water with their nets piled at their feet and their boat aslant at their side, its bow aground.

Then for a half mile or so we were as silent as the hills beside us, until Prenders began, 'You know I wanted to tell you something?'

'Yes, the Bishop said you'd like a talk with me.'

'Well . . . let's begin at the beginning.' He pretended to cheerfulness. 'My name isn't really Prender.'

I let slip no word of surprise, no word at all, but hoped a turn of my head towards him and a smile would do for an answer.

'At least it's only a Christian name. My mother's name actually. . . . Yes . . . my full name is Ivor Michael Prender Garron.'

Garron? Garron? What stirred now in memory? Why had it not stirred only a few days ago when Davy in Baghdad had also let fall that name? But here it was: yes, I remembered a trial in the newspapers some years since—how many? Three perhaps; it had not been noise enough to make the front or middle pages but it had won its headlines along columns further back.

'Yes, I think you are remembering it, Jonny?' There was, all too plainly, an appeal for affection in that 'Jonny'.

'I think I remember a little. But very little.'

'Well, I doubt if you remember that I was Cunningham Professor of Oriental Philosophies at Norminster. That's a narrow subject in any university, even the largest, and Norminster is small, so I seldom had more than one or two students and did all the work alone. Little enough; perhaps four or five hours a week and some obligatory lectures during term, but lecturing I always enjoy—as you may have noticed—'

'I think you're a quite wonderful lecturer,' I put in, since any kind word would be of comfort here.

'Don't know about that, but I did lecture all over the country to silly Literary and Scientific Societies, and this made me fairly well known—which was a pity. Besides I was a professor which makes a fairly tasty dish for newspapers—a professor, and therefore a member of the university's senate, which sounds fine, so when the crash came

—but I'm sorry, we're not there yet. At one time four or five years ago I had only one pupil, a—' he turned his eyes to the distant hills before uttering the next words—'a charming, rather lovely boy. I suppose you can guess what's coming. But I do want you to understand that I really loved him as—I'm afraid—I had loved others before him. Can you understand that it's possible for some of us to love a young boy in exactly the same way as people like you can love a young girl, many years younger, twenty years younger, than yourself?'

Alethea. 'Indeed I can imagine it. And understand.'

'You mean that you have passionately loved someone a lot younger than you?'

I gave his own word back to him. 'Passionately.' And for a moment the old love for Alethea swelled into life again, sinking the heart with its weight, as I thought of the young husband possessing her. I had to ease the bitter heartache by forcing my thoughts back to Prenders and I gave him another word to help him.

'Not only passionately. Illegitimately.'

'She was a girl, of course?'

'Yes.' And how dead a load can lie in a syllable.

'Then by "illegitimately" you don't mean what I mean?'

'What is that? What do you mean?'

'Criminally.'

The pitiless word stopped my tongue from answering. And he, since no answer came, explained, 'I mean criminal according to the law of the land. On my part I find it utterly difficult to think it criminal when there's real love between both. Surely it's hard to deny all love to people like us who can get it in no other way. I accept now that what I had fallen into doing once or twice before—' he raced over this quickly—'was wrong but not with Conal. His name was Conal, a charming Irish boy. With him it was as if we were married, or about to be married. It seemed like that to both of us. Even though I was years older than he. You can imagine that?'

'I can. . . . Yes. . . .'

He brought his eyes away from the lake and looked up at me as we walked on. '*She* was young?'

'Only eighteen.'

'He was eighteen at first. But it lasted years. Four.'

'Yes?'

'And I was forty-two, but we—'

'I was more than that,' I said to help him.

'—but we were happy together. He came to me daily. . . . And yet it was all through him that . . . that I was sunk. He was approached and admitted all, not to betray me, but because he was naturally honest—as honest as the day. Look.' He drew from a trouser pocket a leather wallet—strange place for a bulky wallet, but we were only in open shirts and he had put it there for me. From its least accessible place, closed by a flap, he extracted newspaper cuttings whose edges time had already chipped and browned. 'Perhaps it would be easier if you read some of these. Only a little here and there. It's all rather difficult to tell. No, don't try to read it, walking along. Let's sit down. You needn't read all.'

There could be no emptier place along Galilee's side than this. The steep hills, straw-brown and harsh, fell to the motor road and the beach. Little herbage grew on them and such as could be seen was burnt by the sun. The beach was rocks and stones, flotsam and driftwood, with wavelets, brushed by the wind, curving in sleepily. Sometimes a broader wave would reach towards us and drain away with a long sigh.

Probably Prenders had chosen to sit here because no passers-by were likely to halt in such a place and break our talk or listen.

Sitting hunched on the stones at my side, he took back the cuttings, picked out one, and gave it to me saying, 'I'd like you to read this first, I think. It may suggest that I'm not utterly bad.'

The fringes of the paper, some years old and broken, were yellowing to the colour of the dust about our feet.

As I began to read he tossed white pebbles into the water slowly and, as it were, indifferently.

Headlines from a newspaper's magazine page. First 'Our Youth Today? Delinquent or Devoted?' Then in quotes the unexpected words 'The Front Line'.

It was a report by 'Our Sociological Correspondent'.

'We hear so much in these days about juvenile delinquents and about the lawless and violent behaviour of today's young people, whether boys or girls, that we may come to believe that the majority of our junior citizens are depraved and bad. But is it so? I do not believe it. I just wonder how far the total of delinquents compares, not with the multitude of tolerably well-conducted youngsters, but with the splendid mass of young persons, all over the country, devoting the eagerness and vigour of their youth to fine causes. Be our young people delinquent or devoted, the eager raw material is the same, and it seems clear to me that all turns on how this superb energy and ardour, often so frustrated in our overcrowded cities, is deployed. Or, if you like, *who* deploys it.

'Come with me to the parish of St. Justin Martyr, Cramwell Green, N.E., before, in these days of undoubted thuggery and torture, you lose faith in your human race. "Green" is no word for this over-built area, many of whose decaying streets, though the old Victorian houses are large, could almost be classed as slums, but it is here, among these shadowed purlieus, that the famous Calborne College Mission does its work. St. Justin's is extremely "high", and incidentally this shows that an exalted Anglicanism, almost as papal as the Pope's, can still capture youth—but this is none of my province today. Nor is this famous mission, as a whole, my subject. I want to deal with only one of its activities and the achievement of only one of its leaders. Though the Vicar, Canon Dick Bodley, is the *ex officio* head of the mission, he is the first to say that one part of its work among young people is entirely the creation of Professor Garron who has the chair of Eastern Philosophies at Norminster. "I have delegated all my authority to him," he said to me, "knowing a better man when I see one. He's far abler than myself in this business of winning the enthusiasm and enlisting the help of the young."

'What Dr. Garron has done is to organize the mission's younger members or, rather, the pick of them, both boys and girls, into a phalanx of fresh youngsters who undertake to help in all possible ways those old people who are sick or helpless or blind, or just lonely. They do not go about as members of the mission, but under another name lest any sort of "churchy" character should shut a single door in their faces. Dr. Garron's fine name for them is "The Front Line", a clever name both because all young people like to belong to a secret society with a secret name and because it subtly—and justly—flatters them as picked warriors, a *corps d'élite*. They fight to belong to it.

'The boys go out, usually in pairs, to replaster and repaper some old person's room or repaint another's, and while they're about it, clean the window. They mend radios, or repair the furniture or do the shopping or write letters for the blind. Students, and school children in their holidays, wheel out the old and crippled to the shops or into St. Justin's park. The boys are said to be particularly ready for, and good at, this game. In the nature of things the girls can do the most, washing, ironing, and mending clothes, as well as shopping, writing letters and often reading to the blind. A young and attractive girl can often be a more welcome companion (I write as a man) than any youth. And are they not by nature better talkers and listeners?

'This happy relationship between "Canon Dick" (as he is known to all) and "The Prof" came about because they were schoolboys together at Calborne and went on together to Oxford where they both had distinguished careers, the Professor's the more so. The Professor's department at Norminster is small, which means that he is able to live, most of the time in his old-fashioned house not far from St. Justin Martyr's, near enough for him to allot a whole room to the "Front Line" as their office, which they call their B.H.Q. (Battle Headquarters). Various bodies, such as the Council for Social Service, the Old People's Welfare Association, the Old People's Housing Trust, inform the office, served by a rota of volunteers, of all necessitous cases, and out goes a detailed force of helpers, two probably, as urgently as any ambulance or fire-engine. These young people in the "Front Line" are of all classes and of all ages from thirteen to thirty—the one thing common to them all, apart from their youth and enthusaism, being their devotion to "The Prof".'

I handed the old browned cutting back. 'Magnificent,' I said. And saw that there were tears in his eyes.

'But that's all over and done with now,' he said. 'For ever.'

'No,' I protested.

'Yes. Certainly Yes. Nobody wants an old gaolbird.'

Again the dark and cruel word stopped all speech from me. I had surmised from my dim memories of that trial that he must have served a prison sentence but I did not know it. Until he shot this word across my bows.

I took the next press-cutting from his hand.

A two-column headline: 'Professor Sentenced to Three Years' Imprisonment.' Then 'Charges of Indecency and Grave Offences.'

'At Walton Assizes yesterday Professor Ivor Michael Prender Garron after a plea of guilty was sentenced to three years imprisonment for offences with boys and young men. In the dock with him was Conal O'Terens who also pleaded guilty to similar charges. . . .' My eyes raced over the report, omitting much, because it was too painful to read, with him sitting at my side, tossing stones into the water. I left nearly all of it so as to come at the evidence of Canon Richard Bodley, Vicar of St. Justin Martyr, Cramwell Green, who, called for the defence, spoke of the prisoner's 'magnificent work at their College mission' and told the story of 'The Front Line'. From this I went quickly to the plea in mitigation by counsel for the defence, knowing he must say good things about my friend.

And at last to the words of the Judge, passing sentence. 'Ivor Michael Prender Garron, I have listened to all your counsel has said about your admirable work not only among young people but on behalf of the aged or disabled, and to your vicar's attribution of many fine qualities to you, and I am at least happy to assure you that I shall allow this evidence to weigh with me in passing sentence; but nothing, nothing, can alter the fact that you have chosen to commit these offences with adolescent and immature persons entrusted to your care. This is, and must be treated by this court before the eyes of the world, and for the protection of all young persons everywhere, as a deeply serious charge. According to the relevant Act the punishment for this crime, at its sternest, can be imprisonment for life. But, bearing in mind what I have heard from your counsel and your vicar, and knowing that to a man in your high and public position the disgrace of these proceedings must have served as a terrible penance,

I propose to be as lenient as my duty will allow. You will go to prison for three years. Conal O'Terens, I regard you as secondary in this sad business, and far less culpable than your associate, so very much older than you. You will go to prison for one year.'

I handed the cutting back to Prenders who, taking it, said, 'Fair enough.'

Since I could not comment I turned from the trial and asked if he'd been able to resume work with Canon Dick and the 'Front Line'.

'Oh no. No, no, no. To begin with, I could not have faced them, even if they would have had me—even if any bishop would have allowed me to serve. But that's not to say that when I came home from prison to my house, where, alas, their Battle Headquarters was no longer to be found, a deputation didn't arrive at my door with a wonderful gift. As I say, I could not go out and face the little deputation, but the gift was brought into me. It was inscribed, "For Prof. With the love of the whole Front Line." '

'Good,' I said, looking out across the lake. 'Good kids.'

'Oh, but I imagine it was Canon Dick's doing—still, the children must have all consented.' For sure he was unaware of the deep sadness that rang like a distant bell in that word 'children'.

'And you've never seen any of them again?'

'No. I couldn't. I just sent them a letter with my thanks—and love.'

An inspiration came alive in me. It may have been stirred—I do not know—by the sea before my eyes, the stony shore on which we sat, and the sandalled feet it may once have known. I said, 'Your Canon Dick seems to be a pretty perfect Christian.'

'He is.'

'And you admire him for it?'

'Naturally.'

'And yet you say you've lost all faith in Christianity.'

'Not in Christian ethics. Not in *applied* Christianity. Never, never in that. I still see that nothing else can really save the world and make tolerably decent creatures of our deplorable mankind. In sheer reason I can see nothing else that'll stop that Bomb falling—sooner or later—though what'll really happen, God alone knows. Not in applied Christianity; no. Only the dogmas. No further use for them.'

'That was not so once.'

'Gracious, no! But since then I've been in prison.'

'And that demolished it all?'

Prenders made no reply for some time but just gazed like me across the water at the Syrian hills. They were catching shafts of the sun now, and all their clefts and mouldings were in clear relief above a bright expanse of gun-metal lake. No doubt my question was difficult to answer, so he had picked up a piece of flotsam from the stones at his side, a splinter of wet wood shaped like the blade of a carving knife, and with this he was cutting doodles among the stones and the dust. I left the answer to him, and filled this pause by tossing more pebbles over the loitering ripples into the sleeping water.

At last he said, 'It's quite a day—the day when you are sentenced to years of imprisonment, and they escort you away to prison, and strip you naked of everything you've ever been. In your cell you're no longer quite clear who you are, or what you will be, or what new world you are now alive in. An astounding few hours these. You sit stunned on your stool, and I don't know that one can ever be the same again after this pulverizing shock. You stare at the cell door. It was a new sight to me because I'd been on bail till my conviction. The door's all right for two minutes and then you *see* it. In my ancient prison it was a heavy steel door bristling with steel bolts and with no handle. No handle you could touch or fiddle with. Suddenly the absence of that handle hit me with terror, and when I glanced round at the brick walls I realized that I was locked up in a safe. That door said, "You're locked in a safe"; the bricks said, "You're bricked up in a wall". And from that moment a sickening horror, which was to last for two years, began. Hour after hour after hour, in the daylight or the dark, I was as nearly made mad by it as a man can be. Two minutes, five minutes, after that door first slammed, the horror got me. I only saved myself from dashing my head against the bricks in search of death by pacing up and down and repeating, "I don't give in, I don't give in, I never give in" or "It's the moment that matters, the moment that matters, and at the moment I'm all right." Moment by moment; still all right. On hot oppressive summer days the choking pressure of those close, narrow walls could nearly force a sickness out of me—they did one evening actually make me vomit. In bed after dark I could only bite my lips and repeat a thousand, ten thousand, times, "I don't give in. I'm still all right" as if these words were the only things that held me back from a horror that might burst into madness. Under the blanket my sweat ran and dropped. Can you understand all this?'

'Indeed I can. My worst nightmare is often that I'm bricked up alive, and I only escape from it by waking in a sweat.'

'Well, I *was* bricked up alive. Day after day I thought of suicide. Tear your shirt for a rope. But where hang from? The bars are outside the window. I don't think I shall ever get over my long months of living with and fighting back that horror. To this day, even when a door has a handle, I sometimes crave to open it an inch.'

Hardly knowing what to say, I asked, 'Didn't your religion help at all?'

'No.' A firm statement. 'At first of course I prayed violently to God, hour after hour, and perhaps it helped save my sanity for the first month. But then—the silence. Never any answer. Never any help. "Help me out of this, oh God, if it be thy will. Thy will be done"—and a fat lot of good *that* was! Nothing but the never-ending silence and the gathering conviction that nothing was going to happen to help me. The horror in the long daytime, the worse sweating horror at night, and never the smallest sense of help coming from anywhere, no strengthening of one's mind to bear it, never any lightening of the horror. Not a word, not a sound. Never granted in mercy a callousness so that I could get used to it. So—no God. No one to hear. I decided at last to use my intelligence instead of my hopes and admit there was no one anywhere to hear. So stick it out alone. Prayers are balderdash, a trick for fools. Settle for two years alone with your daily, nightly torment, three years, maybe, if you fail to control yourself and run amok one day—or night. No, Jonny, I may believe in a God, yes, but not in one that cares twopence for me. Or you. Wasn't it he who'd made me as I am—powerless to find and enjoy love except in a fashion that earned me these years on a rack?

Was it any fault of mine that I was born like that? Let him answer for it.'

I could think of nothing cleverer to say than, 'Wasn't the prison chaplain any help?'

'No, but it wasn't his fault. I was in such a state of revolt that he only made me worse. I resisted his help and only wanted to argue and show him that I knew more about the religions of the world than he would ever know. And the more hotly I argued, the more I persuaded myself to deny for ever his God. I had only to look at that door shut on us both, or on me alone after he was gone, for my revolt to flame. Then the dreary services in the prison chapel—oh, my God, the utter dreariness of them after the wonderful, glorious services at St. Justin Martyr's—our High Masses, the Festal Evensongs, the Benedictions.'

The wonderful, glorious services at St. Justin Martyr's—here was the Infidel Lover again. 'He will come back,' the Bishop had said. '*Anima naturaliter Christiana*. One day.' And sitting with him here by the waterside, I believed the Bishop was right. He would come back. He could not live away from his heart for ever. He would come back; most of the way, if never all.

I too perhaps.

Covering any such thoughts, I asked, 'Warders no help?'

'Some of them were not bad fellows but just think what it must do to the best of them, locking up their fellow-men, unlocking them, just like animals in a zoo, peering at them in their captivity, marching them out to labour, sending them round and round on concrete rings in the exercise yard like circus horses—but circus horses are loved, I believe, by their trainers—don't you think it must dull all feeling in time, and even brush it away in most? The wonder is that quite a few are as decent as they are.'

I nodded in some agreement, while he began an apology. 'Oh, but I mustn't make too much of it all. Clearly these black horrors of mine, when locked in, were not suffered by most of the others, if by any of them. And they got better when I was trusted in a cell with two others, carefully chosen men. Company is always balm for any suffering. All the same, in the dark while they were happily asleep, I was always seeing that iron door of the safe and those thick immovable walls—those bricks—and sweating under my blanket. Often I was struggling to get to a stronger emotion than mere selfish fears—to thinking of my love for Conal and trying to send a comforting message to him through the darkness, because he was lying in a cell too.'

It was as he said this that I dared to wonder if, even in an unnameable love like this, the sentence still ran, 'His sins, which are many, are forgiven, for he loved much.'

I asked, 'What became of Conal?'

'He—believe it or not—married a girl . . . while I was still in prison. I suppose he was "cured". He wrote me a letter, telling me all about it and full of affection, but . . . I don't suppose you can imagine what that letter did to me.'

'I can well imagine it,' I said.

'Absurd, but I . . . I just wanted to die.'

'I understand.'

And after wondering whether to speak of her at all, I did tell him about Alethea, because I thought that my sudden desire in the midst of my suffering to get back to some at least of the old faith might drop a seed in him.

'Yes, you must have suffered,' he said.

'Nothing like you,' I allowed.

'I don't know, I don't know, but, anyhow, everything came to an end at last.'

'When was the end?'

'Only just before I met you. That was why we forgathered that afternoon in the old Bishop's drawing-room. He has a heart and the very day after my release he came in person, he, the Lord Bishop of St. Brigid's, and suggested that I come along with him and you others on this jaunt. He didn't preach about it but just called it a holiday. He even asked me to come as his guest, pretending that my knowledge of the East would help, but I wasn't taking that. I have a little money, you see, and Her Majesty the Queen, by entertaining me for two years, had enabled me to save quite a packet.'

I said, 'Thank you so much for telling me all this.'

'Oh, that's nothing, Jonny. You may tell Clemmy too. I think I'd like him to know. Good of you to listen. It'll make no difference between us, will it?'

'God, no!' I exclaimed, and we both knew that those two syllable held the simple truth that, as always after confessions shared, we were nearer to one another than an hour before.

17

The Summing Up

OUR four women, Lady Lampiter, Hester, Jimmy, and Maureen (with Alexander firmly held) stood on this flagged pavement punctuated by grass and weeds, with its broken and recumbent columns, its carven pedestals, its blocks piled upon blocks lying all around it. The pavement lay in a walled garden furnished with pines and palms and tall eucalyptus trees—and more ruins. Beyond the garden walls endless black basalt blocks and shafts, in segments and fragments spread themselves about the arid hills, and among the reeds by the water, to continue the ruins of a large lakeside city where men had lived and traded, and put out to fish with their mended nets, and sat at the receipt of custom.

Neither of our bishops had arrived when Clem, Prenders and I, coming from the hospice, stepped on to this pavement. Since we were all leaving tomorrow from Tel Aviv and its airport at Lod, and these were our last hours in Galilee, we had decided to stand yet once more in this place which, the Bishop maintained, was second only to Golgotha among the sacred places of the world. Golgotha the end, here the beginning. Whether or not these actual paving-stones had known those sandalled feet of Christ, or his eyes had looked on those four Roman columns which now alone stood upright, one could not be certain, said the Bishop. Men disputed their date, some holding that these synagogue ruins belonged to the next century, but let that pass: it was generally accepted by scholars that this was the *site* of the synagogue at Capernaum where Jesus first preached. So, if not the stones themselves, then this air above them had heard before all other places the voice and the doctrine that were to break history in halves.

Here Christianity was born; and here at the suggestion of Solomon Islands we were all to meet for a brief devotion before we left these places, probably for ever.

Clem and I walked forward to join the women, and Prenders came a pace or two behind, carrying perhaps a burden of shyness since both of us now knew his story. From behind us he joked to mask the shyness. 'We're going to pray, are we? Well, I never like to disappoint anybody so I shall do exactly what the atheist Q.C. did when he turned up to plead at a Church court. Studying his brief, he heard the President begin by saying, greatly to his surprise and shock, "Let us pray". His answer to the President, after thought, was "I pray, my lord, but under protest." And the response by an old heathen like me shall be exactly the same.'

'Not heard, I hope,' said I.

'Not heard, no. One wouldn't wish to grieve people. In the spirit only.'

Coming closer to the women, I greeted them with a threadbare and foolish remark, 'Well, all good things come to an end,' but before I had completed it I saw the Dowager's glance shoot towards Prenders, and by the hostility in her eyes and the contempt there I knew that she too had learnt his story. She listened no further to me; she just cast that look on him, then turned about and moved away. She was as ready to humble me as him by thrusting my voice behind her.

How had she come to know? The Bishop would never have told her; neither Jimmy nor Maureen, I felt sure, had known anything about it up till now; the only voice that could have released at last the fascinating tale was Hester's. I remembered detecting in her, on that day in her drawing-room, a kind of stumbling regret that she could not, must not, tell me exciting things about the friend whom the Bishop was bringing on the tour. It was hardly an exaggeration to say that throughout the weeks of our wandering she and the Dowager had not rested from their gossiping, and I guessed that Hester had been unable to let the last days go by without divulging—no doubt 'in the strictest confidence'—the story of Prenders' public disgrace and imprisonment. I could imagine her appeal after this default, 'For heaven's sake don't let the Bishop know that I've told you. He'd never forgive me.'

But Lady Lampiter took pride in her strength of character and her domineering righteousness, and she saw no reason, in the Bishop's absence, to withold from Prenders her opinion of him and of us who probably knew all, since the trial had been public, and yet were friendly with him. Never was a 'cut', an indignant turning away, more deliberate or more convincing.

I was not ready to put up with this.

Prenders had guessed all. He took two steps after her, as if to speak his fury, but halted, turned a white face towards me, and with one fist clenching and unclenching at his side, walked back over those sacred stones and down the ten steps into the garden of high weeds and scattered basalt remains. Among the black remnants he disappeared from sight.

All right. Let him go. I would speak for him.

I took his two steps. And two more. I put myself before her. 'I don't think that was kind,' I said.

'What do you mean?' Clearly she was not accustomed to being addressed in this tone.

'Mr. Prender is an extremely clever man and he saw exactly what it meant—your look at him and your instant turning away.'

'I am very glad if he did. Do you know who—?'

'And I am deeply sorry that he was hurt. He is my friend.'

'Do you know who and what he is?'

'I do.'

'Well, then, I am at a loss to understand how you can condone—'

'Good God, to have a little mercy is not to condone. Mr. Prender has paid his—'

'Do you know that his name is not Prender?'

'It's a name that'll do for me.'

'Oh, please . . .' Hester just breathed. 'Oh, please . . . the Bishop will be here any moment—'

The Dowager gave her no heed. 'Well, then, I'm very sorry, Mr. Palmer, but if you're prepared to have dealings with a man like that, I am not. I am sorry, but I have my standards.'

'I too,' I said.

'I quite agree with Lady Lampiter,' Jimmy put in, playing the jackal to this considerable lioness. Then the Dowager had not scrupled to discuss the matter with her, and beyond doubt with her daughter, Maureen. So the story was in the possession of all. 'Quite agree,' Jimmy said again. The loyal bark of the jackal. 'One must have some standards.'

Furious with her now, because I was sure she had never thought the matter out at all and was merely driven by the desire to agree with a formidable woman and a title, I turned towards her and spoke sneeringly. 'So right you are, Miss Hilder. One must have some standards. I have in fact one or two myself.' Then looked her way no more.

As angry with me for this sneer as I with her for her unsolicited contribution, she announced passionately, 'Lady Lampiter is absolutely right. Absolutely.'

'So you say,' I countered, still rudely declining to look at her. 'So you repeat. But assertion is no argument. Nor yet is reiteration.'

'Well, upon my soul!' she exclaimed, as if this first principle in logic was the rudest thing she'd ever heard. What stronger execration she would have used if the senior ladies had not been there I do not know. I know what I provided her with.

'What is it, what is it, Mummy?' demanded Alexander, pulling on his mother's hand. 'Has somebody said something rude?'

Maureen did not answer; she was too interested in what her mother would say next. And Lady Lampiter, glad of this support from Jimmy on her left, really let herself go. Her heart accelerating, no doubt, with a heightened secretion from her adrenal glands, her body shaking and her voice stumbling, she said, 'I confess I do not understand you all, if you know everything and are prepared to accept it happily. I personally do not shake hands with filth, and nobody's going to persuade me to.'

A good phrase from the Dowager, but I wasn't going to let her get away with it. I used it against her. 'I don't think anyone's asked you to do that. To shake hands with suffering, perhaps, past and present.'

'Just so,' Clem murmured at my side. 'That is it'; and my heart went out to him in gratitude.

Lady Lampiter threw back her head as if to fling from off her frilled and helmet-like hat all this sentimental froth. 'I'm afraid, Mr. Palmer, I'm more interested in the suffering evil-doers inflict than in what they very rightly suffer themselves.'

'And I should have thought that the only thing that matters at any particular moment is that someone is suffering and never mind who or why. Mr. Prenders came with us at the invitation of the Bishop,' I reminded her. 'The Bishop has standards, I suppose?'

'Yes, and I am defeated by them.'

'Very obviously.'

'I must say I feel much the same as Lady Lampiter,' said the voice on her left. 'I do. In every way.'

'Well, then I'm sorry for you.'

'Sorry? For me? God above, I—'

'Oh, dear, oh dear . . .' Hester sighed, looking towards those steps up which the Bishop would come, and speaking to the air rather than to us. 'Oh, I should never have spoken. It . . . it slipped out.'

'Mr. Prender is in many ways a very good man,' I dared to say, addressing only Lady Lampiter, the captain in this fight, and leaving Lieutenant Jimmy where she stood. 'A better man than I am. His life, as a whole, has been far more unselfish than mine.'

'Good?!'

'Yes, good.'

'Well, if you call that sort of thing good—'

'I must say I find Mr. Palmer's position difficult to understand.' Jimmy was determined not to be by-passed. 'I certainly do. Very difficult.'

'Then again I'm sorry for you.' I was in no mood for the courtesies. 'It should be simple enough to a good intelligence. If one big sin is enough to make a man bad, God help us all. Me and you and all of us.'

'There was more than one—' began the Dowager.

'Well, *ten* big sins,' I almost shouted at her. 'I haven't got through life without ten of them. Nor, I suspect has anyone here.' I stressed the 'anyone' that she might include herself in it. 'At heart Mr. Prender is a good man. I know it.'

And here Maureen spoke. '*I* agree with Mr. Palmer,' she said, and nothing has ever pleased me more. Once again I had misjudged the total quality of one of our company. I even felt a brief love for the girl who, in this quarrel, had suddenly come in with forgiveness for Prenders' sins—and of me, apparently, for mine. Her mother, hearing her, said, 'Good lord, I don't know where we're getting to.'

'Getting an inch or two nearer Christianity,' I suggested.

'What is it, Mummy?' Alexander demanded again. 'Is Mr. Palmer being rude?'

'Be quiet!' was all the reply he got, for now Clem intervened, speaking more gently and wisely than any of us. 'I agree with you, Lady Lampiter, and with Jimmy, that we must have some standards. But standards can differ, you know. There are standards of compassion and forgiveness.' He said this with the friendliest smile and followed it with words whose aptness delighted me. Looking round at the tumbled columns, the broken capitals, and the piled blocks now throwing their shadows on these pavement flags, he said, 'And this is a good spot on which to proclaim them.'

'Exactly, exactly!' I endorsed with enthusiasm, thinking suddenly, and in the same moment, that this was no fitting place for a violent quarrel, but that it had heard much controversy once before. I spoke, musingly, to the air around me, but for all to hear who cared to. 'How some people can do some things in some places I do not know.'

'It was a place of healing too,' Clem added softly but in the hearing of the Dowager, though he too was looking at no one in particular, 'And there's no healing in hate. Or in mere contempt.'

'*Exactly*,' I repeated, louder and less impersonally than he. Less kind than Clem, I said it, fully intending the Dowager to think it designed for her.

'Ah . . . pah! . . . nonsense!' Lady Lampiter stuttered and stumbled, pushing these disabling ideas aside. 'Of course we must forgive, and all that . . . whenever possible. I know my Christianity, I hope—but there are some things which are beyond forgiveness.'

'There are none,' I said.

'Of course there are. I have no use for softness and sentimentality towards outrageous sinners. This compassion—'

'Mummy, doesn't she like Mr. Palmer?'

'—and forgiveness can be carried much too far, in my view.'

'But unfortunately not in the view of Jesus Christ,' I retorted. 'Seventy times seven. Though perhaps you have no great use for him at times.'

In an effort to bring us all back to sanity and calm Clem intervened again with a small laugh and the words, 'Perhaps I prefer Jon's standards of compassion and forgiveness because I have such frequent need of them.'

But I had no desire as yet to be sane and calm. My asperity was by no means exhausted. I attacked her with all the trite and obvious questions. Did she never say, 'There but for the grace of God . . .?' Or remember 'Forgive your brother, not seven times, but seventy times seven' which must be something of a strain? Or ask herself how far she was in a position to cast the first stone; which inevitably led me to the woman taken in adultery and to the words, 'Neither do I condemn thee. Go and sin no more.'

But here a revelation: she instantly revealed, though unconsciously, how pleased she could be if one record of Christ's forgiveness was open to a query and might be doubted. 'And *that* story,' she declared with a note of triumph, 'happens to be an interpolation in St. John's gospel. It was not written by St. John at all.' So? She was glad, was she, that these lovely words of pardon might never, perhaps, have been spoken. 'Perhaps you did not know that, Mr. Palmer.'

'I certainly know it. Anybody who's made any study of the gospels knows it. But it's a story that rings with truth. And it pictures for me the one master I'm prepared to worship.' (Thus, out of the abundance of the heart the mouth, even in a fury, will sometimes speak.)

'For me too,' said Clem softly.

'And furthermore,' I flung at her, since she deserved to be steamrolled flat, 'it's almost certain that none of the fourth gospel was written by St. John. So what does it matter who wrote this bit?'

'Of course St. John wrote it,' she affirmed.

'Oh . . . well . . .' I sighed and, shrugging, looked helplessly towards Clem. How could one argue with women who just asserted what they wanted to believe rather than established it?

'Oh, Mummy, who of 'em is it that's been rude?'

'You keep quiet. It's nothing to do with you.'

'But I want to *know*. Is it Mr. Palmer?'

'No one's been rude.'

'Then why is Granny so angry?' asked the sensible child.

'No one's been rude.'

'Oh, come, dear Maureen,' I thought. 'Don't lie to the child. I *was* rude, and fully intended to be, and I'm thoroughly pleased about it. I've felt much better ever since. A bit shaken, maybe, though otherwise fine.' But I had no time to deplore her answers further because just then I heard footsteps and, turning, saw Prenders coming back. Probably he'd gone walking alone among the scattered black basalt remnants outside the garden, and then decided that 'he'd be damned if he'd run away from the face of any old hen'. No Lady Lampiter was going to drive him away with a filthy glance. Almost certainly he was returning clothed in anger rather than ease, but never had this unhappy man touched me more than now as he came slowly towards us again over these pavement flags. And was it possible that another of us was feeling something like this? For now there unrolled a scene that astonished me.

Maureen—Maureen of all people—*my* Maureen—quickly dropped Alexander's hand and walked towards him, taking with her a charming smile. 'Come along, Mr. Prender,' I heard her say. 'You mustn't desert us. Where have you been running off to? The Bishop wants us to be all here together on our last day, and we must have *you*.' And she touched his hand with her fingers rather as if she were calling home again a straying child. It was no more than a touch accompanying the merry words, 'We're not letting *you* escape us today,' but it reminded me or the way she had touched my knee, in different mood, in the car on Mount Lebanon. It could have been, of course, that she had a need to differ when possible from a punishing mother; it could even have been that she had none of her mother's attitude to sin; but there appeared to be more in her action that either of these. It had all the look of a woman ministering to someone who'd been hurt. Bless you, Maureen.

Resolved to be with her in this friendly approach, I followed and in my turn spoke easily to him as if nothing had happened. 'There's a wad of things I'd like to ask you, Pren, about this site and these ruins. They're clearly Hellenistic, are they not?'

As I spoke I realized that Clem was standing with us.

And Alexander. But he was not come to demonstrate forgiveness and Christian charity. 'What *was* it, Mummy?' he persisted, seizing her hand. 'What was it Mr. Palmer said?'

'Never you mind.'

'But I want to *know*.'

'Well then you'll have to want. We none of us get all the things we want in this world. Stay here with me, and be quiet.'

So Alexander never knew; and meanwhile Lady Lampiter, and her ally, Jimmy, were left alone with all the hot indignation that had been theirs. I suspected that Jimmy's was less warm than the Dowager's because her support had been social flattery more than heartfelt agreement. She, I thought, liked to be where the power was, and here, of a sudden, were three of us against one, which more than counterbalanced the prepotency of the Dowager. I was right, for, sure enough, as we approached, she deliberately gave Prenders an amicable smile, a smile that was the very statement of social welcome.

She had crossed the floor of the house. Quietly and without fuss she had attached herself to the majority party. And Lady Lampiter, as we all rejoined her, could only stand there like a lonely statue, carved in black basalt (a volcanic rock) and representing 'No Compromise'.

§

Our two bishops arrived and, after wandering with us around the ruined shafts and capitals, Bishop Brakewaite assembled us at the western end of that pavement, near the four upright columns supporting the remains of their architrave, and announced, 'We're going to have a few minutes of devotion here where we end our pilgrimage. I propose to ask Freddy to lead us in it and to sum up for us what our thoughts and feelings should be—' was it in his present contrite mood and humble admiration for 'Freddy's' goodness that he stepped down from his leadership and left the younger bishop to occupy his place? 'Come, Freddy. We all want to hear from you.'

Freddy, with us standing around him, spoke well, his secure, untroubled faith and his deep piety directing him. For me and, I think, for all, judging from the way their eyes stayed on him, he raised the magic from this untidy lakeside garden till it brooded and shimmered above all the wild grasses, the ferns and moss, the weedy pavements, and the litter of monumental stones from centuries long gone.

Here we were, he said, in this small acre of Capernaum, and it was hardly irreverent to imagine that Christ in his heaven often thought of this place. For beneath the flagstones of this pavement were the foundations of his own synagogue and probably some of the stones on which he stood. Probably not a stretch of this garden which had not known his feet. And Peter's feet for certain, and Matthew's, and those of Zebedee's sons. Remember: the very water that lapped the wall of this garden had brought his doctrine ashore for us, as he sat in a boat, teaching the people. That hill there, beyond the high ruined wall and the tall eucalyptus, had heard the words, 'Blessed are the merciful for they shall obtain mercy. Blessed are the peacemakers—' I glanced towards Lady Lampiter but this particular reminiscence didn't appear to be troubling her. We were not to worry, he continued, if at present we could not properly order and assess all the wonderful places we had visited and all the thoughts that could and should be drawn from them. There must now be a whole storehouse of memories deep in our hearts and minds, some of which might have temporarily sunk down into forgetfulness—but not to worry! This was a valuable equipment within us which God could use as and when he wished. Never mind if a hundred distractions and all the cares of the world when we were home again overlaid this fine store; the use of it would often be, not our work, but God's; he would call to the surface again any part that we needed and that would help and inspire us. And now, clasping his hands before him, he spoke a Bidding Prayer. 'Let us remember where we stand. Let us offer thanks for all that was given here to the world. Let us pray to God for all who have or shall come to this place. Let us ask pardon for the imperfections in our search for his spirit in this his homeland, and let us commit ourselves anew, however imperfectly, to him, here on his own home-ground. Finally let us humbly gather up all these our petitions and praises into the words which he gave us—and which, we may feel sure, he himself often used when alone in his home here, perhaps before retiring to sleep, or in company with his disciples by the lake, or alone again on one of these hills around, when he'd withdrawn there to be in full touch with his Father'—whereupon we all bent our heads and said the Paternoster.

I observed that Lady Lampiter spoke all of it quite easily, not even stumbling at its uncomfortable suggestion that we could be forgiven only as we forgave. Her Amen was firm and loud, even deliberately loud, and I had a feeling that if it was addressed upwards to Heaven (as it certainly was) it was also directed a little sideways towards Mr. Palmer and those who had agreed with him.

But of course one does not know. Who could know what these haunted stones were doing to any one?

§

On our last night at the Beth-muri Hospice there was a remarkable sunset. It seemed, at first sight as we were called excitedly into the garden to look at it, almost too good to be true. One long rose-feathered cloud stretched over the lake from the distant Syrian hills to those behind our garden. It had the long pointed shape of an angel's wing slowly outspreading, and it lay from end to end of a sky brightly blue above it and below. Here and there the mountains opposite threw back its rose-grey tints, while the lake, a sheet of steel, reflected them. And all over our warm garden the shrill, whirring song of the cicadas may have been their mating calls but sounded like a general salute to this fine over-arching sunset, under an immense blue night.

Of course, in any other land, east or west, given the same conjunction of sky and cloudscape and still evening water, the scene would have been no different, but this was Galilee; one could look to the lake's northern brink and see there a strip of dark trees which housed the ruins of Capernaum; and how could one avoid being lyrical about so legendary a sea, and likening this brief embellishment to a poem of sanctification?

18

Homeward

So it was all over, the pilgrimage, the search in pursuit of new understandings, and we were filing into the aeroplane at Lod. Within the plane the picture was much the same as it had been twenty days before. There was the Dowager leading Hester toward the front seats ('*I'm* not afraid of fire') and chattering with her all the way. There were our two bishops in seats on the other side of the gangway, evading perhaps the likelihood of unending feminine talk for the next eight hours. There, behind them, were Maureen and Alexander, the boy having fought to be well in front so that, when the cockpit door was open, he could see what he called 'the driver'—which might have upset the Captain, had he heard it. There was the Springing Jimmy sitting alone, and gallantly parading an absence of vexation that no one had cared to sit with her.

Remembering Prenders' irrational need to be near a doorway, no matter how tightly sealed, I led him and Clem in a casual manner towards back seats, but he instantly detected my thought and out of Clem's hearing said, 'Dinna fash yersel', Jonny. Not going to be too bad. And I'm going to get better of all this. It's only a legacy of prison. I knew nothing about it till that first day in a locked cell. It'll go gradually. Better already, since I've been able to talk about it to a sympathetic friend. As I told you, it's always easier in company, and easier still when one of the company understands, like you.'

'Well, at least take the window-seat,' I laughed.

'Do you mind if I do?... no ... tell you what: I'll take this window-seat behind you and Clemmy.'

Clem and I then competed in self-sacrifice, each urging the other to take the window-seat, and Clem conquered in the fight, probably because he was the more truly unselfish, though I, sitting down by the window, insisted properly, even volubly, even too frequently, that we changed places later.

This let me have the last sight of land. As the plane took off and roared towards the sea, I don't remember if it was Clem or Prenders —probably Prenders, the ever informative—who reminded us that Tel Aviv was one with Joppa, and that it was from the port of Joppa that Jonah took ship for Tarshish, 'nearly wrecking the whole outfit because he was flying from the presence of the Lord'.

Since I had long forgotten this I said only, as Tel Aviv or Joppa withdrew into the past behind us, 'Oh, dear,' having no witticism ready.

Clem said, 'Well, if the Lord sends a mighty wind, we'll throw out Alexander.'

But Prenders objected, 'Oh no. Not the poor kid. Throw me out. I'm the obvious Jonah. Ask Lady Lampiter.'

Clem, looking before and behind him at the interior of the plane, so long and so crowded from head to tail, changed his opinion. 'I don't feel we need worry. I'd say all of us already were in the belly of the whale, and it'll vomit us out on *terra firma* at London Airport.'

I stayed looking back at the long coastline. There it lay on the sea, the coast of Israel like a sentence out of world history and perhaps the greatest sentence of all. What names in that sentence: Judah, Israel, Caesarea, Carmel, Galilee. . . .

I looked till we were far out over the sea and nothing more of the East was in sight, and then Clem and I fell to discussing whether the places we'd visited, the things we'd learned, and the emotions we'd felt had made us any different from what we'd been three weeks before. Thinking of the Bishop, though not telling Clem his story, I asked, 'Has anything really happened to us? Do we now know any more than your Great Bell of Bow?'

Clem replied, 'I do not yet know if I know any more—and that,

I hope you noticed, is a sentence in a perfect dactyllic metre. It would make a nice new chime for Bow Bells: "All that I know . . . Is that I long more than ever . . . To feel that I do." How's that?'

'I don't know but it just about sums me up as well.'

Prenders' eyes were now shut, and he was almost certainly asleep, for his breathing was nasal and heavy, so we spoke softly and agreed on one extraordinary fact: that the best help which had come to us had come from the endless but admirable loquacity of an avowed unbeliever. Prenders' rushing outflow about the sixth-century enlightenment all over the world, and about the Deutero-Isaiah and the Zoroastrians and Hindus and Sufis, had seemed to illuminate doubt and 'unknowing' (which were not the same as disbelief) with something of the light of Faith itself.

'Yes,' Clem agreed with me. 'There's no God but God, and Prenders is his prophet.'

'There still hangs in my mind,' I continued enthusiastically, 'and always will, the memory of that camel train passing under Bisitun and leaving a cloud of dust behind it, and old Prenders quoting the most perfect statement on God Transcendent and Immanent I'd ever heard—from Rumi, wasn't it?—"Gaze not left or right, Only his dust is here, and he in the Infinite." He went on with something very wise from the Upanishads about not knowing being better than knowing. I forget how it went, but—'

A voice behind us provided the words, probably with pride. ' "Who says that Spirit is not known, knows. Who claims that he knows, knows nothing." '

I looked round. Prenders' eyes were still shut but there was a grin about his lips. He must have heard all.

'Thank you,' I said.

And he pursued, eyes still shut, 'All mystics say the same. You should read *The Cloud of Unknowing*. No one really knows who wrote it, but it expounds that if a God can be known by reason or thought he cannot be God, but only some easy symbol for earthbound minds. "By love he can be gotten and holden" it says in its most famous sentence, "but by thought never." '

Offering no more, he apparently continued his search for sleep.

'Thank you,' I said again, but his eyes stayed shut.

By now we had left the sun of the East behind us and were cleaving through a white cloud of the West. This enveloping cloud, though shutting from sight all but itself, was not dense; it was thin and of a soft luminous texture as if composed of light as well as of vapour. Immediately I thought it made a pretty fair picture of the 'cloud of unknowing' at which Clem and I seemed to have arrived, a cloud certainly, but strangely lit up by the wisdom of Prenders.

Talking as our plane speeded on, I submitted to Clem a theory of mine, very much within a cloud of unknowing, but long held without benefit of Prenders. It was this: that in our present order of existence we must accept that apparent incompatibles were *both* true, and that in some other dimension they would be seen to be in a harmony as part and parcel of one another, forming a unity.

'Such incompatibles as—?' demanded Clem.

'Well, good and evil, pleasure and pain, beauty and ugliness—or if you want to soar into metaphysics—finite and infinite, free-will and determinism, time and eternity. There's no escaping these absolute incompatibles in this world, but—'

'But you should read Nicholas of Cusa,' came the voice of the sleeper behind me. 'He said all this five hundred years before you. In his *De Docta Ignorantia*.'

'Well, maybe he did,' I said, turning round and addressing the unopened eyes, 'but I arrived at it without help from him. And who was he, anyway?'

'A fifteenth-century cardinal, famous as a mathematician and political economist, which makes his mysticism all the more remarkable.'

'And what did you say his book was?' asked Clem.

' "*De Docta Ignorantia*".'

'Which means—?'

Prenders now accorded us the courtesy of opening his eyes. He stared at us as if trying to supply us with the best translation. 'Well . . . "Instructed and Unashamed Ignorance" is the best I can do for you. The exalted ignorance in which alone you can apprehend truths that transcend reason. He describes how one day, travelling in the seas of Greece, he suddenly saw that all your incompatibles are only such in the context of this spacio-temporal world. In the unity and infinity of God they all coincide. He calls this the Coincidence of Contradictories. Perhaps you are a reincarnation of him. In one of his finest passages he says, "The place wherein Thou art found is girt around with the coincidence of contradictories, and this is the wall of Paradise wherein thou dost abide." All of which is more or less what you've just said to us—to which I listened with interest. I congratulate you.'

Strange how some dim idea of one's own, when another surprises you by saying it was long ago held by a wise man, seems to spring alight and alive, though only a kind of dream-shape before. Self-congratulation danced in my mind.

Clem, on the contrary, was frowning as if at a difficult idea which had never approached his mind before.

So Prenders quoted another sentence from his mystical mathematician and economist. 'He says the door in the wall of Paradise is guarded by the proud spirit of reason who must be vanquished first or the way will never lie open.' It was as though this Prenders who hotly declined any mystical religion for himself, was eager that we should have one. He drove on in his efforts to work a salvation for us, though he himself was beyond saving. He admitted this. 'Happy to be a signpost,' he explained, 'while I myself am a castaway. You know your Willie James, I suppose?'

'You mean,' Clem asked, 'the William James who, as someone said, made his books on psychology as readable as novels while his brother, Henry, made his novels as unreadable as books on psychology?'

'That's the boy, Clemmy. And in his *Varieties of Religious Experience* he tells how when anaesthetized by nitrous oxide he had mystical experiences which he, though a hard-brained intellectual, was prepared to regard as significant. He saw then that all the opposites in this world that bewilder our thinking were not just contrasted species of one genus, but that the better of the two species, the good one, was also the genus, absorbing the opposite into itself. More or less, you see, what Nicholas of Cusa and Jonny of Palmer, Sans and Someone both say. And, as I told you, Zoroaster. A good company.'

'I think perhaps I see what they're getting at,' said Clem. 'Up to a point.'

It was less than appropriate that, precisely at this stage the aeroplane should go roaring out of cloud into open sky with the full sun above it and the ocean of white vapours below. Inappropriate because I was now almost proud of my luminous cloud of unknowing. It was the place in which Nicholas of Cusa—and Prenders—said I might, indeed must, dwell, a cloud of ignorance instructed and unashamed. Seemingly Clem was thinking exactly the same, for he said, 'This is where the good bishop and the Dowager dwell, forever untroubled. All sunlight and certainty for them.'

'And the Springing Jimmy,' I added. 'She flies about splendidly here. Well out of sight of us down below in the clouds.'

§

So it ended; we were all home again and dispersed like bagatelle balls, each to his familiar and humdrum slot. And what had it done for me in my slot? The Bishop with his easy faith had believed that something was given to him by the lake, some word from his master, but no such healing 'miracle' had been granted me. And yet I had gathered something: a kind of liberation, a new restfulness; peace in an ignorance which leaned ever and unshakeably towards things one wanted to believe. Relieved of the burden of dogmas too heavy, I was ready, on the advice of Prenders and all his saints, to commit myself to this clouded trust.

That, I thought at first, was all.

Poor Prenders, brilliant, lost and wandering. I remembered words he had once let slip about 'the dreary services in prison after the wonderful, glorious services at St. Justin Martyr's', and I decided I'd like to have a look at one of these. So I wrote asking him which Sunday would be the one to see a St. Justin's Mass at its best; and I received this impudent reply: 'For shame, Jonny. Are you not aware that the seventh Sunday after Easter is always Pentecost or Whitsunday, that next Sunday, as ever was, is this same seventh, and that the Feast of Pentecost is a Primary Double of the First class? So go next Sunday and you'll get something good. Give my love to Canon Dick if you see him. But I trust, my good Jon Palmer, that after your recent visit to the Holy Land you will take your palm along with you as the emblem of your penitence, full forgiveness, current state of grace, and consequent rejoicing. Yours ever, "Prenders".

'P.S. I think often of Babylon and Bisitun.'

'Primary Double of the First Class' conveyed nothing to me, even though I had once been a ceremoniarius; but it seemed to promise 'something good'. Prenders was far ahead of me in these matters.

Only a few hours after the receipt of this letter Clem dined with me in the club and over our table, over excellent *entrecôtes* and a good club claret, I suggested brightly that he too should come along to old Prenders' church and see what games they got up to there.

'No, Jon,' he answered, with a most confident shake of his head. 'No, Jon, no. I've no use whatever for your High Church goings-on. If I'm anything, I'm Broad with leanings to Low. I want simplicity and quiet in my worship, and sometimes I think I ought to have been a Quaker. They've carried simplicity so far that they've nothing left but silence.'

'But, my dear chap,' I protested, 'as a good High Churchman you can have all the simplicity and stillness you need in a Low Mass. Go to Low Mass and then, with my consent, you can give High Mass a miss.'

Hardly listening to this objection—and indeed it wasn't worth listening to—he continued, 'The only time I found myself—by mistake—in an ultra-High church—it was in Brighton, I need scarcely say—I came away thinking, "Well, I don't know what all that was about. I simply don't know what they were up to." '

'I would explain,' I offered, smiling indulgently. 'You come along on Sunday. It's a Primary Double of the First Class.'

'What does that mean?'

'I don't know.'

'Probably Double Trouble for me. It's just not my meat. If it helps some of you, I'm all for your having it, *in toto* and with knobs on, but it's no good to me. All that paraphernalia and pantomime just gets between me and God. Maybe that's because, as I've told you before, I'm not an artist but only an accountant.'

'And that won't wash. Because, as *I've* told you before, you're a bit of a poet.'

'Thank you very much.'

'Don't mention it. I don't accept any of that nonsense. Let's have some more wine.' I re-charged his glass and while I waited for the wine steward, said, 'Now look, listen, and learn. Are you telling me that at the recent coronation of our most religious and gracious queen, you'd have done away with all the robes of the bishops, the uniforms of the Gentlemen-at-arms, and all the pageantry and music and singing and trumpets and drums? Of course you wouldn't. You were thrilled to bits by it, and so was the whole world. Well, why the hell, if you rejoice in all that ceremonial around an earthly monarchy, can't you accept it when it's offered to God? Or look again: we were both good soldiers in the war, and didn't we attend some funeral services with full military honours—the band playing Chopin's funeral march in the procession to the cemetery, the flag of Britain honouring the coffin, the Last Post sounded by the trumpeters, the last shots fired over the grave by the firing party, and the Reveille when the world must begin again—my God, were we moved? We all, including you old prots, crave poetry; and ceremonial is great poetry. It *isn't* pantomime, stupid. It's poetry. And you all love it—except in church.'

Forgetting the food on my plate, absent-mindedly refilling and neglecting my glass, I raved on about High Mass as a superb poem which gave us more, much more, than its words or its music or its visual beauty could express. I argued, with the Buddhists, that magnificent ritual could bore through to deeper and richer realms in us than anything mere intellect could reach. It could raise a numinous ecstasy that transcended reason and understanding. And religion should do no less. Its business was with things deeper than thought.

To this he countered, 'I suppose it can do something for some people, but only if they start by believing quite a little—'

'As you and I do,' I interrupted.

'—but to the man who believes nothing, the atheist and the anti-clerical—it's just abracadabra. I've an atheist friend who gets really hot about it. He calls it disgusting trickery by power-hungry priests who draw upon all the arts to give their ridiculous beliefs a moving beauty that overthrows reason and sense. What annoys him is that you Catholic Christians, Roman or Anglo, are the finest salesmen in the world. You've got the most skilful admen of today beaten into a corner at their own game.'

'And so we have,' I triumphed, forgetting I was no longer a Catholic, 'because we've learned how to do it over two thousand years. I accept every word your friend says. We do it all marvellously, so why not come along and see them doing it at Prenders' old church?'

'Prenders, atheist and rebel, is hardly the best advertisement of it,' Clem argued, though gently enough.

And I answered, 'We don't know yet.'

§

But there was no persuading Clem to come to a High Mass, and I went alone to St. Justin Martyr's. I did not suggest that my wife should come with me, though in her loyalty she would willingly have done so. I just recorded how one of our pilgrims had 'gone off the deep end about the services at his church', and said I'd like to go and see what they really amounted to, while she took the children, as usual, to the Children's Service in the little grey church on the hill.

And I got into my car and drove the twenty miles to Cramwell Green, that grey neighbourhood in north-east London which, according to Prenders' newspaper article, was the parish of St. Justin Martyr and the field of the Calborne Mission. It was a curious dim neighbourhood that I found. The article had described it as 'slummy' but if this was so, these long streets were slums in tall houses. The high, grey, stucco'd houses in their first few years had known comfortable middle-class families, with cap'd and apron'd servants but now, behind the crumbling stucco and suffering brick-work, had decayed into tenements. Conceivably the present inflating of wages had lifted them from the 'slums' suggested in the article, but only yesterday this must have been an area of the poor and struggling, and in parts was still so today. I passed more than one African face as I drove my car slowly along. Pleasant faces, these dark ones, but they showed how far the neighbourhood had slipped from what it was intended at first to be.

Some of the houses were already condemned and empty, awaiting the demolition gangs. The front windows of these condemned houses were smashed—why not?—by stones from the happy young; those of the upper floors showed through their jagged gashes a dark emptiness within; those on the lower floors were screened from entry, and from further outdoor sports, by sheets of corrugated iron.

This was London, palpably London, that crazy mixed-up city, so splendid and lovely in some parts, but here the greyest, weariest, and most melancholy capital in the world. A drizzling rain had stopped only an hour ago and the paving flags before the basements were as greasy as they were grey. Here were dulness and greyness after Jerusalem and Tiberias, the white and sun-bright cities of the East.

A steeple ahead. That must be St. Justin's. And what a disappointment. An edifice as outmoded and apparently forgotten as the streets over which it was built to watch. In all its details it was ready-made, reach-me-down Gothic, from walls and windows and gable ends to the point of its steeple; and all its greyness was darkened by a hundred years of London soot. I parked my car in a side-street and walked with a saddened heart towards its north door, fearing a gloomy arcaded cavern within.

But—I passed through an inner door, and never was disappointment so instantly allayed. Walls, window-embrasures, columns, arches—all things from floor to vaulted roof were white, and as white as if painted yesterday. The capitals of the pillars were picked out in gold; the pews, once no doubt a dismal brown, were now dove-grey and pale olive green. And as it wanted but six minutes to eleven and the last bell was ringing in the steeple, all the theatre beyond the chancel arch—choir, sanctuary, altar, reredos—was under light. A candelabra with thirty candles brightly glimmering hung beneath the rood. Eight candles on silver candlesticks stood paraded before the choir stalls as for a great service. On the footpace beneath the altar a robed acolyte with a long taper was lighting the altar candles. High above all a single sanctuary lamp burned red.

The church was not full, but it was a large church, and the number of people in the centre pews amounted to a good congregation for these irreligious days. While the majority were women, I was pleased to see that more than a few were young people, girls or youths. Were some of them, perhaps, those who'd had their places in Prenders' Front Line, and what had happened to that honourable company now? Were these the remnants of it?

Being tall, I like always an outside seat in a pew, and I began to walk to one I could see in the third pew from the front. Does it say anything for the native modesty of humans that in any public meeting or service that is free they will never, if they can help it, seat themselves in the two front rows? I had not gone four paces up the nave when I saw—yes, Prenders: Prenders in the last pew but one. He was not kneeling in prayer as some already were, but sitting back like one who'd come to watch.

Doubting whether the strange fellow would wish to meet me in these circumstances, I pretended not to have noticed him. (In the end this doubt seemed justified; he must have preferred to be alone and ungreeted by me or any other, since, after the service, he slipped away unseen.) But in the single minute it took me to walk from the back of the nave to the front, I remembered—whether suitably or not, who can say?—the night falling under Bisitun, and the stars glittering above us, while Prenders quoted some of the Sufi's poem about the sinner who looked back on his way to hell, and its lovely closing words, 'Bring him back for he never lost hope in me.'

With this line playing in my memory I took my seat.

Two minutes afterwards the lighting of the sanctuary—altar, footpace and pavement—brightened further, a clock struck in the tower, and the bell stopped.

The congregation rose. From the sacristy came the thurifer swinging his thurible and leading in procession the crucifer with a taper on either side, the choir, the torch-bearers for the Canon, the ceremoniarius alone and resplendent in his robe and lastly, as a fine *coda*, the subdeacon, deacon, and priest in their historic vestments, red for Pentecost—tunicle, dalmatic, and cope.

All went towards the altar; stood facing it; then, after the chanted words, 'Let us proceed in peace', swung one and all towards the congregation, and burst into the Pentecostal *Salve, festa dies*, singing it in plainsong as they came down in a bannered procession amongst us.

'Lo, in the likeness of fire, on them that await his appearing,
He whom the Lord foretold suddenly, swiftly descends.
    Hail thee, festival day. . . .'

I confess my breath was caught back, as it always had been in the old days; an emotion welled up in me almost from the spring-source of tears, while my body remained rapt in a stillness; I guessed—no, I knew—that Prenders, far behind me, was experiencing hardly less; and I thought of him in his grey prison chapel, watching the 'dreary services' there and longing for all of this. For poetry in the heart of drabness. The great poem of the Church in our tarnished world.

Proceeding in full unison round the south aisle and up the nave, all paused at the entrance to the chancel; the plainsong reached its close; the organ burst into strong harmonies, and as the procession ascended the chancel steps to take their separate places in choir or sanctuary, they sang the *Veni Creator Spiritus*.

'The wonderful, glorious services at St. Justin Martyr's' Prenders had called them, and while the words were facile, they were exact. For me, as this service went on—the resplendent ceremoniarius guiding it all, the tall tapers burning, the cloud-blue incense lifting, the voices soaring, the silences, the torch-bearers, four and four, assembled along the pavement for the Sanctus, the Humble Access, and the Consecration, the far-away bell in the high tower only just heard as it rang thrice at the Elevation of the Host and thrice again at the Elevation of the Chalice for the world to hear, while the thurifer incensed host and cup with his three double swings, the jingle of his thurible chains the only sound in the church—oh, I knew that

Prenders was one with me in his longing to accept it all again—if only he could, if only he could. . . .

'I didn't know what it was all about,' Clem had said. 'I simply didn't know what they were up to.' But *I* knew. It was about the ever wonder-filled truth that life is far greater than we know; that things are not what they seem to scientist and materialist, but far more than they seem; that none of our good sceptics and humanists can know what powers were once evolved in a man who at last ful-filled our human nature, with all its potential, by dedicating it in complete obedience to his God who was Love—and so what then? Well, perhaps, it was only some of us who could experience it like this; others it affected differently; many men, many natures, and while for Clem this high ceremonial was no more than an un-rent temple-veil between him and the Holy of Holies, for others of us, such as Prenders and me, it was a numinous glory filling the temple and making us feel (in a variant of old Omar's words) one with Yesterday's Two Thousand Years.

Not, alas, that in the face of all this beauty I was worshipping. Love it as I might, I was still an outsider and as I knelt or stood I was only watching and thinking. All through the service I was only thinking.

§

Now it was the Communion of the Faithful, and as I watched the people going up to the altar rails I was still only thinking dreamily. My mind wandered away to many other things than the wish that I could, once again, go up with them.

Their progress towards the sanctuary was slow because they were many—old, young, hale and crippled—and it was all very different from the days of my youthful faith, when I myself might have been up there within the sanctuary as acolyte, thurifer, or even ceremon-arius, and when we boys held it a profanity that anyone in full health should take the sacrament other than fasting. Much had happened in the world since I stood up there on the footpace in proud robes. I watched and went on woolgathering.

Then, all of a sudden, I was aware of a steady direction in my thoughts. It was as if I were being impelled along this straight path from behind or perhaps drawn along it from in front because there was a light in the distance. I had been recalling how Solomon Islands, in the ruins of Capernaum's synagogue, had said that, now after our pilgrimage, there must be a deep storehouse of memories within us, any one of which God would call to the surface when and as he wished. And the memory which had come to the surface and sent my thoughts in this new direction as I knelt here was that of my lonely walk down the slope of Olivet, trying to picture Christ coming down it for the last time—to accept the dreadful cup which he knew stood before him. I was thinking, How could one do other than love this young man coming with his disciples down that rough white track from Bethany, when the one thing about him of which we could feel certain was that he was coming determined to *be* the Suffering Servant of Isaiah; to bear our griefs, carry our sorrows, take the chastisement of our peace upon him, and so show the world what God and love really were. Coming towards this tremendous purpose against odds in himself, it would seem; remember 'Take away this cup from me, but no, thy will. . . . Why hast thou forsaken me, but no . . . it is finished, it is done, it is achieved.'

How other than love him and (a new half-resolve) range oneself with him as these people, young and old, simple and unlearned or wise and scholarly, were doing?

And while I was wishing I could do just this, there came the most extraordinary thought of all. The difficulties of an adequate belief were great, but old Prenders, sitting far behind me, Prenders the unbeliever, the apostate (or so he said), the angry rebel, had eased them all for me in his strange places—among Babylon's ruins or under Bisitun, or in the aeroplane coming home. He had shown Clem and me that there was an ultimate faith somewhere beyond 'not knowing'; that one could be 'swallowed up in God's sea, Past faith, past unbelieving, Past doubt, past certainty', that all the perplexing incompatibles could be held, as it were, one in either hand, because, while we could not understand this now, they were reconciled, and coincided, in the unity and infinity of God.

Thus Prenders. That a so-called infidel should have scattered all these enlightening ideas before me—was this, perhaps, my equivalent of the Bishop's little 'miracle' by the shore of Galilee where, he believed, help had been deliberately granted him?

The stream of communicants was dwindling, and as the last of them were coming from the back pews, I wondered for a second or two if I should see Prenders going up with them. He did not go past my watching eyes and, curiosity conquering, I turned my head shamelessly round to learn what he was doing in his last row but one. He was not sitting back to watch comfortably. He was kneeling, either in reverence for these sacred moments or, more likely, in a courteous consideration for the reverence of others.

§

The last notes of the *Agnus Dei*, sung by choir alone, had died away, and now those of the congregation who had remained in their pews were singing on their knees, softly, Newman's hymn,

> Firmly I believe and truly
> God is Three, and God is One. . . .

Those incompatibles. Like Clem I could not say 'Firmly I believe and truly' but I did remember Prenders in the aeroplane, quoting from behind shut eyes Nicholas of Cusa's words, 'The place wherein thou art found is girt around by the coincidence of contradictories, and this is the wall of Paradise wherein thou dost abide'; and I suspected, as always, that this might be the truth.

> And I next acknowledge duly
> Manhood taken by the Son. . . .

Perfect God and perfect Man. Incompatibles. But again came words of Prenders (these had been uttered in a Galilee taxi between Cana and Tiberias): 'The Church itself is the Queen of Agnostics,' he had said, and when I asked what on earth he meant, he answered, 'It's simple enough, chum. Have you never grasped that the Church's creeds are no more than her high fences protecting certain divine mysteries which she doesn't pretend to be able to explain and will not allow her children to explain? Every one of them who's tried to explain the *how* of Christ's godhead and manhood—Arius, Sabellius, Nestorius, Eutyches—she has condemned as a heretic. In other words, she says, "Here are the facts, chums, but they are inevitably incomprehensible to our present limited understanding." You see? Just like you and the Great Bell of Bow, she prefers to say "I do not know." '

The hymn ended, the last few communicants trickled past me to their pews, the organist was playing gently his variations on the hymn's melody till the priest should be ready to say the Paternoster, and it was in these quiet moments that I came to a decision, and a happy one. Belief in an unknown God has never been any difficulty to me. As surely as the materialist and humanist believes in a rational order of the universe which can never be fully known, but will not fail him, so surely I believe in a God who can never be fully known. Each of these axioms, after all, is a transcendental faith, and looks rather like the same thing, some of us calling it Nature's Laws, and some of us calling it God.

But on this Sunday in Prenders' old church there was still nothing easy about a full, orthodox faith in that young man on the Bethany road, whom I could but love; and my decision was this, as we waited on our knees, silently, for his own Paternoster.

'Surely,' I decided, 'the only thing to do is to give oneself to a love one feels, and leave all else with the God unknown.' Next time, then—or perhaps one day—I would go up with the people and share with them in their communion. I would go in a kind of blind love and trust, asking pardon all the way for any unworthiness in a faith so unsure. I felt very happy in this thought, happy, too, in the recollection that it would put me, more or less, side by side in a loyal, if halting, faith, with my good friend, Clem; and even as I dwelt on it, there leapt into my mind three magnificent words of Aristotle's—Aristotle whom no one had ever yet rebuked as sentimental, Aristotle the earthbound philosopher whose feet were ever on the ground rather than among the stars. His God whom, as an austere philosopher, he must hold to be impassive, immutable and immobile, was none the less able, though in stillness and rest, to move all things; and his words for this were: κινεῖ ὡς ἐρώμενον: 'he moves us—' or, if you like—'he draws us as a belovéd.'

If these words were the truth for me about that young man on the Bethany track, they went for this service too. It drew me as a belovéd. I remembered Clem saying that perhaps he ought to have been a Quaker because their silences would suit him so much better than my High Church goings-on. Well, I was perhaps a Quaker too, in this different sense: that Quakers demanded no certainties from their followers. But if I was such a Quaker I was also one who, untypically, loved and needed services like these in St. Justin Martyr's: majestic parables of God's love given to men, and their love returned to him with every beauty they could offer. An Anglo-Catholic Quaker, let us say. Believing much, if less than all. While hoping all.

Such was my decision that Sunday morning in the old church of Prenders, my teacher.

Am I then home again at last? I do not know. Perhaps I shall never know. I hope and trust and do not know.